CASINO CARIBBEAN

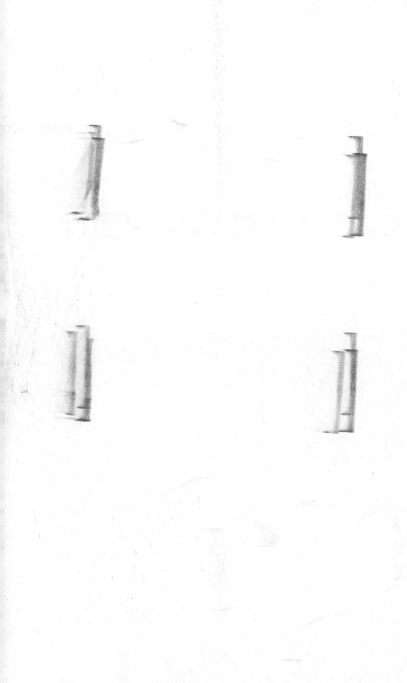

GRAHAM TEMPEST

CASINO CARIBBEAN

AN OLIVER STEELE THRILLER

B

A BRIGHTWAY BOOK

CASINO CARIBBEAN
A Brightway Book

Brightway Publishing Inc.
522 Hunt Club Blvd, #316
Apopka, Florida 32703

© Brightway Publishing Inc
Text copyright © 2010 by Jeremy Stone

Created for Brightway Publishing Inc by
Berry & Co (Publishing) Ltd
47 Crewys Road
London NW2 2AU

Designer Anne Wilson
Cover design Ed Berry

ISBN 978-0-9845153-0-1

Printed in Singapore

PROLOGUE

At the age of 28, Frankie Leon decided it was time to stop pushing inferior cocaine in South Florida and get into something respectable. So he set to work and started an Internet casino.

Respectable is a relative term. An Internet casino is the kind of business where thousands of chronic losers pay good money to sit at home and play poker, or some other game of chance, on their personal computers.

A New Yorker from Long Island, Frankie was a liberal arts graduate, the son of law-abiding, middle-class parents. Plump and pimply, with a permanent five o'clock shadow, he had an irritating mannerism of blinking through his thick spectacles. Behind his back, he was laughed at as a yuppie dealer by people in the business – and there were plenty of them – who did not wish him well. He had started out young, selling carefully measured sandwich bags of marijuana to his teenage school friends. After less than a decade, he had accumulated a fortune worth several million dollars, mostly in cash. But respectable it was not. His mother in Long Island, overweight like her son and twice the size of her skinny husband, Lou, would telephone him:

'I worry about you, Franklin, down there in Miami. How do you live?'

'I'm in sales, Mom, I'm doing well. Don't worry.'

'Are you eating okay?'

'Sure.'

'What you need is a wife.'

The casino became highly successful. This was no surprise to Frankie, who had never lacked self-confidence. As he had sat thinking, at the outset, in his air-conditioned mansion in Coconut Grove, a lushly wooded quarter of Miami, watching the brilliantly coloured parrots flutter and swoop around the mango trees in his garden, he had been struck by the key feature that the on-line casino game shared with drug dealing: it was a cash business. If a player had a gambling habit and a Visa card with a $20,000 line of credit, he – and most players were men – could drop some serious money. Why not with Frankie?

He started to form a clear picture in his mind of what he wanted. It involved clothing a basic money-making gambling programme with some colourful 'virtual reality' scenery that would make it irresistible to the solitary gambler.

So, over the next two years, he developed and implemented his plan.

His first step was to buy a casino licence. This particular licence was issued by the government of Antigua and Barbuda. As part of the British Commonwealth, Antigua falls within the authority of the Eastern Caribbean Supreme Court. The authority wielded by US courts in Antigua could be summed up very simply: there was none. Frankie liked that.

Then he had to set about building the business. Things went slowly for a while but hit their stride when he found the right computer programmer. He had needed someone to design the software that would turn his imaginary casino into electronic fact and had interviewed a dozen candidates without finding anyone who grasped his vision.

Then he met Judith. He had spotted her resumé on Monster.com and called her in. A 25-year-old, black-haired, pale and elegant, she came to the interview wearing a pinstripe suit and high heels, unusually smart for a programmer. To Frankie's taste she was too intense, he was more at ease with less assertive women.

She had been working for a Californian firm, writing video games for football fans – creating images of brutish athletes battering each other violently. She had been going out of her mind so she posted her resume on the Internet. She had either quit or was fired – exactly which was unclear. Judith also suffered from an unfortunate character defect – one that had brought her stay in Silicon Valley to an untimely end – but Frankie would not find out about that until much later.

'I need a "virtual reality" card-playing programme, something that makes people feel they are there,' he explained.

She frowned. 'Feel they are *where?*'

'Las Vegas.'

She thought for a moment, wrinkling her pretty brow. 'Downtown or the Strip?'

'Downtown. It needs to be funky. I want them to smell the smoke, chat with the dealers, joke with the guy in the next seat. They should have a sense of Las Vegas the way it used to be.'

'Free drinks for the players?' she asked drily and flashed a brief, brilliant smile.

'All but.' He noted the facetiousness but approved. He had interviewed a bunch of candidates already and none were picking up on his mood the way she was. It intrigued him that she was good looking as well.

'Is this something you can handle?' he asked.

She shrugged. 'Sure. There's nothing novel about the graphics. I've done it before. Footballers, gamblers, you name it – the software is similar. As for the card playing, the programmes for that are already out there. I'd have to talk to some casino people about the details but that should be easy enough.'

'When are you available?'

'Now.'

She had hesitated almost imperceptibly but Frankie caught it. Not a good sign, he thought. 'What happened at your last job?'

'I quit.'

'Why?'

'Personal reasons.'

He shot her a glance. 'Okay if I call them for a reference?'

She paused again. 'Sure.'

He tapped his pencil absentmindedly on the desktop. 'Do you

have any samples of your work that I could look at?'

'I can bring some in tomorrow.'

'Why don't you do that?'

He stood up.

After she left, he called her last employer in San José.

A happy-voiced female human resources specialist, super-friendly in a Californian way, told him Judith had worked there for 'about a year.'

'How was her work?'

'Outstanding. One of our best programmers.'

'Did you fire her?'

'Of course not. It was mutual.'

'She says she left for personal reasons,' said Frankie thoughtfully.

'There was an agreed parting.' The woman's friendliness was evaporating.

'May I speak to her supervisor?'

'I'm so sorry, all references are handled by this department.'

Much less friendly now, Frankie noticed. He tried another tack. 'Let me speak to your supervisor.'

'She's out today.'

It was like dealing with the telephone company. He gave up.

Next morning, Judith marched into his office, lugging an Apple laptop with an oversized screen.

'What's that?'

'Just a few ideas I put together.'

As he watched, she booted up the computer and guided him through a questionnaire that defined a player's physical appearance. She kitted Frankie out with a computer avatar, an on-screen manikin with a body type and facial features – eyes, nose, hairstyle – matching his own.

Coached by Judith, he walked into an Edwardian-style casino and saloon, with bedrooms upstairs. Encouraged by a smiling dealer with a luxuriant moustache, he sat down to play blackjack. In the background, ragtime piano music mingled with the anachronistic din of slot machines and a cheerful hubbub of conversation. The video sequence did not flow well. Large areas of the screen were plain blue and the screen went blank between the scene of his arrival and the card-playing. But the general idea came across vividly.

'I'm impressed,' he said, despite himself.

'Of course.'

He blinked and looked at her face; it was expressionless.

She said: 'This is just a start – crude cut-and-paste stuff. Polishing it to perfection is much harder. That takes time.'

'How much time?'

'Six months.'

He was disappointed. 'That long?'

She shrugged. 'At least. There's no point in my trying to kid you. If I lied now, you would just get angry later on and fire me.'

He digested that. 'Got anything else?'

'Sure.'

Guided by Judith's nimble fingers, the Frankie Leon character stood up and walked away from the blackjack table. In the hotel lobby, he climbed the stairs, walked down a corridor and knocked on a bedroom door. Inside, a smiling showgirl in '90s costume – what there was of it – was reclining on an ornate four-poster bed. She beckoned him in. The scene grew progressively more explicit as he watched. The loop ended with uninhibited sexual gymnastics.

He grinned. 'You're hired.'

She looked at him. 'Whoa! What about salary?'

He shrugged. 'Ninety … no to heck with it, a hundred thousand.'

She sneered, briefly unattractive. 'At two hundred we might have something to talk about.'

He was taken aback. 'How much were you making before?'

'That's my business.'

She knew she had him.

He sighed. 'Okay!'

'You'll get your money's worth.' She spoke tartly, but the brilliant smile was back. Frankie found the speed with which the smile came and went disturbing.

'Well, I certainly hope so. Because otherwise…' He deliberately let the threat hang in the air.

But she was as good as her word. Assistant programmers were hired and, six months later, she delivered a programme that was years ahead of the competition.

Casino Caribbean was born.

A player could log on in the privacy of his home and, in moments, be there at the tables ready to play. After first authorizing the use of his credit card, naturally. Gambling on-line was like real life, only better. There were no travel expenses to get to Las Vegas or some dreary Indian reservation in the middle of nowhere. And, of course, there were the erotic scenes. Of its kind, the programme was a masterpiece.

Business exceeded his expectations. Word spread. Business boomed and growth was exponential. After a year, Casino Caribbean's sales were approaching a $100 million a year. In the second year they reached $180 million. After three years, sales hit $400 million a year and were still growing. Frankie could hardly believe it himself.

Most of the Casino's customers were American, because that was where the money was. The rest were spread around the world. Gambling ignores national boundaries. Time zones were no problem, the system's computers worked 24 hours a day with surprisingly little human supervision.

By now Frankie had moved to Antigua and was living in luxury. Seriously wealthy, he was making money so fast his drug earnings looked like pocket change. The good times would roll forever, he thought – well, at least for a few more years, if he was in a more cautious mood.

But after a while, small things began to go wrong.

And then, of course, came the killings.

CHAPTER 1

FORT LAUDERDALE

OLIVER STEELE, a forensic accountant with a troubled past, was in Fort Lauderdale on business. He had come to visit and, if possible, to help a compulsive gambler named Larry Smith who had recently spent his way through his entire life's savings. It was lunchtime.

Made restless by the cloying humidity, Oliver decided to drive down Las Olas Boulevard eastward to the beach where a light breeze gave some relief from the 90-degree heat. He found an open-air sandwich kiosk under a couple of dusty palms and sat down, ignoring the adage 'never sit under a palm tree in case a coconut falls on you.' The metaphorical coconuts had already fallen. Looking back over the past five years, he found it hard to believe the mess he had made of his own life and career. By now, with any luck, he should have been a partner in a respected accounting firm with a good salary, an attractive wife and a couple of precocious kids. Instead he was broke, far from home and an undischarged bankrupt. So here he was at thirty, on the beach in more ways than one, fit and good looking with a great tan, but none too happy.

He was honest enough to admit that the first culprit in all this was himself but he also knew that Charlie Southampton, formerly the senior partner of Southampton and Gray, Chartered Accountants, of 55 Bishopsgate in the City of London, now serving a five-year sentence for embezzlement, had helped to put him there. Until he met Charlie, he had been on a fast track for success. A scholarship to

Balliol College, Oxford, a first in classics and a full blue for squash, coupled with the benefit of an English mother and an American father, gave him the right credentials for a life in business, and when he decided to train as an accountant, the handful of firms to which he applied were all favourably impressed.

That was when things began to drift off course. He should have joined an international megafirm, endured three years of tedious training and added an important line to his CV. Instead, he joined Southampton and Gray, a minnow compared to the other firms interested in his services. Why? It came down to ego. Oliver was ambitious and Charlie was a master of subtle flattery. At the interview, he was expansive. No hard handshake and steely glare. Instead, a wave to the drinks tray, a large gin and tonic and then his opening gambit: 'I'm not getting any younger,' confided in a friendly rumble between sips of his drink. 'Someone will have to take over the reins here. You'll have to do a stint in the trenches, of course. We all did, but it won't be too bad.' He winked a watery eye. Of course, the Old Bunningtonian tie, black with turquoise and silver stripes, worn by both men helped to ensure an easy communication. Oliver was hooked.

And, indeed, the next three years passed painlessly enough. Charlie Southampton liked his weekly game of squash and an articled clerk with a squash blue was an added plus. Oliver had the sense not to pretend that they could play on level terms but by giving Charlie a six-point start they could have a half way decent game. Occasionally he let Charlie win. His reward was an entrée into a society that extended to dinners at the Southamptons' flat in Onslow Square and weekends at their Sussex estate. There he played tennis with daughter Serena, too, whose boyish figure and short tennis dress seemed to offer other more interesting games at some unspecified future date. Three years on, Oliver felt he was almost one of the family.

So it was not a total surprise when Charlie called him in just after his finals and told him that he was to become a junior partner. He brushed Oliver's thanks aside. 'I'm sure you'll do the firm proud,' he said cheerfully, pouring the usual G and T. The creases on his mottled face had deepened noticeably in three years.

'Any advice for a new partner?' asked Oliver

'Use your head.' Charlie paused. 'And be loyal, of course; that's important.'

Oliver would soon learn just how seriously Charlie meant him to take that admonition. Three weeks' later, Charlie beckoned him into his office at 6pm on a Friday, when everyone else had left. An empty glass and a pile of papers sat in front of him on the big mahogany desk.

'Do us a favour, need your John Hancock on something.' He pushed a folder across the leather desktop. Inside were two unsigned sets of an audit report of the kind that it was the firm's bread and butter business to generate. Each set had been collated and stapled, and an envelope prepared and franked ready to post. All that remained was for the reports to be signed and mailed.

Oliver's first reaction was to decline, politely. It was never wise to sign something you had not studied. He looked at the name on the title page, and then at Charlie, who nodded.

'It's the UMAT account, a somewhat tedious cross I have to bear.'

UMAT, the United Association of Machine Tool Manufacturers and Traders, was a trade association with a budget of a million pounds a year, solid businessmen trying to sustain an industry under pressure from its Far Eastern competitors. It had assets of several million pounds. Charlie might grumble about the work but in fact it was an entity he had promoted himself with a view to earning a generous audit fee every year and another fee for keeping the books.

'It needs a partner's signature but I can't sign since I am on the board. Harry Blunt usually does it but he's on holiday. It needs to go out tonight.'

Charlie looked a bit pink around the gills, thought Oliver, but that was par for the course on a Friday afternoon. The older man may have noticed some reluctance in Oliver's face because he held up a hand, which shook slightly. 'Bit unfair to ask you to sign sight unseen, eh? Why don't you take a peep at the bank reconciliation, the papers are in the file. Money in the bank, balance agrees with the statement from Barclays. Everything is in apple-pie order.'

Oliver opened the file and glanced at the working papers. They supported Charlie's comments. Feeling slightly ungracious, he signed the reports and pushed them over to Charlie.

'Thanks, old man. Now, how about a nip to start the weekend?' He poured Oliver a drink and refilled his own glass.

The following week, the trouble began. At a board meeting, which Charlie did not attend, the directors unexpectedly decided to sell shares to the value of roughly a million pounds. The proceeds were to be spent on advertising. It was a reasonable business deci-sion. The problem was that the shares turned out to be missing. They had been sold on the instructions of one C. Southampton. Had Oliver conducted even a reasonably diligent audit before signing his name to the unqualified audit report, he would have noticed their absence. From there on, the descent was swift. It turned out that Charlie had been gambling at Crockfords and losing heavily. Ironically, many of his outings had been with his colleagues from UMAT, most of whom were pretty well heeled and enjoyed a little gambling with their pal Charlie. Charlie had tried to make matters better by doubling up but only made them much worse. Desperate, he ended up helping himself to UMAT's cash. It had been going on for several years.

The upshot? Charlie went to prison. So did the other partner, Harry Blunt, whose signing of the audit report in past years was deemed criminal conspiracy. Oliver escaped jail on account of his youth and inexperience but he had to suffer a judicial tongue-lashing he was unlikely to forget. 'Unbelievably careless' was some of the milder language the judge used.

Worse was to come. In a civil suit, damages were awarded against the three partners – Charlie Southampton, Harry Blunt and

Oliver himself. Southampton turned out to have been heavily indebted for years, his properties mortgaged to the hilt, his net worth zero. Blunt, a free-spending yuppie, was equally impoverished. The firm had insurance but due to an oversight, Oliver's name had not yet been added to the list of covered partners in the files of the insurance company so he found himself on the hook for a million pounds. He went to see a distinguished bankruptcy lawyer, Victor Aronson, QC, in Kings Bench Walk, who explained that, with care, he could probably be discharged for a much smaller amount. Quixotically and against his advice, Oliver insisted on remaining fully liable.

So he emerged an undischarged bankrupt and a negative millionaire. The firm of Southampton and Gray ceased to exist. That was two years ago. Since then he had repaid a few thousand pounds out of his earnings but he still had a very long way to go to make full amends. One might say, he reflected sadly, that gambling – not his but Southampton's – had been his downfall. Now he was setting out to help another gambler in distress and the irony was not lost on him.

He gazed out to sea. It was hurricane season in Florida. Gulls wheeled above the white-yellow sand. He winced in irritation at the jarring screech and rumble behind him as the traffic barrelled northwards on Atlantic Boulevard. Chewing on a hamburger and watching the slight swell on the ocean, he felt oddly sad. There was plenty to like about Fort Lauderdale. The bright enamel colours were still as pleasing as when he had come to live here three years ago as a 'forensic accountant,' a kind of financial investigator which was the path he had chosen to follow since the debacle at Southampton and Gray. But he had grown restless and moved south to the island of Tortola after less than a year.

It was the urbanization that got him down. He caught an unwelcome whiff of automobile exhausts mixed with suntan oil as he finished his meal and drove his rented car back to town to revisit

Larry Smith. He wanted to ask the headstrong retiree, who had bet and lost every penny of his and his wife's money, for the paperwork relating to his debts. He would need it if he was going to help.

CHAPTER 2

TORTOLA

*T*HE DAY BEFORE, Oliver had received a summons from his biggest client and fellow Tortola resident, the reclusive Carlton Tisch.

'Come and see me,' said Tisch, typically terse.

'Why?' asked Oliver, irritated. He had promised himself a day's scuba diving.

'I want to talk to you.'

'I was on my way out to the reef.'

'This is work. The fish will have to wait.'

Occasionally Oliver asked himself why he had quit a town like Fort Lauderdale with a half-way decent social life in favour of a mountainous Caribbean island with barely 24,000 inhabitants. It made more sense, though, when he took into account Tortola's fabulous white beaches and its booming financial services industry.

The island was a tax haven. It was home to thousands of offshore companies. Although it was a British colony, the US dollar was the official currency and businessmen from both sides of the Atlantic felt at home there. In Roadtown, the island's modest capital, salt-caked yachtsmen rubbed shoulders with the bankers and accountants striding down Main Street in navy pinstripe trousers (but without jackets, not in 85-degree heat).

There was a good reason why Tortola's pristine beaches were often deserted: there were no direct flights, either from the United States or Europe. Visitors from USA had to change at San Juan in Puerto Rico and finish their journey by propeller plane. Which was just how Tortolans liked it, by the way. If you didn't like flying in small airplanes, that was too bad – you chilled out and caught the ferry from neighbouring St. Thomas.

The road up to Carlton Tisch's estate was rutted and full of potholes. As Oliver's jeep bounced along the path, a grazing goat looked up for just long enough to glare resentfully at him before resuming its lunch. When he reached the deceptively rustic villa on its rocky point, he parked on the tree-shaded gravel drive in front. The house, while not large, was built high on a cliff commanding a superb view south over the sparkling blue Sir Francis Drake Channel. He walked round the island-style building onto a patio facing the ocean and came face to face with Carlton Tisch.

He never felt quite at ease with Tisch. The gulf between them was too great. Like Oliver, Tisch was deeply suntanned but any physical resemblance ended there. Where Oliver was an even six feet, Tisch needed Cuban heels to reach five feet. While Oliver walked easily with the balanced gait of a sportsman, Tisch tended to strut jerkily, like a chicken. And yet, as Oliver knew, the little man was strong physically: an expert sailor who could also hold his own on a tennis court. And he had persistence in spades. Perhaps that was what made Oliver uneasy; so far he had got by using charm, the odd-well chosen Greek or Latin quotation and an easy smile on his mobile, cherubic face. There was nothing cherubic about Tisch whose habitual expression was a challenging glare. Quote the classics at him and you got a 'God give me strength' and a rolling of the eyes or at best a sardonic grin.

Tisch was sitting out in the sun, in grubby week-old jockey shorts, chewing a pencil and jotting fitfully in the margin of his wife's *House and Garden*.

'What are you doing?' asked Oliver.

'I'm buying a business.'

He did not look capable of buying a business unless it was a very small one. Watery blue eyes and grey stubble said 'beachcomber' of uncertain age. His short, skinny body was tanned nut-brown, his chest a thicket of grey curls. 'Large or small?'

'Depends on your standards.'

'How much is it worth?'

'Do you mean, how much is it *really* worth, or how much am I paying for it?'

'Both.'

'If I tell you, you must promise not to buy any shares before Tuesday,' Tisch leered.

Oliver sighed. 'I promise.'

'We're offering nine bucks a share but they're worth sixteen.'

'How many shares?'

'Altogether? A hundred million.'

Oliver rubbed his chin. 'Let's see, nine from sixteen is seven, seven times a hundred million. That's $700 million profit.'

Tisch nodded.

'That's a lot of money for an afternoon's work.'

'I'm only in for a quarter of that personally.' Tisch sounded defensive. They had had this kind of discussion before.

'Well, I guess that makes everything all right,' said Oliver sarcastically.

'I'm creating wealth for the economy,' Tisch said.

He looked Oliver straight in the eye, holding the pose for a second, then looked away, grinning.

Oliver sighed.

'What I don't get is, if it's so easy, how come everyone doesn't do this?'

Tisch shrugged. 'Maybe they just enjoy working eight hours a day, five days a week.'

Arrogant jerk, thought Oliver, who was a sometime investor himself, but not on Tisch's scale. He knew there was more to the process than Tisch liked to pretend.

For one thing, he had probably rendered the transaction risk-free by lining up allies in advance – big stockholders willing to vote in favour of the bid. Without that, Tisch could be left holding a pile of stock bought using borrowed money and facing serious losses.

'Is it a profitable business?' Oliver asked.

'It will meet our projections.'

'How do you know? Have you kicked the tyres, checked out the nuts and bolts so to speak?'

'Sort of.'

Oliver looked sceptical. 'Or have you just read a few pages of figures?'

'You don't know that.'

Tisch sighed a 'Lord help me' sigh. 'Let me try and explain. This business has four factories and a hundred retail outlets, okay?'

'If you say so.'

'Of which one plant and a dozen outlets are losing money.'

'So?'

'So we set up a "restructuring reserve" to cover the cost of closing the loss-makers. We backdate the reserve, of course. That puts the blame on the previous owners.'

Oliver half understood. 'So you make those losses go away?'

'Yes but we go one better: We set the reserve good and high. Then we bring any unused reserves back as profit the next year.'

Oliver looked shocked. 'Is that legal?'

'Sure it is.'

'But it would have to be a good faith reserve, right?'

'Of course.'

'Not just something to help you cook the books?'

Tisch stared at him coldly. Then he laughed and clapped him on the back.

'That's not why I wanted to see you.'

'Well?'

'I have a job for you. You doing anything right now? Let's go sailing. Hop in the truck.'

He was a bad driver, alarmingly fast. Oliver hung on nervously as the vehicle bucked and bounced over the rutted path down to the marina. But twenty minutes later they were out in blue water, running before a healthy breeze, with a line out for bass or snapper. Or anything, come to that. The boat, *Goneril*, Tisch's passion, was trimmed. There was no sign of bad weather, no feeder bands from Hurricane Daisy. Those would come later. Daisy was less than 36 hours away, a Force Five according to the TV weather men. And Tortola was slap in the forecast path.

Tisch fished two Budweisers out of the cooler and handed Oliver one.

'Are you a gambler?'

'Depends what you mean.'

'Horses? Football?'

Oliver laughed cheerfully. 'I can't tell a tight end from a horse's ass. I enjoy a game of blackjack, though.'

'How often?'

'I go to Las Vegas maybe twice a year. Or Atlantic City. It depends which coast I happen to be on. I kill a couple of days playing cards. I may lose a thousand dollars.'

'Ever win?'

'Rarely.'

'You're hardly a high roller. More of a minnow.'

'I accept the characterization.'

'That may be an advantage in this particular case.'

'What case?'

'I need you to do a couple of days work for me.'

He had Oliver's attention. June in the Caribbean was conducive to bouts of island fever – the need to leave, go anywhere as long as it was off the island.

Besides, two days probably meant two weeks – Tisch had a grandiose way of seeing things only in terms of results and usually underestimated the time required. He would think of a solution and consider it done, instantaneously.

Tisch produced a watertight metal box from which he took out a Monte Cristo cigar which he lit. His voice dropped to a mutter.

'A friend of mine, Larry Smith, is in trouble.'

Carlton Tisch had a mannerism that infuriated Oliver. Whenever the little financier was expounding a line of thought that he particularly wanted his listener to understand, he tended to speak quieter and quieter, lowering his voice until it faded away completely in a mumbling diminuendo. You had to say 'Speak up, Carlton' loudly, usually more than once, whereupon his eyes would flash resentfully at being made to repeat himself.

The wind whistled in the rigging, drowning out whatever the small man was trying to communicate.

'Speak up, Carlton,' said Oliver patiently.

Carlton scowled. 'If you will just pay attention.'

With occasional pauses to check the fishing lines, he explained, 'Larry used to work for me. He ran a garden tools business that I bought when the owners had some huge family quarrel. I got a good price.

Tisch always got a good price, thought Oliver.

'Larry is an upstanding kind of guy. Straight back, military moustache, likes to cuss but popular with his employees. Hot second wife, 35 years his junior. Last year he retired and moved to Fort Lauderdale. He has just one problem – he loves to gamble. While he was still working, he kept the urge under control. But with time on his hands, the bug bit. He got involved with an on-line casino, placing big bets from his home computer. Things went downhill fast. In no time he had maxed out his credit cards – over $100,000. His wife called me, at her wits end. I talked to Larry and it turned out things were really bad. After the credit cards, he had also managed to clean out their joint checking account.'

'So now they're broke?'

'They limp along. He still has his pension and social security. Madeleine intercepts the cheques and uses them to buy three money orders – one for the mortgage, one for his life insurance and one for her Jaguar payment.'

'She sounds like a fortune hunter.

Carlton laughed. 'She also knows Larry.'

'How is their relationship?'

'Not bad, considering the financial strains. But now the casino people are pressuring him for a major repayment.'

'How major?'

'Fifty thousand by next week.'

'Or?'

'Or they send the enforcers.'

'Does he have the money?'

'No.'

'Have you considered lending it to him?'

A silly question. Carlton's eyes flickered. Putting his own money at risk wasn't how he worked, he was not cast in the Robin Hood mould.

'What do you want me to do?'

'Sort it out,' Carlton said. He gave Oliver a half smile.

'Why me?'

'Why not?'

'Am I supposed to single handedly intimidate a gang of violent criminals?'

'No. But you can follow a financial trail, which is what it will take. And you are young and energetic. And we need to do something about this.'

Oliver sighed. 'Where is all this happening?'

'The Smiths live in Fort Lauderdale.'

'Well, that's a relief, at least it's warm there. The last time I worked for you I ended up in Philadelphia,' Oliver complained. He craved the warmth of the sun and was never comfortable without it.

'You are still living comfortably on the fee from that job, may I remind you?'

Oliver shook his head. 'I have never trusted Philadelphia, not since they moved the statue of Rocky from the Art Museum steps.'

'Now you're whining,' said Tisch curtly. 'Everything turned out well.'

I suppose he's right, thought Oliver grudgingly. The target in that affair had been the CEO of a major hedge fund. The man was a pillar of the community, a patron of the local symphony orchestra and so on but he had been cooking the books for years. He had managed to fool everyone. Everyone except Carlton, that is.

Carlton had smelled a rat because he was a bit of a rat himself. He had sent Oliver to Philadelphia where Oliver got to know a young woman in accounts receivable and bought her a few drinks. She apparently nursed a resentment about a non-promotion because the floodgates opened. Apparently the CEO had been manipulating the bad loans reserve every year in order to justify huge bonuses for himself. The woman provided names and numbers.

Armed with this information, Carlton Tisch stood up at the annual stockholders' meeting and asked a question. That loose pebble started an avalanche that swept away the CEO and half the board of directors. The stock price plunged and never recovered.

Oliver's pay cheque was generous. Tisch apparently thought he was worth the fee but Oliver had not quite understood why, so he waited until after a good dinner and an excellent bottle of claret and confronted Tisch point blank.

'You owned stock in that company. The price tanked. Why are you happy?'

Tisch shook his head. 'I sold in time.'

'Isn't that insider trading?'

'I'm not an insider, just a stockholder.'

'What about your friends? Did you tip them off?'

Tisch frowned. 'I would prefer to say that they received good investment advice.'

Tisch's friends were pros. They would have bailed out quietly, early on. There was a jerk on the line. Tisch reeled in a young two-foot bass that thrashed wildly until he unhooked it and threw it back.

'I don't understand one thing,' said Oliver thoughtfully.

'What's that?'

'Larry Smith's creditors. The lenders. Are they supposed to just forgive the debt, give Larry a free pass?'

Tisch scowled. 'And your point is?'

'Well, isn't that asking rather a lot? Your friend Smith really does owe the money.'

'Gambling debts are not legally enforceable,' Tisch growled. 'He needs help, damn it. Whose side are you on?' Tisch grew pale under his tan when he was annoyed.

'I'm not convinced,' said Oliver.

'Shakespeare said, "To err is human, to forgive divine".'

'I think that was Alexander Pope and I doubt if he had gambling in mind.'

Tisch threw up his hands. 'I frankly don't care. We've got to get the man off the hook.'

He was visibly irritated – he had a low threshold of patience – but Oliver wasn't ready to concede.

'It won't be easy if it's an Internet operation. How do I find the physical address of a computer web site? Where do I start?'

'Talk to Larry.'

Oliver was feeling a growing lack of sympathy for Larry. 'I can't get excited about your friend, frankly. He got himself into this.'

'So do it out of sympathy for his wife.'

'Why? She married the jerk.'

'Do it for me, then.' Carlton tried unconvincingly to look pathetic. 'His daughter is quite a looker by the way,' he added slyly.

Oliver raised an eyebrow.

'Twenty five and ripe.' Carlton, who was 60, considered himself an authority on younger women – he had recently married one. Mimi Tisch, née Entwistle, wife number three, was from Huddersfield in Yorkshire, a bunny girl whom he met at the London Playboy Club a year earlier and had married within a month. The pre-nup was rumoured to be generous so he must have fallen heavily. Since then he had tried repeatedly to fix Oliver up.

'Bimbo?'

'Nope. Degree from Princeton.'

'Degree in what?'

'I don't know,' Tisch said exasperated. 'I don't ask these things.' But he could see Oliver was intrigued.

'At least check her out.'

Oliver decided it was time to back off. He had made his point but Tisch's friend was in real trouble and the financier was obviously upset.

He sighed.

'I suppose I'm not all that busy at the moment.'

Tisch whipped out a shiny mobile phone and grinned. 'Satellite job, works anywhere.'

He dialled a number.

'Larry, this is Carl. I have someone I want you to talk to.'

There was a long pause.

'About your situation.'

Another pause.

'Trust him? Of course I trust him.'

Oliver overheard sounds of annoyance.

'Just talk to him, okay?'

Tisch handed Oliver the instrument. Oliver refrained from tossing it overboard. 'Hi,' he said.

'What do you want?' An older voice, quavering.

Oliver muttered something bland about wanting to help.

'Impossible,' barked Smith.

Oliver sighed. Obviously little would be achieved by phone.

'Can I come and see you?'

There was reluctant agreement. But it was not an encouraging start.

An hour later they were back at Tisch's house. The traditional appearance of the island-style home concealed a very un-traditional framework of steel struts and piles anchored deep in the living rock and built to withstand the strongest of hurricanes.

They sat on the terrace, watching afternoon sun play on the blue waves. Mimi Tisch came out of the house in a white tennis dress and planted a friendly kiss on Oliver's cheek.

'Off on one of Carl's crazy projects?'

'That's about it.'

'Well, stay out of trouble,' she said cheerfully.

'If I get into trouble, I'll call Carlton.'

'Don't call,' said Tisch.'

Oliver went home to pack, nursing a minor resentment at being enlisted in a cause he did not support.

At home, he switched on CNN. An earnest announcer was issuing warnings about Hurricane Daisy. At that very moment Daisy was destroying property and taking lives on Montserrat with winds gusting up to 160 miles per hour. That made her a Class 5, the worst. She was driving north at twelve miles an hour.

A week earlier, hurricane Charlie had sideswiped Tortola, leaving snapped power lines and mountains of debris. On Cuba, it had killed fifteen people. Now, Daisy was due in a day or two.

On either side of Oliver's house, his neighbours were busy securing loose items. There were logs and branches left over from Charlie that could become deadly projectiles in a high wind Oliver opened his front door – the wood-frame house was at sea level just a block from the beach – and stared out at the ocean. The water was choppy but not yet frightening.

He envied the Tisch family their fortified retreat up on the hill. They would be safe and sound, come the hurricane. That was Carlton, always compulsive, always prepared. He would literally be staying cool thanks to a Honda standby generator and a hundred gallon propane tank.

He closed the door.

Moments later it flew open unceremoniously and a young black woman bustled in.

'Hi, Oliver.'

'Hi, Rose.'

Rose, who was young and pretty, was his cleaner. The neighbours probably thought something was going on between them but Oliver had more sense. Rose was from a large Tortola family. One brother was head of the fire department; another worked for the Governor, big strapping guys. Inter-racial romance was fine with Oliver and probably with Rose, too, but Tortola was a small island. A falling out could be embarrassing.

Still, he enjoyed watching her work. The strip of golden flesh between her shirt and the waistband of her jeans inspired pleasant thoughts. She also cleaned for Mimi Tisch; he wondered idly if Rose had the same effect on Carlton.

She finished mopping the kitchen floor and straightened up. Hands on hips, she glared at him in mock exasperation: 'All this travel! If you had a wife, she'd soon put a stop to your gallivanting.'

He grinned. 'That's why I don't have one. I'm married to my work.'

He spoke with irony but it was true. He saw himself as shining a cleansing light into murky corners of a financial world. He resented the fact that many so-called financial advisors were no more than sharks, deceiving others for gain. When stockbrokers conned small savers into heavily fee-laden funds, it made his blood boil. And as for the pseudo hedge funds, investment *flavour du jour* that charged huge fees for unfulfilled promises, call it salesmanship or whatever you wanted – to him it was stealing.

It was time to go. Before leaving the house, he googled 'Casinos' and 'Internet.' He got several thousand hits. He printed out a few pages that looked promising and stuffed them in his bag to read on the aeroplane.

Fred Entwistle, Mimi's dad and Carlton Tisch's father-in-law, drove him to the airport. A dour Yorkshireman of fifty or so, with sandy hair and a bland face, he did odd jobs for Carlton. He was obsessively careful with money and reputedly still had the first penny he ever earned. He drove an elderly Chevrolet with all the windows down, flooding the car with warm evening air.

He also had a powerful curiosity.

'Business trip, is it?'

'Something like that.'

'Must be nice to understand finance, you being an accountant and all.'

'It's okay.'

CHAPTER 3

MIAMI

A T MIAMI AIRPORT, Oliver rented a car. Then he checked into his favourite Miami hotel, the Mutiny in Coconut Grove. From there he drove to Versailles, the gaudy, bustling Cuban restaurant on 'Calle Ocho' – West 8th Street – a popular eating place of the Cuban American community.

At the brightly lit restaurant he ordered roast pork slathered in garlic with sweet-fried plantains, black beans and rice. Around him, several generations of Cuban Americans animatedly discussed the hated Fidel Castro and the shortcomings of life in the United States. It reminded him very much of his student years in London when Polish friends would take him to Daquise in South Kensington to rub shoulders with ancient Polish aristocrats suffering the same pangs of nostalgia.

Afterwards he stood outside on the pavement and sipped sweet black Cuban coffee from a tiny china cup in the warm night air. He would drive the remaining thirty miles to Fort Lauderdale in the morning.

CHAPTER 4

INTRODUCING MADELEINE SMITH

L ARRY SMITH lived in an expensive subdivision on the outskirts of Fort Lauderdale. A chiselled granite plaque outside wrought iron gates displayed its name, Forest Lake, but oddly enough there was no forest and no real lake, just rows of almost identical villas with pillared porticos and well-watered lawns backing onto a man-made retention pond with a fountain in the middle. Nothing looked more than five years old.

Oliver pressed the doorbell. The opening bars of Dixie – 'I wish I was in the land of cotton' – pealed from within, electronically generated. The contrast with his Hispanic surroundings the night before was total; he was definitely not on Calle Ocho anymore.

A well-dressed young woman opened the door. She smiled at him, a gracious country-club kind of smile.

'Mr. Steele! Hi, I'm Madeleine Smith. Welcome to our home.'

He shook the proffered hand – long and white, with scarlet nails – and noted the weak grip. But her glance and the touch of her hand triggered an electric reaction in Oliver that startled him. For a moment he could not figure why; then he realized her striking resemblance to a girl he had loved a decade ago.

Whenever Oliver took stock of his sex life, he came to the unde- niably vulgar conclusion that he wished he had slept with more women. He realized he shared this regret with much of the world's male population but he felt it strongly anyway. He had had a number of relationships, typically lasting for a year or so before his partner got tired of waiting for him to make some kind of commitment but now, at the age of 30, he had no serious attachment. He did have some good female friends who played a significant part in his life and who must have had generous natures because they were still willing to take his phone calls despite his chronic vagueness about his relationship with them, but there were also some, he reflected wryly, who would have nothing whatever to do with him.

The girl Virginia, whose memory Madeleine Smith evoked so powerfully, was in the latter group. She was dark, shapely and the great-granddaughter of a South African mining magnate. He had met her at a Commem ball in his final year at Oxford, to which she had come as the partner of someone else, but the attraction had been visceral and they had consummated their union in his cramped college bedsitting room by the grey light of dawn the following morning. Unfortunately, besides being eighteen, voluptuous and possessed of a wicked grin, Virginia was accustomed to an expensive lifestyle; even before his fall from financial grace, he had found her to be a costly proposition. For some time they had met regularly, usually for an expensive dinner and a mutually satisfying romp afterwards without much in the way of conversation. But when, shortly after the debacle at Southampton and Gray, he attempted to explain to her his reduced circumstances he encountered a definite chill. It became apparent that for Virginia he was now damaged goods, both as a provider of amusement and as a potential marriage partner. Shortly after dinner, in a frosty atmosphere, he had returned her to her flat in Belgravia having learned a sobering lesson.

So, as he met Madeleine Smith now, he felt conflicting emotions. The jolt of physical attraction tugged one way, the warning that beauty is as beauty does and was not always friendly towards him, tugged the other. He swallowed, reminded himself to concentrate on the job at hand and stepped across the threshold.

Madeleine Smith was well dressed in a silk blouse and tailored skirt; she was also carefully made up, maybe a bit too carefully for so early in the day. Was that in his honour? Anxiety lines edging her brown eyes hinted that all might not be tranquil in Forest Lake.

'Let me take you through to Larry.'

He caught a whiff of alcohol on her breath as she ushered him into a heavily decorator-influenced hallway. A bottle of Johnnie Walker and a sherry decanter stood on a tray on the Chinese lacquer dresser. The decanter was half-empty, the stopper missing. A mother of pearl dragon glared at Oliver from the dresser.

At the rear of the house, she knocked on a closed door.

'Come.'

The word was barked rather than spoken. She showed Oliver into a suburban father's den with bowling trophies, a computer, photos of Smith with a woman, presumably his first wife, and two laughing teenagers. There was another, larger, picture of Madeleine alone in an expensive leather frame.

Smith was handsome in a conventional way but older than Oliver had expected. He turned away from the computer, oddly furtive and Oliver wondered if he had blanked the screen to hide what he had been doing.

'You boys want coffee?' Madeleine asked.

Smith shook his head irritably.

She hovered as if hoping to be included, then gave up.

'I'll leave you two to get acquainted.'

Smith waved Oliver to a chair and glared enquiringly at him.

Oliver nodded pleasantly. 'Carlton says hi!'

Smith was dressed as if for golf in tan shirt and slacks but he looked somehow out of place without a business suit. His face was red, either from the sun or from hypertension, and his hand shook slightly as he teased a cigarette from a pack of Marlboros. A big ashtray was empty but ash had spilled onto the tooled leather desktop as if it had been emptied recently. His mouth was set in a frown, but he spoke civilly enough.

'How is he?'

'Well. Doing a lot of sailing.'

'Did he send you to straighten me out?'

'He says you're in a spot of trouble.'

'He's a worrier. I know, I used to work for him.'

'I work for him, too. Most of the time, when he worries, he's right.'

Smith shook his head dismissively.

Oliver got the impression he was wavering between denial and acceptance. Finally the words came.

'I had a run of bad luck.'

'How so?'

'It's a long story. How much time do you have?'

Oliver shrugged. 'It would help to know the history.'

'You want to know how I got so messed up?'

He had only smoked half the Marlboro but he crushed it and lit another. He tapped the computer keyboard and the screen sprang alive in a blaze of colour.

Oliver leaned forward to look.

It was the home page of a casino web site with slot machines, flashing lights and coloured buttons.

Smith grinned sardonically. 'What's your pleasure?'

A row of coloured tabs along the top border bore the names of various games – poker, blackjack, roulette. Just below that, there was a row of national flags; by pressing a button Oliver could also play in French, German, Japanese or Mandarin. Payment could be made in dollars, euros or yen.

'Will I need money?'

'You can practise for free.'

Oliver looked at him.

'Yeah, that's how I got started.'

'Are there any limits on spending?'

'On this site, no. Some of the other places have a $5000 dollar limit.'

'Per player?'

'Per credit card.'

'How many credit cards do you have?'

'Eleven.'

'Eleven?'

He smiled guiltily. 'I had them for the business. I just kept them after I retired.'

'How does your family feel about your gambling?'

'My wife's ready to shoot me.'

'And your kids?' Oliver nodded at the photo. 'Is that your daughter?'

'Yes,' Smith said. There was a silence. 'She doesn't live here.'

But he seemed willing to talk. Maybe it was easier with Oliver than with his wife.

'Do you play on more than one web site?'

He nodded.

'I suppose by playing several sites you can max out your cards?'

'You got it.'

'Carlton said you tapped into your checking account, too?' Oliver probed gently.

'That was on a different site. They offer "cash only" gaming for people with problem credit.'

'How did you find that site?'

'I didn't. They found me.'

'How?'

'I got an e-mail. They have ways of finding suckers, I guess.'

'Did you write cheques to them?'

'I signed a electronic check authorization. It's like auto-paying your insurance or your phone bill.'

Oliver winced. 'So they could tap straight into your bank account. For how much?'

'Whatever I owed them.'

'It was a joint account and yet your wife didn't know?'

'She doesn't read bank statements – she leaves that to me.'

'Well she certainly knows now. When did she find out?'

'When her cheques started to bounce.' He grimaced. 'Her hair-dresser, her women's group…'

No wonder she was angry, thought Oliver. Her shame must have been total.

'But why is the casino still chasing you? I thought you were cleaned out.'

'When I ran out of cash they let me borrow.'

This was getting increasingly depressing. 'How does that work?'

Smith's mottled face was a study in embarrassment.

'I signed promissory notes. On the Internet.'

'How can someone sign their name on the Internet?'

'Well, I checked a box on the screen. It's the same.'

'Is that legally binding?'

'They said so.'

Oliver stared at him.

Finally Smith said, 'Stupid, huh?'

'How much are you in for?'

'There's the credit cards for $110,000. Plus $70,000 on the notes. Plus late fees.'

'Carlton thought you only owed $100,000.'

'That was last month.'

'What sort of threats have you been getting?'

'Nothing I can't handle.'

'Can you be a bit more specific?'

'They want fifty grand by the end of the week.'

'Or what?'

'They didn't say.'

'In what form do they want payment?'

'Cash or certified check.'

'Can you pay them anything?'

He shook his head. 'The well is dry.'

There was silence in the room except for the soft hum of the air conditioning.

Finally, Oliver asked 'Do you ever intend to pay?'

Smith gave Oliver a withering look. 'Of course, I always pay my debts.'

'Well, isn't that nice! Where will you get the money?'

'Sooner or later my luck will change. I'm due.'

Oliver flinched at the denial, it was hard not to. Here was a man prepared to destroy his finances, his family and his life. It spelled addiction. It really did not matter whether his problem was greed, faulty synapses in the brain or just sheer wilfulness. If you stripped away the psychobabble and got past the hand wringing, you saw the ugly truth – he was a hard case, an addict.

A thought struck Oliver.

'Can I see one of the notes?'

The lender was Security Financings Ltd, an Antigua corporation. It was a demand note, so the lender could call it in at any time. The interest rate was high – although no higher than some credit cards. As Oliver had feared, the borrower also had agreed to pay legal costs and collection expenses. That was ominous.

'I don't see an address. How do you get in touch with them?'

'They said they would call me.'

'I don't like the sound of that.'

He bristled. 'I was in the military; they don't scare me. I'm not even being shot at.'

That could change, Oliver thought. But he said, 'I'd like to help.'

'What exactly can you do?'

'I'm not sure,' Oliver said.

He wrote down the Internet address of the website where Smith had signed the promissory notes.

As he left, Smith was turning back to his computer.

Madeleine Smith emerged from the kitchen as he was making for the door. She stood near him on the doorstep, their faces close together.

'Is there anything you can do?', she asked.

'To change him? No.'

She sighed. 'Addicts don't get better until they really want to, right?'

'Maybe he could try a twelve-step group, like Alcoholics Anonymous?' said Oliver. 'There are groups for everything nowadays.'

Even as he spoke he bit his tongue remembering the Johnnie Walker bottle. He foresaw testing times for the Smiths.

'How much do his kids know about this?'

'Not much, they aren't often here. Larry Jr. is at business school in California. I didn't want to worry him.'

'What about the daughter?'

'Kathy? She has an apartment down at the beach. She may suspect something but she doesn't know. She probably just thinks Larry and I had a fight.'

'Do you often?'

'What?'

'Fight.'

She blushed. 'Before this, never.'

He wrote down his phone number. 'Call me if you think of anything else.'

He had had enough of the Smith household for one morning. He drove around until he saw a pay phone that still boasted a tattered Yellow Pages and got the address of an Internet cafe. He went straight there and paid two dollars for an hour of computer time.

He was a bit uneasy about becoming a customer of a gambling web site. He did not have an addictive personality but there was always that slight fear of straying onto a risky path, of losing control. However, some research was necessary. So, sitting at the computer, he logged on to the same website Larry Smith had used. He would do a little gambling. By duplicating what Smith had done he might get some ideas.

He had to accept the casino's terms and conditions, six pages of them. He agreed to use his real name. He promised not to use the service for any fraudulent activity including money laundering. If the casino suspected him of any of these things, his access might be terminated. They didn't say it would be, just that it might, artful wording suggesting a fairly permissive attitude. The agreement would be governed by the laws of Antigua and Barbuda. Whatever, he thought. He said 'yes' to everything.

Then they wanted his credit card number. He took a deep breath and gave it up.

After that, it was easy to enter the simulated blackjack room and play. The graphics were lifelike and he soon got into the spirit of things. A video-animated dealer greeted him with a smile. He authorized three hundred dollars on his credit card and the dealer pushed a pile of brightly coloured chips across the green table towards him and said 'Good luck y'all' in a Texas drawl.

At first he had good luck – after a quarter of an hour he was ahead a hundred dollars. Then the dealer started drawing picture cards and no matter how carefully he wagered, splitting aces and doubling down at the right time, his pile began to shrink. His luck was running out.

Or was it? What if luck had nothing to do with it? Was he being systematically cheated by a computer programme where the odds favoured the house excessively? Even though Carlton Tisch was footing the bill, he lost his taste for on-line blackjack in a hurry.

Before exiting the casino website he scanned its screens carefully, looking for a physical address but, beyond the references to Antigua, he could see nothing. He still had a few minutes of computer time left, so he surfed around some of the other gambling sites. A name jumped out at him: Security Financings. It was the same outfit that had issued Larry Smith's promissory notes. Apparently they served more than one casino. They were offering unsecured loans to 'sportsmen with problem credit.' It was a way for people who still had not seen the light to borrow more money and extend their playing time; mugs like Larry Smith in other words.

The concept was stomach-turning, but he sensed that it could provide a starting point for him. There might be some kind of registry or other agency on Antigua with information about the company.

His computer time ran out. He walked out of the air-conditioned Internet store into the baking noonday sun and drove east to the beach. He ordered his hamburger and gazed into space.

A total stranger at the next table, a man of about forty, waved at him. Apparently Oliver was staring at him because he grinned and said, 'Go for it!'

'Excuse me?'

'Whatever it is, go for it.'

He was wiry, with a leathery face and John Lennon glasses. He wore a grubby yellow T-shirt with a map of the Florida Keys.

'Have we met?'

'No. But you look real conflicted about something.'

Oliver laughed. 'Just planning what to do next.'

'Gotcha. Give it a whirl anyway.'

'Maybe I will.'

'There you go.'

The man stood up, jammed a John Deere cap on his head and drove off in a battered truck, honking farewell.

Oliver finished his food, got in his car and drove back to Forest Lake and the Smiths.

When he approached the Smiths' home for the second time that day, a black Lincoln Town Car with smoked windows was parked outside. It had not been there earlier. It was blocking Madeleine Smith's freshly polished Jaguar, which, in turn, was blocking the garage door. Unsure who would be leaving first, Oliver parked his car so as not to hinder the Lincoln's exit.

The air shimmered in the heat. A tiled roof over the small *porte-cochère* provided shade but very little cooling. Walking toward the house, he saw that the door was open, ajar by a few inches. He was surprised. This looked like a safe neighbourhood but in his experience people who lived in air-conditioned homes kept their doors and windows closed in June. As he was about to press the bell, he noticed the wood gleamed raw where the lock had splintered away from the hollow cavity door. Suddenly he could feel his heart pounding in his chest and a prickling of sweat on the back of his neck.

Better take a look, said an inner voice. Be careful, though, it added. So, rather than ringing the doorbell and waiting for an answer, he tiptoed over the threshold. There was nobody in the Mexican-tiled hallway; he padded quietly across it, determined but nervous.

Thinking that if the Smiths had unwelcome visitors, they might be armed, he looked around for something with which to defend himself. Nothing suggested itself as a weapon except a long, thin Giacometti-style bronze statuette, two feet high on a marble plinth. He gripped it by the throat, hefted it, and took a tentative practice swing before edging closer to the living room now. He could hear someone sobbing but the noise did little to prepare him for what he saw when he pushed open the door.

He recognized Larry Smith and his beautiful wife but not the third person, a heavily built man with a shaven bullet head. He wore a dark grey suit, white shirt and black tie, and would have passed for a respectable businessman were he not crouched aggressively over Madeleine Smith, the source of the frantic cries. Her face was a mask of terror. She cowered on the brocade-covered sofa, naked above the waist, and her back pressed hard against the cushions as she shrank back from her assailant. Her silk blouse, clearly torn off her, lay on the rug. To Oliver it looked as if the scene had been in progress for some time. Her husband, secured to a chair with duct tape, was watching helplessly, more duct tape covering his mouth. Blood dripped from a cut on his forehead. It had flowed down his cheek, across the tape and onto his shirt, forming a clotted dark red pool on his chest. His eyes rolled and his elderly shoulders heaved.

Madeleine's assailant had his back to Oliver, but at the sound of his footfall, he turned and straightened. He lunged for Oliver and sent him flying with a shove. Off-balance, Oliver fell to one knee on the tiled floor, dropping the statue which slid away out of reach but he recovered, rising to his feet quickly, fists at the ready. As the two men circled warily, he sized up his opponent. Bullet-head's face was expressionless, which in itself told Oliver that he was dealing with someone with no time for cheap theatrics.

In his boxing days at boarding school, whatever success he had was due not to technical skill but to his ability to deliver a single crushing punch with his right fist, delivered with the pinpoint timing of a perfect golf shot. It was a gift: you either had it or not and sometimes, at least, he had it. He cocked his wrist and launched a massive blow towards the point of his opponent's chin. That, at least was the intention. Landed cleanly, the punch would have dropped Bullethead like a stone but he twisted his head at the last minute and it caught him on the side of the chin. It was still hard enough to stun the heavily built man and he fell like a sack of potatoes.

Oliver turned and held out a hand to Madeleine Smith. She gripped it fiercely and as their eyes met, her lips formed a silent 'thank you.' He helped her stand, then went over to the old man in the chair and started to tug at the strips of grey duct tape around his wrists.

But he had underestimated the toughness of Bullet-head. With his back turned he barely heard a last-minute warning cry from Madeleine as something hard crashed into his skull. He slipped on the glazed floor and fell awkwardly, his head hitting the tiles. He had a sense of his assailant making for the door before grey clouds swirled round his throbbing skull and obscured his vision. He struggled desperately against the seductive urge to pass out but after a few seconds he lost the unequal battle and collapsed.

When he recovered consciousness, he was lying flat on his back on the cold tiles of the Smiths' living room. His head throbbed painfully. The Giacometti statue lay in a corner in pieces – the bronze figure separated from its marble base.

Madeleine was trying to untie her husband but making little progress. She was clearly not good with duct tape.

Oliver hauled himself upright and tottered over to them. 'You need scissors,' he muttered.

She seemed not to hear. Her blouse was still lying on the floor. She picked it up and wrapped it round her shoulders, with a sideways glance at him, before going into the kitchen and reappearing with some household shears.

'Are you okay?' she asked Oliver.

'No, my head hurts, but thanks for asking.'

He turned to Smith. 'Hold still.' He snipped the tape away from Smith's mouth.

The old man was as white as a sheet. His eyes were rolling in his head. He opened his mouth, but his wife spoke first. 'Happy now?' she snapped.

He flinched. After a second, he muttered:

'Where's the nitro?'

She rummaged in her purse. 'He had bypass surgery last year,' she said. Finding a tiny bottle, she slipped a nitro-glycerine pill under his tongue. She had a look of 'how on earth did I get involved in all this?'

'What in God's name was that about,' she asked Oliver.

'You tell me.'

'That man just broke in. It happened so fast. I heard a crash at the front door and suddenly he was in the living room.'

'Well, I guess we know who sent him,' said Oliver.

'He asked for money. I told him there wasn't any but he wouldn't listen.'

'And things went downhill from there? Well, he's gone, so apparently he felt he had made his point.'

'He was just trying to scare us,' said Larry Smith.

'Did a decent job by the look of things,' said Oliver. 'Sorry about the Giacometti,' he added.

'It's only a copy,' said Smith.

'Oh, for God's sake.' Madeleine snapped. She ran out of the room.

'I apologize for my wife,' said Smith.

'No problem,' said Oliver. He looked around. 'Well, I need to leave but I want to take one of those loan notes you signed.'

Smith tottered next door, rummaged in his desk and handed Oliver a manila folder.

'Here, take the whole file. Where are you going?'

'To work on your case. I've got a few ideas.' He paused. 'Do you keep a gun in the house?'

Smith nodded. 'A shotgun. I used to hunt.'

'Keep it handy. Use it if you have to. It sends a message.'

Madeleine reappeared, dabbing her eyes with a Kleenex.

Her husband had sat down on the sofa. He looked shrunken and old. Oliver felt sorry for him but somewhat less sorry for Madeleine.

She walked Oliver to the door.

'Thank you so much.'

'I didn't do anything.'

'If you hadn't come by...'

In the silence, both their imaginations were working.

She laid a hand on his shoulder but did not meet his eye. They were pro forma thanks, he thought, she says it but she doesn't mean it, she's thinking something else.

He moved towards his car. 'Better get your husband to hospital, have him checked out,' he said irritably.

Driving back to Miami airport he chided himself for being so critical. He was probably expecting too much. Everyone was overwrought.

He had to admit to himself that he was finally intrigued by the whole case. He was not emotionally engaged with the Smiths; he had not warmed to them despite their predicament. But it was a job and an intellectual challenge. It might take his mind off his own bankruptcy. Professional pride was starting to nag at him to do whatever he could.

The problem was, he lacked information. Well, he told himself, when all else fails just march towards the sound of the guns. When he got back to Miami he saw there was a non-stop flight to Antigua that evening. When he got to Antigua he would hang out in a bar with his ears open, so to speak, follow a few leads, hope to get lucky. Not much of a battle plan but he'd give it his best shot.

Airborne, he took stock. Despite the day's excitement, he foresaw an interesting mental challenge without a whole lot of surprises, he told himself. He relaxed and decided not to worry about it.

But he was mistaken.

CHAPTER V

ANTIGUA

CARLTON TISCH had a rule: he always stayed at the best hotel in town, so when Oliver worked for Tisch, he usually did the same thing. However, the two men disagreed totally about the meaning of 'best.' Tisch equated it with 'expensive,' Oliver preferred charm and character so, being in need of somewhere to stay, he headed confidently for the Antigua Star.

The hotel overlooked a white sandy beach on a gently curving bay. Its long white buildings were no higher than the surrounding palm trees. Oliver's spacious room was decorated in natural wood. A private balcony and terrace overlooked the bay. Fans spun slowly overhead – air conditioning was unnecessary thanks to the sea breeze, warm but not humid, that wafted in through beach-side windows.

He slung his grip on the bed and phoned Carlton.

'Tisch.'

The bark was discouraging. He was probably in his studio – he painted small watercolours, surprisingly sensitive.

'I'm on Antigua,' said Oliver. 'I've been thinking.'

'Congratulations.'

'Some deception is needed here. I need a cover story.'

'No problem. Pose as a journalist researching the casino industry.'

'That wouldn't work. This is a shady industry. People won't help an investigating journalist, they will assume that he just wants to dig up dirt and make them look bad. I would just get the cold shoulder.'

Carlton grunted, apparently he accepted the logic. 'What do you suggest?'

'How would you like to be in the casino business?'

The silence from the little financier was deafening.

'Not for real, just as a cover,' said Oliver hastily. 'Then I can say I represent an investor. People could call you for a reference.'

'I don't like it.'

'It would solve a problem for me.'

'And create one for me. Internet betting is illegal in the States, or did you forget?'

'Got a better idea?'

Tisch thought for a minute.

'Why don't you use Kon?'

Carlton liked to joke that every businessman needs a Kon Feaver. Kon was Carlton's friend from the old days, a genial, bow-legged 50-year-old, five foot ten and well proportioned with strong, muscular limbs. He had been many things in his life – Israeli air force pilot, professional soccer player, prisoner in an Egyptian jail. At present he was the nominal chairman of a Cayman Islands investment group controlled, discreetly, by Carlton himself. He usually kicked around in khaki shorts and grubby sneakers, a gold Star of David nestling in his greying chest hair. There was a twinkle in his eye and a bounce in his step. He was completely loyal to Carlton. He was also chronically broke, so it was simply not worth anyone's while to sue him. Consequently, whenever Carlton decided to venture into something a bit risky, Kon would step up and sign on as figurehead president. He would make the perfect "investor" in a fictitious internet casino.

'That works,' said Oliver.

'Want his phone number?'

'I can reach him through the New York office, can't I?'

Carlton maintained a handsome townhouse on Manhattan's Upper East Side. It appeared on the books of one of his companies as a "corporate office" but was decorated in suspiciously residential style, very much to his and Mimi's taste. Carlton's young assistant, Ken Horowitz, had a tiny office in the basement. Ken's job included redirecting phone calls to various parts of Carlton's sprawling empire.

'Don't go through the USA,' said Tisch hurriedly. 'I'll give you Ken's mobile number.'

Oliver wrote it down, and paused. 'I don't recognize that area code.'

'It's Curacao.' Carlton's tone did not encourage further enquiry.

Oliver breakfasted on fresh mango, sitting on his veranda by the ocean. Then he chatted with the hotel concierge who suggested that information about Antigua businesses was probably available from the Registrar of Companies at Government House. So, full of optimism, he fired up his white rental car and drove into town. What he found was a Georgian building in 17th-century Colonial style – cool and dignified, it was everything that a Government House on a Caribbean island should be. There was just one problem; it was not an office, but the personal residence of the Governor General and closed to the public. Clearly not what he was looking for. So much for the bellman's advice.

There was a guard outside, a big sergeant in white tunic and shorts. Approaching him and feeling slightly foolish, Oliver said, 'I think I'm at the wrong place. I wanted to inspect the documents of an International Business Company.'

'And why shouldn't you, mon?' grinned the guard, courteously tolerant of fools. 'But not here.'

'Any idea where I can do that?'

'Have you tried the FSRC?'

'Which stands for?'

'That would be the Financial Services Regulatory Commission.' In his deliberate island accent, the words rolled off the tongue like music, each syllable receiving its due weight.

'Is that far?'

'Oh, it's some way.'

Oliver's heart sank. 'How far is some way?'

'Out towards the airport, along Parham Road.'

That sounded better; the airport was only six miles away. There was something to be said for islands, Oliver thought.

'Look for the First Caribbean Financial Centre, it's in there,' said his saviour.

Ten minutes later, he reached the modern bank complex and walked into the lobby of the FSRC.

A smiling island girl nodded from behind the desk.

'Morning, sir.'

'I need company information.'

'Registrar's office.'

An elderly gentleman worked the elevator. His black pate shone as if polished. Stroking a white moustache, he politely directed Oliver down a corridor.

The buxom female clerk was all business.

'Company name?'

'Security Financings.'

She was back in moments with a manila folder. Oliver's heart leaped.

'Copies are a dollar a page,' she said dryly. 'That's Eastern Caribbean dollars, it's about thirty seven cents American.'

She indicated a small copying machine in the corner.

His optimism subsided when he opened the folder and saw how thin the file was. Just a single sheet. He learned that Security Financings was an 'International Business Company' with three directors but the file did not list their names. It had an authorized share capital of 10,000 bearer shares but, again, no names. It did list the original incorporator of the company, one Jasper Demon, attorney-at-law, and its registered office, which was also the Law Offices of Demon and Demon in St. John's. He went back to the clerk.

'May I inspect the company's annual report?'

She shook her head. 'It's not required to be filed.'

'Then can I see a balance sheet?'

'Not required.'

'How about the names of the directors?'

She shook her head, smiling.

'Don't tell me,' said Oliver. 'Not required.'

'Correct.'

He gave up.

'Here's a question you *can* answer: Where can I get lunch? Somewhere with good fresh seafood?'

'On Antigua all the fish is fresh.' She thought for a moment. 'Try Johnny's Crab Shack.'

'Is that far?'

'It's down town, by the jetty. From here, fifteen minutes.'

Oliver paid his EC dollar and left clutching his single page. At least he had the incorporator's name. The incorporator might be just another tight-lipped lawyer, but it was a start.

The woman behind the counter waited until Oliver was safely out of earshot, then picked up her telephone.

'Cousin Neville? You know that list of companies? The ones where you asked me to call you if anyone enquired? Well, I have something for you.'

Oliver spotted her using the phone from the corner of his eye and wondered idly why; he thought no more about it until later. He had planned to head straight for the restaurant, but on his way out he noticed a sign that said 'Division of Gaming, 2nd Floor.' On an impulse, he walked in, sporting his best smile.

'Looking for information,' he said brightly. 'I'm starting an Internet gaming business.'

Well, he might have been, who was to know? He held his breath, but there was no problem. With a flourish the clerk handed him a bunch of fact sheets. The first one was about taxes. He scanned it quickly while the clerk watched him.

A 3 per cent tax was payable by operators on their "net win", defined as the difference between the gross stakes laid and the winnings paid out. Well, that was clear enough. It was pretty low if he compared it to the rates paid by US corporations to Uncle

Sam. He read on. The next paragraph stated that there was a maximum cap of US$50,000 per month on taxes. He read that out loud to the clerk, to be sure he understood. He got a nod, '$600,000 a year, that's not pocket change.'

'I should think not,' said Oliver. But, privately, he was thinking just the opposite. It meant that once a company's net gain exceeded twenty million dollars, not too unusual for a mature global business, there was no more tax. So the tax was regressive, favouring larger companies – something to keep in mind.

Meanwhile, also on Antigua, the grey-suited enforcer who had visited the Smiths in Fort Lauderdale was reporting back to his boss, Frankie Leon. They stood, talking, in the panelled hallway of Leon's grey stone 18th-century manor house a few miles from the capital.

'How did it go with the old guy?' asked Frankie.

The enforcer lied, something he did automatically, out of habit. He did not tell Frankie that he had run out of the Smith's house without concluding his business, namely to terrify Larry Smith by inflicting a fate worse than death on the man's nubile wife. He did not consider the details to be any of Frankie's business.

'I gave the old goat a good scare. Roughed his wife up a bit. They got the message.'

'Collect any money?'

The enforcer shook his head in disgust. 'Nah. They don't got none. Prob'ly gonna lose their ritzy house some time soon. One thing, though...'

He hesitated, trying to phrase it with the least discredit to himself. 'Some fella busted in while I was questioning the Smiths. I saw him off.'

'What kind of guy?'

'Young fella with an accent, could have been British.'

'Okay.'

Frankie did not attach much importance to this information although he stored it away in his mind.

But, later that morning he got a phone call from his assistant, Neville Morgan, a smiling, dark-skinned Antiguan in his thirties who said: 'I just heard from my cousin at the FSRC. Someone is enquiring after Security Financings.'

'Tell me more.'

'That's all I know. He pulled the file and made a copy of the Articles. He didn't learn much; those files are a joke.' Neville laughed shortly. 'The guy looked pretty disappointed. He sounded British, by the way. My cousin thought he might be a journalist researching a story, he had that nosy attitude.'

But at the word British, Frankie put two and two together. Instant rage engulfed him. Someone once said "only the paranoid survive" and Frankie had not got where he was by being sloppy. First, a Britisher caused trouble at the Smiths' home in Fort Lauderdale and then, the very next day, someone who could be the same person came sniffing round Frankie's finance company. The connection was too obvious to miss. His mind immediately envisioned the worst-case scenario, where some offence of a non-financial nature such as the hazing of Larry and Madeleine Smith could be attributed to him and used as a lever to pry him loose from his comfortable hideout in Antigua. Tax and banking secrecy was one thing –criminal offences involving violence were another story. They posed a significant danger of extradition to refugees like himself.

'Fix it,' he told Neville. Neville murmured something unintelligible.

'Now,' barked Frankie.

Neville went away and made a phone call.

Oliver parked down town and strolled towards the water. He was clearly in a prosperous area, buoyed by tourist dollars from cruise ships and hotels. The shop windows displayed Cuban cigars, Swiss watches and expensive perfume as well as the ever-present T-shirts.

He had only walked a couple of blocks when something – he did not know what – made him look behind him.

If the young woman was trying to avoid being noticed, she was doing a poor job. When Oliver stopped, she stopped. When he started walking again, so did she. On an island where ninety per cent of the population was black and many of the rest were Mediterranean, Syrian or mixed race, she was not exactly inconspicuous. Her appearance was pure corn-fed American and none the worse for that. She was dressed in holiday mode – maroon tank top and short white shorts – and there was a pleasant swing to her walk. There was something familiar about her face behind the big sunglasses, but he struggled to place it. He stared directly at her but she avoided his eye, feigning interest in a display of straw dolls.

He shrugged and went into Johnny's Crab Shack, an open-air establishment by the water with wooden tables on a deck overlooking a fleet of colourful fishing boats. Shown to a table, he sat and looked around approvingly. It had the look of a serious fish place with a bottle of Johnny's Special Tartar Sauce on each table and a comforting smell of frying shrimp in the air.

The next time he saw the girl, he was nursing a pre-lunch rum Collins. She walked straight up to him but then hovered nervously, apparently hoping for an invitation to sit down. 'Mr. Steele?'

He half rose. 'Have we met?'

She smiled shyly. 'Mind if I join you? I'm Kathy Smith.'

So that was it. Larry Smith's daughter. He had no idea why she was here but his instinct was that she was an unwanted complication.

'What's good to eat here?' She picked up the huge menu.

'Try the shrimp.'

'I think I'll have the eggs Benedict.'

'What are you doing here?'

'Welcome to you, too,' she said. Shy, maybe, but with a mind of her own.

The gunshots came just as she was giving the waiter her order.

There were two reports, from the direction of the street. Her water glass splintered into a thousand fragments. A china dish of celery stalks disintegrated, scattering food everywhere. A bloody scratch appeared on her tanned forearm. In all the excitement, neither of them noticed that the waiter had staggered and was sinking to the ground, blood spreading across his white-shirted stomach.

A few minutes later, the police arrived. An ambulance came also, siren wailing, but it was too late for the luckless waiter who bled to death in minutes. Photographs were taken and his body was driven away. Paramedics applied a bandage to Kathy's arm where a glass shard had grazed the skin. Johnny's Crab Shack was closed for the rest of the day to the chagrin of its flustered manager.

Neville had the uncomfortable task of telling Frankie what had happened.

'Our shooter missed the guy. He hit a waiter instead.'

Frankie looked thunderous.

'You sent some jerk who couldn't shoot straight?'

Neville spread his arms in a gesture of resignation and apology. He was an expert at deflecting Frankie's bursts of anger. The best thing was not to offer excuses but just to act resigned and remorseful.

Frankie did not ask about the health of the waiter so Neville thought he had better mention it.

'The waiter died,' he said.

'So what, I should care?' Frankie was furious about the failure of the mission.

It did not occur to him just then that, despite a history of considerable violence, this was the first time he had ever given an order that directly caused loss of life. In other words, even if he had only been half-concentrating when he instructed Neville, he was guilty – in just about any jurisdiction – of murder. Nor did he reflect on the irony that he had committed the act not in the course of a specific crime but simply to protect his way of life, to preserve the more or less legal status quo.

CHAPTER 6

AT THE POLICE STATION

*I*NSPECTOR TOM TRURO, a well-dressed young Antiguan with a weary, humorous face, straightened his Jermyn Street silk tie.

'Are you two travelling together?'

'No,' said Oliver.

'Yes,' said Kathy at the same time, and went pink.

They were sitting in the inspector's office at St. John's police station.

Oliver started to explain. 'The thing is...'

She said, 'We're friends, but we bumped into each other by chance.'

'When?'

'Just before.'

'Before the shooting?'

'Right.'

Truro took off his dark glasses, folded them carefully and stowed them in the jacket of his pale grey suit.

'What exactly are you doing on Antigua?'

'I'm a financial consultant,' Oliver said, before she could speak.

'And you are here on business?'

Oliver nodded. 'My client is considering a new venture here.'

'In what field?'

'An Internet casino.'

The temperature fell several degrees.

'It's an industry that Antiguan law encourages,' Oliver said gently.

'At the political level, that is true.'

Oliver was about to say something sarcastic about governments that charged a hundred grand for a casino licence but he bit his tongue. To cross swords with authority before he even got started might be unwise. 'You don't approve?'

Truro sighed. 'Do you know what the population of Antigua is?'

'Two hundred thousand?' Oliver guessed.

'Eighty thousand.'

'Your point being?'

'This is a small community. Our legislators may not have realized that the effect of a controversial industry would be so marked. A little bad influence goes a long way.'

'Bad influence?'

'This is not the first incident.'

Clearly a touchy subject. 'Any ideas about the shooter?' Oliver asked.

Truro stared at Oliver for a long time. Finally he stood up.

'Stay out of trouble. We shall be in touch if we need you.'

Outside, Kathy and Oliver looked at each other.

'We still haven't had lunch,' Kathy said. She touched her bandaged arm thoughtfully. 'Where can we go?'

'Somewhere indoors. I still feel rather exposed.'

'You think you were the target? What about me?'

'Whatever,' said Oliver. The bullets had roughly bisected the short distance between them.

'What about your hotel?'

'Fine.'

Kathy ordered lobster salad, the most expensive dish on the menu. Oliver wondered if she would leave him with the bill. He ordered a plain hamburger, even though Carlton was paying. Still, at least the hotel dining room was almost empty and besides being classier than Johnny's it was shielded from passing eyes so he felt less vulnerable.

'You haven't explained why you are here.'

'To help my father.'

'That's why I'm here.'

'Good. Two heads are better than one.'

Oliver wondered about that.

'I suppose you know what's going on with your dad?'

'Of course. My stepmother thinks I don't know, but it's so obvious. I've walked in on him gambling more than once. Neither of them wants to talk so I can tell something is wrong.'

He wondered if she knew about the threats. If she didn't, he would rather not be the one to tell her.

And now a death was involved.

For the life of him he could not understand why Smith's case had led to such violence. Unless killing was just a matter of no concern to the people involved.

He looked at his watch.

'This is fun but I have to go and see someone.'

'Who?'

'The attorney for the company that lent your father money.'

He bit his tongue too late – she was instantly alert.

'When do we leave?'

'We?'

'I want to help.'

'Thanks, but I don't think so,' he said. He felt rising anxiety.

She did not pout exactly, but she looked thoughtful. He changed the subject.

'What did you say your degree was in?'

'I didn't.'

'What was it?'

She sighed. 'International taxation.'

'I'm impressed. I hope you'll be sensible about this. No use our butting heads.'

She contemplated her plate. She had long eyelashes. 'Got it.'

He signed the bill. 'Glad we're clear. Any plans for this afternoon?'

'I'll just work on my tan, I guess.' She looked out at the beach.

Kathy had graduated from UCLA with excellent grades in finance. Her first job was with Pferck, the international drug company at their world headquarters in Menlo Park, California.

As a young woman with a good degree and a cheerful attitude, she did not find it hard to get hired and she soon became a popular, if junior, member of the office. She liked the competitive atmosphere and was not averse to the heady feeling of power that went with being near the tip of the pyramid in a huge multinational. But after a while the novelty started to wear off. Being naturally impatient, she chafed at being a cog in the system with little real influence. She was also appalled at all the politicking that went on. So often, it seemed to her, egos and influence trumped common sense when it came to making major decisions.

So she quit and went home to Florida where she scratched a living advising much smaller companies on how to structure their international tax affairs. That was where she got to know the IRS agent Charlie Green when he was sent to audit one of her clients. He was basically good natured and easy to talk to, a useful quality in his line of work, and over lunch one day – at which, to avoid impropriety, he insisted on paying his share in accordance with the IRS rule book – she described her problem.

'My dad's being taken to the cleaners by an offshore Internet casino.'

'How does that make you feel?'

'I'd like to strangle the owners and dance on their graves.'

'Seriously, what do you plan to do about it?'

She shrugged. 'How can I get the bastards off his back?' She explained the situation.

Green sighed. 'Realistically, we can't do much to help so long as the people who run the casino stay overseas. It would be a different story if you could coax them back onto US soil. That achieved, the IRS would do the rest.'

'How would I do that?'

'That's the challenge.' He stroked his chin thoughtfully. 'It would need some ingenuity but I can think of one or two ways it might be done.'

♦

CHAPTER 7

THE FLACKS ARE IN TOWN

OLIVER AND KATHY were not the only visitors to Antigua with an interest in casinos. At that very moment three businessmen from the rocky Mediterranean tax haven of Gibraltar were having a meeting in a suite in the same hotel.

Wilf Flack, president of the Flack Entertainment Group, was listening patiently to Norrie Flack, his uncle and fellow shareholder. Norrie was also Vice President in charge of security. Their computer guru, Ron Rigby, was with them. The Flacks had come to the island to buy an Internet casino.

Uncle Norrie stood up, walked to the window and stared out at the swaying palms. He was getting restless. They had been on Antigua for a week.

'Damn coconuts,' he muttered. 'I am so sick of coconuts.'

'We'll be going home soon,' said Wilf tightly. His uncle was starting to get on his nerves.

Both the Flacks were skilful in their fields. Wilf's was finance. A studious young man with black framed glasses, he was a chartered accountant and a Harvard MBA. Uncle Norrie, a glum-looking individual, built like a weightlifter but run to fat, was also skilled, but in violence. He liked to resolve issues using superior force and he did not have much patience with his nephew's bloodless approach to business.

The Flacks were cockneys, raised in London's East End, but they had recently uprooted their operation lock, stock and barrel and expatriated themselves to Gibraltar to avoid taxes. This had not pleased Uncle Norrie, who suffered badly from homesickness, but it had greatly increased the group's cash flow.

Wilf wanted to buy Casino Caribbean from Frankie Leon. An Internet casino was the next step in his game plan for the family business. He was well aware of Frankie's background as a former drug dealer. Frankie's reputation would have discouraged some people from doing business with him, but Wilf looked past that. If you came up in the betting business around Bethnal Green, shadiness went with the territory and Frankie had something he wanted.

But after a week on Antigua, Uncle Norrie was increasingly fidgety. He yearned for the racing pages, decent beer, snooker at the pub. Anything was better than sitting around in hotel rooms, waiting.

Wilf was just as keen to conclude negotiations but he possessed much more self control. He was the third Flack to run the business. His grandfather, Wilf senior, was still alive but retired – nowadays he spent most of his time chasing young nurses round his Canary Wharf penthouse, but in his day he had been both ruthless and smart. He built up a chain of betting shops in a part of London where nothing came easily. His son and heir, Ted, died young of injuries sustained in a gangland riot. Ted's brother, Norrie, was passed over for promotion when a family conclave pronounced him just too much of a rough diamond to be put in charge. That left grandson Wilf to take over the reins.

Wilf might have been young but he was no fool. He had planned his approach to Frankie Leon very carefully. At the first meeting with Frankie, he had aggressively questioned the accuracy of the casino's financial statements.

On one level, his questions were negotiating points. But they were also a stalling tactic. He wanted to buy time for his programmer, Rigby, to analyze the Casino's computer programmes. Wilf could see that the programmes were the key to the casino business. If he could just hack into Frankie's computer system and build a 'carbon copy' of the setup he could get for free something that had cost Frankie months of work and millions of dollars to develop. Then he would not need to buy the business at all.

At their next meeting, he intended to press Frankie to let Rigby review the source code, the algorithms that underpinned the impressive graphics and made the whole thing work. Rigby had a near-photographic memory and was capable of memorizing large chunks of computer code. Wilf wanted Rigby to spend time with Judith Barcat, the designer of the system, for that purpose.

But, since he knew his request would probably be refused, he also wanted to try and break the code by other means. At that very moment Rigby was sitting in the corner, typing furiously. He hummed to himself, mouth open as he worked. His face was spotted with liverish freckles and pale from a lifetime of frowning at screens. A luridly patterned shirt spilled out of cheap pants, revealing rolls of fat. His colleagues had learned to keep their distance to avoid the aura of sweat.

'How are you getting on with that?' asked Wilf, for the tenth time.

Rigby brushed back his greasy red hair. 'I'll have this thing cracked in a few m-m-minutes.' He had a slight stutter. Nonetheless, he was supremely confident of his ability to make computers do anything, with or without their owners' permission. A gifted hacker, his talents were offset by a startling naiveté about everything else.

That means he'll need a few days, thought Wilf.

'Stay focused, I can't stall them much longer.'

Uncle Norrie was listening.

'Why don't we just go in and do the bastards?' He took a large knife from his pocket, a switchblade, and set to work grooming a fingernail.

Wilf sighed. 'Don't forget the image, Uncle Norrie. We're the good guys, coming into town to clean up the business, okay?'

The phone rang and he grabbed it.

When he hung up, he was excited. 'Leon wants to see us. Let's go.'

Things were moving and thank God for that. The truth was, Wilf was missing his wife and children. He even missed Gibraltar with its down-at-heel colonial atmosphere. But now he felt better. He might have been less comfortable if he had known that Uncle Norrie was working behind his back, making other arrangements. They included hiring local muscle, young Antiguans with guns and clubs, ready to take the initiative if need be.

Frankie Leon, from Long Island by way of Coconut Grove, was fifty pounds overweight. He had built up a hugely profitable business over the last five years and was not the type to spare himself the good things of life.

He had come to Antigua following some unpleasantness in the United States, something about a tax audit. The less said about that, the better. Suffice it that he needed to find a different line of business. On-line gaming had appealed to him strongly. In fact, he could not understand why more entrepreneurs were not piling onto the bandwagon. Things had gone slowly at first. Getting the computer programmes written and debugged took time.

A year went by while Frankie's funds dwindled. But finally his programmer Judith and her staff finished the fine-tuning, bringing things to the point where almost no human input was required. All was ready. Casino Caribbean went live.

Gamblers could play in privacy, sitting at their computers around the world, but mainly in the United States, where people had frighteningly easy access to funds. Most of the big banks would cheerfully give a credit card to anyone, whether they could afford the repayments or not.

It was hard to believe how easy it was, marvelled Frankie. Gamblers willingly released the most intimate information about their personal finances and, from then on, they were pretty much at his mercy. The reason, of course, was that they had the bug. Frankie never gambled and he despised people who did. Time and again he had seen gamblers get into financial trouble but that was their problem. The casino's terms of business were clear. Money to cover their wagers was charged to their bank accounts or credit cards, and credited to Casino Caribbean's account daily. Bettors might become over-extended but the Casino always got paid.

Sometimes the bettor won. When that happened, he could promptly receive a draft for his winnings – he just had to ask. But most bettors did not ask. Why quit when they were beating the system? Usually they soldiered on, eventually losing and getting deeper into debt.

Frankie was content just to offer casino games – poker, blackjack and other numbers-based games like keno and roulette. They were low maintenance in the sense that the odds could be programmed in at the beginning and not adjusted unless the house wanted to tip the scales more or less in its favour. The house had control. That appealed to Frankie. He did not run a sports book – betting on football or racing. That was more labour intensive. It involved regular inputting of external results. And the house had less control.

At first he hired veterans from Las Vegas to help him establish the odds. But he realized after a while that their continued presence was unnecessary. He gave them nice bonuses and sent them home, secretly relieved that he could get rid of them before they got too friendly with the computer staff. He was paranoid about being cheated and if anyone was going to rip him off, he reckoned it would be the programmers, either by conspiring with outsiders or by some highly technical scheme buried under thousands of lines of computer code. He paid them well to ensure their loyalty, but he also had them watched day and night. Trust was a luxury he could not afford. The drug business had taught him that.

Recently, Frankie had started to think about an exit strategy. Business was great but the good times would not last – good times never did. Congress was trying hard to outlaw the industry. One day the banks, their US assets vulnerable, might bend to federal pressure and stop handling gaming transactions. That would leave Frankie and his peers in the industry high and dry, at least as far as doing business with American bettors. Before that happened, he must fold his tent and steal away. The danger was not imminent but he should be prepared.

A few weeks ago the Flack Entertainment Group had approached him. He had checked them out; they were big in Europe and had survived fifty years in a tough business so they probably knew what they were doing. They had recently moved from England to Gibraltar, a known tax haven, and they seemed very keen on the Casino idea. Maybe they had not read the American newspapers?

He had already held one meeting with the Flacks and they had asked a lot of questions. Afterwards, he still was not sure how well it had gone.

The three visitors had sat across the table from him, an odd bunch. Frankie focused on Wilf Flack, physically unimpressive but apparently the leader. Slim, clean shirt, striped tie, could be from one of those British private schools, he thought.

Frankie himself was seriously overweight since he took no exercise of any kind. He had a bland moon face with five o'clock shadow most of the day. He took off his thick glasses and smiled round the table as graciously as he knew how.

'So when do you want to take over?' As a salesman, he liked to use the presumptive close where you assumed the prospect was ready to buy and just wanted you to take his money.

'I'm not sure yet that we do.' Wilf Flack was courteous but blunt.

'Then why are you here?'

Wilf smiled. 'The Flack Entertainment Group is expanding. We operate one of the biggest Internet sports books in Europe. You should check out our website.'

Frankie shrugged. 'I never look at other people's websites.'

It was a silly lie and they both knew it. Wilf inclined his head as if to say, 'Please yourself' and continued, 'We are ready to add a casino division. It will be a logical fit – punters who have won a bundle on the St. Leger may like to try and double it playing poker.'

'St. Leger?'

'An English horse race for three-year-olds.'

Frankie frowned. 'Why approach me rather than one of my competitors?'

'We've looked at others, trust me. We like your style, your presentation. Your screens are appealing. The commands are intuitive. You give the gambler an enjoyable experience.'

Wilf paused. 'If he enjoys losing money, that is.'

Laughter round the table – a joke among professionals.

'What makes you think I am interested in selling?'

Wilf spread his hands. 'You answered our letter.'

Frankie nodded acknowledgment. The fact was: he was a trader. For him wheeling and dealing were the thrill, not running a web site. The casino was minting money but it no longer excited him. It was a static thing, running smoothly, without drama. That might be fine for other people but not for Frankie.

Business was still growing, but for how long? So it seemed like a good time to cash in. He reckoned it was like selling anything – you picked your time, made your best deal and left before the music stopped.

'It took a lot of money to put this operation together,' he said.

'And we're willing to recognize that,' said Wilf sincerely.

'A billion,' said Frankie.

There was silence, broken by Wilf. 'I'm sorry, what did you say?' He smiled in disbelief.

Uncle Norrie scowled. Rigby looked out of the window.

'That's my price,' said Frankie. 'A billion dollars. Cash. For that you get everything – the programmes, the people, the real estate. The licence, of course, too; a fully self-contained business.'

'You must be mad.' Uncle Norrie spat out the words, his face dark. He pushed back his chair. 'Let's go, Wilf.'

Rigby stood up nervously.

Wilf raised a hand. 'Hold on, chaps. Frankie meant no offence, I'm sure. Just starting the bidding, right, Frankie?'

Frankie scowled.

Wilf scribbled on a yellow legal pad. 'Let's see. I'm calculating what it would cost us to start from scratch. We don't want to do that, mind you – we're impatient people and we'd prefer to move quickly. But we might have to. So let's do the math, as you Americans say. There's the licence for a hundred thousand. Then there is the building. Add on a few months worth of overhead expenses.'

He looked up apologetically. 'Doesn't amount to much!'

'There's a lot more to it than that,' said Frankie grumpily.

Wilf raised an eyebrow, taking care not to smile. He had turned the discussion round. Frankie was now defending his price. The trader in Frankie appreciated the manoeuvre. Wilf was wilier than he looked. 'Look, if you have to start from scratch, it will take you a year just to do the programming.'

Wilf turned to Rigby. 'Is that true, Ron?'

At the mention of programmes, Rigby had stopped looking out of the window.

'Take me a m-m-month,' he muttered.

'That's absurd' said Frankie.

'Don't be so sure,' said Wilf. 'Ron's awfully good. Works like lightning, never comes up for air, do you Ron?'

Frankie shook his head. He was no manager but he knew one thing for sure: all programmers lied.

'That's what we used to think. We had a junior programmer just like you,' he indicated Rigby dismissively. 'I had to fire him. He could never grasp the difference between a draft and a finished version. Yes, you could write the basic procedures in a month but they wouldn't be worth beans. This stuff has to be immaculate.'

'Tell you what,' said Wilf. 'I'll give you $10 million for the programmes. A generous sum. Add another $10 million for the house and a bit for other start-up costs. $25 million altogether, payable over three years. It's a good offer.'

Frankie scowled. 'No, it's not. I gross that much in three months. You would be buying the business with its own cash.'

Wilf looked genuinely surprised.

'$25 million in three months? You gross $100 million a year?'

Frankie shook his head. 'Much more. Probably $400 million by the end of this year.'

Rigby whistled and Uncle Norrie frowned at him.

'That's gross income, right?'

'Sure.'

'What's the net profit after expenses?'

Frankie did not answer. Offhand, he could not remember. He just knew there was a heck of a lot of money coming in. The casino was a cash cow and he wasn't going to let it go cheap.

On the other hand, there were those damn US legislators.

'I'll give you $50 million,' said Wilf, 'Over five years.'

'Five hundred,' said Frankie. 'Over three years. And I'll sign a non-compete agreement.'

'For how long?'

'A year.'

'Five years.'

'Three.'

'We'll need to see a profit and loss statement,' said Wilf.

'Of course.'

'And a balance sheet.'

'Okay, but you'll have to sign a confidentiality agreement.'

'No problem.'

'I'll send them round to your hotel.'

Everyone stood up, looked at their watches, shook hands.

Outside, waiting for a taxi, the Flacks stood and talked.

'What do you think?' asked Wilf.

'Too easy,' said Norrie. 'Got to be a catch.'

'My thoughts exactly.'

'I really could knock off those programmes in a month,' said Rigby.

They both ignored him.

Indoors, Frankie telephoned Ritchie Codrington, the genial retired St. John's police sergeant who was his chief of security. Although he was now in a legitimate business, Frankie was still very security conscious. Very few people knew what went on inside his organization and he wanted to keep it that way.

Above all he did not want the world to know how much money he was making. There were people in Miami – very unpleasant people – who still claimed he owed them money and he had no wish to attract attention. Discretion was the watchword.

He had originally hired Codrington to keep an eye on the programming staff. The software was uniquely valuable and he did not want some corruptible programmer leaking codes to a competitor. He liked the non-threatening old sergeant and could control him easily. But he also hired some younger, rougher characters. Such characters were not hard to find on Antigua where unemployment was high. Working for Frankie, with his permission to carry unlicensed firearms, was a lot more fun than driving a tour bus. Their job description was hazy but it reflected Frankie's paranoia and his desire for privacy.

To Ritchie he said:

'I don't trust these people, I think they're trying to screw me. Keep a close eye on them.'

'No problem,' said Ritchie. 'I'm on top of it, mon.'

CHAPTER 8

JASPER DEMON, ATTORNEY

OLIVER STEELE liked the look of the Law Offices of Demon and Demon. They consisted of a pleasant white-washed mansion with a pink tiled roof on the outskirts of St. John.

In the air-conditioned waiting room, a female secretary was talking on the phone, drinking coffee and typing, all at the same time. He was struck again by how handsome Antigua's women were.

She waved at a closed door. 'He won't be long.'

Oliver sat down and leafed through *Newsweek*.

Another man was also waiting, so they sat side by side. A pale individual in heavy glasses, he wore a dark suit, white shirt and striped tie. The tie looked familiar to Oliver. After a few minutes, he broke the silence.

'Is that a Bunnington tie or just something with similar stripes?'

His neighbour beamed.

'It's Bunnington. Were you there?'

'I was indeed. Oliver Steele, Masefield House. The only American in a sea of British schoolboys.'

The man stuck out a hand. 'Wilf Flack, Blenheim. Maybe we were contemporaries?'

An onlooker would have been baffled by the cryptic names passing to and fro but they made perfect sense to the two men.

'There was a Flack who was Head of School my first year,' said Oliver.

'That's me.'

'Captain of cricket?'

'Guilty.'

'Two years in a row, I think.'

Flack smiled modestly. 'I was lucky. But tell me, what was an American doing at an English boarding school and speaking BBC English?'

'My mother was English.'

'Ah!'

Neither man asked the other what brought him to Antigua. If they had, it might have avoided significant bloodshed. But it would have been unBunningtonian. Instead, they reminisced about boarding schools, rugger and the sadistic proclivities of English schoolmasters until the buzzer rang and Oliver was ushered in.

Jasper Demon stood up. As they shook hands, Oliver realized with a shock that he was staring straight over Demon's head – the blue-chinned lawyer was barely five feet tall.

Neatly dressed in shirt and tie, he waved Oliver to a sofa and sat down opposite. Bookshelves full of leather-bound legal texts lined the walls of Demon's office but his coffee table was strewn with back numbers of Cosmopolitan and Playboy.

'Coffee, Stella!'

Coffee appeared. They stirred in sugar, eying each other.

Demon looked about forty, with a small pot belly. He was bright eyed and alert.

'First time in Antigua?'

'First in a while.'

'Enjoying it?'

Oliver nodded enthusiastically. 'Very much. Wonderful place.' He thought it simpler not to mention the dead waiter at Johnny's.

'How can I help you?'

'Do you form International Business Companies?'

'Sure do.'

'Did you form one called Security Financing?'

'Possibly.'

'Only possibly?'

'I'd have to check. We do a lot of them, it's our bread and butter.' He reached for the phone but Oliver stopped him.

'No need. Your name is in their file at the Regulatory Commission's office.'

Demon laughed. 'Their enormous file. All of half a page, right?'

'Precisely.'

'What do you need to know?'

'Are they a good company to deal with?'

'Oh, I'm sure they are.' A smile played at the corner of Demon's mouth.

So much for not recognizing the name, thought Oliver.

'We may be getting into the interactive casino business.'

'And you want to help your bettors get loans?'

Oliver nodded. He was not hoping for too much. Most attorneys were tight lipped when asked about an existing client but the prospect of a substantial new client might loosen even a lawyer's tongue. He pressed on.

'My researcher came across their name while he was surfing for casinos on the Internet. Several casinos use Security Financing.'

'I daresay.'

'How would you describe them?'

Demon frowned. 'In what way?'

'How do they earn their income?'

'They make loans. I assume you knew that already.'

'Are they what is called a hard money lender?'

'Meaning?'

'A lender of last resort, one that charges very high interest.'

'It's possible. I just handled the incorporation. What exactly do you need from me?'

Oliver smiled. 'An introduction. When we get our website going we shall need someone like that.'

Demon stared out of the window. 'I don't mean to be rude, but who is we?'

Oliver produced his card. 'I represent the Pyramid Group of Grand Cayman. We make private equity investments. You may know Kon Feaver, our president.'

Demon shrugged and deliberately let the card fall onto the table where it brushed the thigh of July's Playmate of the Month. Oliver was starting to wonder whether he could do business with Demon. He seemed a tough piece of work.

'I just want to find out if they are good business partners. The best way I know to do that is to talk to their customers, the people that send business their way.'

'Their biggest customer would be Casino Caribbean.'

Bells went off in Oliver's head.

'Okay. And who owns Casino Caribbean?'

Demon shook his head. 'From there you're on your own, I can't help you any more.'

'Why not?'

He shrugged. 'It might not be appreciated. Casino people can be very sensitive.'

'You already told me they work with Security Financing.'

'That's different. That information is already available on the Casino's website.'

Oliver was getting exasperated. 'Why is the owner's name such a big deal?'

Demon spread his hands. 'It just is. Some casino owners would kill me if they thought I was being disloyal.'

'You don't look easily intimidated.'

'I'm not, but it is a very tough industry. If you plan to get into that business, you should know that.'

Oliver realized he would not get much further. He stood up.

'Thanks for the coffee.'

'You're very welcome.' As Oliver left, Demon picked up his card and studied it thoughtfully.

Outside, who should be sitting trading girl talk with Demon's secretary but Kathy Smith. She looked fresh and appealing in a halter-top and straw sunhat.

'Hi, darling!' she said brightly.

'What the heck are you doing here?'

'Didn't want to overdo the tanning, not on the first day. This sun is fierce. So I thought I'd join you for a drive, dear.'

Oliver reluctantly played along with the cue. They left together arm in arm but he was not pleased at being manipulated.

'How did you get here?'

'By taxi.'

He unlocked his car. 'Get in.'

She lit a cigarette. It was pink with a gold foil filter. He glanced at the pack, it was emblazoned with the Russian imperial eagle – Sobranie, a brand some of his more pretentious Oxford friends used to smoke. He hadn't come across it in years. He considered Kathy, frowning slightly. A tax expert who smoked Russian cigarettes? And who kept turning up where she was not wanted?

He concentrated on navigating the unfamiliar streets. After a few minutes he spoke.

'I would really prefer you not to follow me around.'

She grinned. 'It's your magnetic personality.'

'I don't think it's helpful.'

'Sorry,' she said. Then, after a pause, 'What did you find out?'

'Not much,' Oliver conceded.

'Typical attorney?'

'Pretty much.'

'Did you find out who owns Casino Caribbean?'

'He knew but he wouldn't say.'

'It's someone called Leon.'

He looked at her.

'Who?'

'Frankie Leon. He lives in Conway Hill, about ten miles from here.'

'How in the world do you know that?'

'Demon's secretary was on the 'phone to him. I overheard, I was only two feet away.'

'You eavesdropped?'

'No. Well, yes. It's what you needed, right?'

'Maybe.'

'So you could say "thank you" or "I appreciate it"…or something along those lines.'

He shrugged.

'You're welcome,' she grinned.

It irked him to admit that without her he would be nowhere.

'So what next?' she asked.

'I'm thinking about that.'

'Let's go out and see the guy.'

'And ask him what?'

'You'll think of something. Tell him to leave my father alone.'

He pondered. 'I don't suppose you got his address?'

'Not exactly. But Conway Hill can't be a big place. It's out along the coast road. By the way, can I make another suggestion?'

'If you must.'

'Ditch the rental car. Take a taxi.'

'Why?'

'Rented cars isolate you from your surroundings. You need to get in touch with the community. You need information. Taxi drivers are sources of information.'

Annoying she might be but she did have a point, he thought grudgingly.

So back at the hotel they boarded a taxi. The driver, a dour Negro with a neck overflowing his collar, looked at them.

Kathy smiled. 'We want to visit a Mr. Franklin Leon. His house is in Conway Hill. That's ten miles north of here.'

'I know where Conway Hill is,' said the driver.

'Think you can find the house?'

'No problem.'

He drove off rather fast. Oliver and Kathy exchanged glances. She shrugged.

Twenty minutes later, when they had just passed the same clump of palm trees for the third time Oliver leaned forward.

'How are we doing?'

The driver peered out of the dusty window.

'It's around here somewhere. What was that name? Lewis?'

'Leon.'

'Leon, right. Been here several years. Runs some kind of business.'

'Are you sure you know where you are?' asked Kathy.

The driver bristled. 'This is Conway Hill.'

Just ahead was a tiny roadside kiosk, strategically situated in the middle of nowhere. Its palm-thatched roof sheltered a miscellaneous collection of merchandise from the sun. There were oranges, candy bars, flyblown magazines. Next to it was a red post box.

'Pull over,' said Kathy. She got out.

An old man with a face like brown parchment sat in a frayed deck chair, watching the store. He nodded at her, screwing up his eyes against the afternoon sun.

'We're looking for the Leon house. Can you help us?'

He smiled and shook his head.

'Is that a yes or a no?'

'No, ma'am. But I know someone who can.'

She looked round; there was nobody.

The old man whistled loudly and shouted 'Winston!'

A child aged about ten wobbled out from behind the kiosk on a red bicycle.

'Can you help these good people?'

'Yes, sir.'

'Where is Mr. Leon's house?' asked Oliver.

'Don't know.' Thumb in mouth.

'I thought you said you knew.'

He shook his head. 'Din't say I knew. Said I could help.'

He took his thumb out of his mouth and indicated the dusty mail box at the edge of the dirt road.

'Man coming.'

As if on cue, an elderly mail van approached, stopping in a cloud of dust. Emerging, the driver opened the mail box with a large bunch of keys.

Kathy gave him her best smile. 'We need directions to the Leon residence.'

'Follow me, darlin,' it's my next stop.'

'You're brilliant.'

They followed the van along the main road until it turned off towards the sea on a dirt track that wound through thick palm groves. Half a mile further on, they stopped at a pair of massive wrought-iron gates, flanked by a crumbling gatehouse. Through the iron bars Oliver could make out a grey manor house reminiscent of antebellum homes of the Deep South.

The place had a slightly sinister air; he suddenly realized that it was one of the island's old sugar plantations, the slave-based mainstay of Antigua's economy in the 18th century. He shivered involuntarily.

The mailman indicated a mailbox in the wall of the gate house and pushed the mail through the opening. 'This is as far as I go.'

'Do you ever go all the way up to the house?' Oliver asked.

He shook his head. 'My orders are to stop here.'

'What if they have to sign for something?'

'I call them on the intercom.' He indicated a loudspeaker grille just above the box.

'Ever see Frank Leon?'

'Sure. Sometimes he will walk out here and sign.'

'What's he like?'

The mailman shrugged. 'Heavy-set young gentleman. Could stand to lose a few pounds. New York accent.'

'How would you recognize a New York accent?' asked Kathy.

The mailman grinned. 'I have cousins in Queens, I know what New York sounds like.'

Oliver and Kathy stood looking at the mansion.

'Are you thinking what I'm thinking?' said Kathy.

'Don't do it,' said Oliver.

'Come on, what's to lose?'

'Plenty.'

'What's happening?' asked the mailman.

'She wants to ring the bell and have the owner come down here,' said Oliver.

'But he doesn't need to sign for anything.'

'It would take too long to explain,' said Oliver.

From his taxi, the cab driver coughed noisily. He had been sitting waiting for them and looking cross. He looked pointedly at his watch.

'Do you think he wants to leave?' asked Kathy.

'He's a surly fellow, take no notice,' said the mailman who had taken a liking to Kathy.

'Do you know him?' asked Oliver

'He's my cousin.'

'Can't stay here all day,' the driver muttered.

'Oh I'm sure you're missing thousands of dollars' worth of business,' said Kathy sarcastically.

'He does have a point, though,' said Oliver.

He shepherded Kathy into the cab and they headed back to St. Johns.

By the time they arrived at the hotel, it was starting to get dark.

'I think I'll go and phone Carlton,' said Oliver. 'Do you want to meet for supper? We can make some plans.'

'Sure,' she said.

'How's it going?' asked Tisch, at the other end of the phone.

'Quite well. We found the owner of the Casino, a guy called Frankie Leon. We went and looked at his place from the outside, it's pretty substantial.'

'You work fast, I'm impressed.'

'It's easier once you are here on the island,' said Oliver modestly. 'I'm guessing most people would not make the effort to get on a plane and come here.'

'Did you get his name from company records?'

'From his attorney's secretary, actually.'

Oliver told himself he would give Kathy the credit at some future date, but not now.

'The thing is, what should I do next?'

'Put some pressure on him.'

'Yes, but how?'

'Everyone has their weak spot. You'd be surprised. Find out everything you can about him and shoot it over to me. I'll see if any skeletons are rattling about in his closet and we'll take it from there.'

'How's the weather in Tortola?'

'Wet and windy. The hurricane is getting closer.'

'Sometimes they weaken when they reach land,' said Oliver.

'Sometimes, but not always. This is a big one.'

'How fast is it moving?'

'Four miles an hour. At the moment it's passing to the west of St. Kitts and moving north so it's just a day from here.'

'Better haul *Goneril* out of the water,' said Oliver.

'I already did.'

'Well, good luck.'

Oliver knew Tisch had lived through several hurricanes, which probably accounted for the anxiety in the little financier's voice.

He went down to the restaurant expecting to meet Kathy but there was no sign of her. After five minutes, he went to the house phone and called her room. There was no reply. He was surprised, but he assumed she had fallen asleep. He returned and ate supper alone.

CHAPTER 9

KATHY'S NEW PLAN

HE WAS IN HIS ROOM AFTERWARDS when the phone rang. It was Kathy.

'Where the heck are you?' he asked.

'Outside Leon's place. Just left there actually. I spoke to him.'

Oliver swore under his breath. 'That's exactly what I asked you not to do.'

'I know, but I got some great information.' Her voice was low but she sounded excited. 'He's a real freak, by the way.'

'Why am I not surprised?' said Oliver.

'Listen, I need a ride home.'

'How come?'

'Well, I got here by taxi. The driver was supposed to wait but he must have given up because when I came out later he had gone.'

'You've got a heck of a nerve.'

'Aw, come on,' she wheedled.

'Where exactly are you now?'

'Outside the gatehouse. You're a star, I won't forget this.'

'You'd better not.' Obviously he would have to go and fetch her but he was getting a bit tired of Kathy Smith.

The air was getting cool. He grabbed a sweater and drove the Peugeot out along the coast road. The highway was narrow and tricky to negotiate in the moonlight. It did not help that, in his exasperation, he was driving too fast. Once or twice he nearly ran off the verge and down the cliff into the ocean.

But by the time he approached Leon's mansion he had calmed

down. He stopped the car a hundred yards short of the gates and approached on foot. His sneakers made no sound on the sandy dirt.

The mutter of crickets and an occasional night bird's call surrounded him, the normal sounds of a tropical island after dark. There was a full moon and no cloud; once his eyes got used to the conditions, he could see almost as well as if it were day. Everything was as it should be.

Except, Oliver realized, no sign of Kathy.

He peered around. This was where she had said she would be.

'Kathy?'

Silence.

He called again.

Was she lurking somewhere in the bushes? He wouldn't put it past her.

He scanned the dusty ground but all he could see in the moonlight was a pattern of car tracks made by whatever vehicles were last there. The gatehouse was bathed in moonlight, the iron gates shut and bolted. Through the bars he could see lights in the main house some fifty yards away. More light came from the windows of an outbuilding.

He was almost ready to give up when a glint in the dust caught his eye and he bent down to look. It was a mobile phone with a silver finish. He picked it up. It could have been hers. She must have a phone, how else could she have called him? He slipped the unit into his pocket.

He was returning to his car when his eye caught a movement, just a darker shadow in the shadows. It was near a cluster of palms by the side of the road.

A chill gripped his stomach, a primitive reaction.

'Kathy?'

He moved towards the shadow but when he arrived, there was nothing there. Had his eyes played a trick on him?

The blow came suddenly.

The back of his head exploded; he staggered and fell. The last thing he remembered before oblivion took over was the tops of the palm trees spinning in a slow circle far above his head.

The throbbing began at the top of his skull and shot down through his face and jaw so that, as he turned his head, he let out a cry of pain. He blinked gingerly and looked around. The mere act of focusing was agony. He was alone, lying on the concrete floor of a high-ceilinged shed. Moonlight filtered in through dusty panes set high in the walls. As his eyes adjusted, he made out heavy machinery and what looked like vats or boiling pots. The air smelled musty. He guessed that he was in one of the buildings he had seen from the road through the gates of Leon's compound. Queasily, he tried to assess his situation. His wrists were tied tight together. Strong twine cut into the skin painfully.

His legs and ankles, on the other hand, were free; by distributing his weight carefully he was able to haul himself slowly upright, fighting waves of nausea. He stumbled as far as the door and leaned up against it. That was the best he could do, still groggy. The heavy wooden door was apparently locked from the outside; he would not be leaving unaided.

He was still trying to clear his head when he heard voices. The door flew open, pushing him aside and light flooded the room. A man and a woman entered.

The woman was slim and dark haired, smoking a cigarette in a holder. She was about thirty, attractive in a dark cocktail dress that emphasized her pale arms and shoulders. In other circumstances, Oliver's spirits would have been uplifted – she had a style that appealed to him. Her eyes met Oliver's for a moment but without displaying the least hint of sympathy. No help there.

Her companion was tall, shaven-headed and black. He was good-looking and athletic, in his thirties, wearing a pale blue business suit, white shirt and black tie. His broad shoulders tapered to a narrow waist; smiling, but with an air of menace, he resembled the great Cuban boxer, Teofilo Stevenson.

Oliver cleared his throat.

'Mind telling me what this is all about?'

The man helped Oliver up and propped him in a sitting position on a grimy wooden bench.

'My turn first. What are you doing here?'

'Here?'

'You were lurking outside Mr. Leon's front gate after dark.'

'I was not *lurking*.'

The man frowned. 'Behaving suspiciously.'

'I was out walking. It was a nice evening.'

The man produced a brown leather wallet which Oliver recognized as his own.

'You have a Florida driver's licence. Your name is Oliver Steele. What do you do for a living, Mr. Steele?

'I'm a consultant.'

The man smiled.

'And who exactly are you two?' gritted Oliver, trying to sound calm. His wrists hurt and his head throbbed, but he was determined to try and take the initiative.

'A fair question. My name is Neville Morgan, I am Mr. Leon's assistant. And this is Judith Barcat. Judith is our Vice President of IT.'

'IT?'

'Information technology. Computer systems. The things you came here to steal.'

'Steal?'

Neville laughed. 'You've no idea what I'm talking about?'

'None whatever.'

Oliver was confused. It annoyed him that the man clearly thought he was lying. There was something going on here that he was not getting. But instinct told him that to discuss the real purpose of his visit – Larry Smith's gambling debts – with anyone but Leon would only compound confusion.

He cleared his throat.

'We are talking at cross-purposes. I just have two questions. Where is Kathy Smith, and when can I meet Franklin Leon?'

Neville looked puzzled.

'I don't know where Kathy Smith is. But I'll give you one more chance to explain what you want from Mr. Leon.'

Oliver had assumed that Kathy had been abducted by Leon. If not, where was she?

Neville was watching him curiously. The silence lasted a while. Finally Neville sighed and turned to the woman.

'I guess it's time to try another way.'

The woman smiled. 'My turn?' she asked.

The smile lit up her face. She was remarkably beautiful.

Neville nodded. He turned to Oliver.

'A word of advice: Judith thinks like one of her own computers. To her, everything is either black or white, on or off. It makes her perfect for her job designing information systems. However, she sometimes has trouble with human relationships.'

'I see,' said Oliver, although he did not. He was trying to figure out what had happened to Kathy.

'Once again,' said Judith, 'Why are you here?'

'To talk to Frankie Leon.'

'About what?'

Oliver smiled but said nothing.

She returned the smile. To Neville she said, 'String him up!'

Neville looked uneasy, as if he knew what was coming.

'Do it,' she snapped. The brilliant smile did not waver but she sounded irritated.

Neville shrugged. He lifted Oliver off the bench with one muscular arm and dragged him, still groggy, towards a piece of rusting iron machinery in the middle of the room. It stood about six feet high. Neville deftly hooked Oliver's wrists over a projecting screw. With his toes brushing the concrete floor, he was completely helpless.

At that exact moment, Kathy was having a heated argument with Norrie Flack. She was not getting her point across. They had met only an hour ago and the relationship had gone downhill fast since then.

Kathy first become aware of the Flack Group while she was standing on the front step of Frankie Leon's crumbling mansion, talking to him. The topic of conversation was one that Oliver would never have guessed. Suffice it to say that – much to Frankie's surprise – they had found some common ground.

As they were parting, Kathy noticed something odd. From the corner of her eye, high in the thick foliage of a tree just inside the weathered brick wall that surrounded the estate, she saw movement.

The trunk of the tree was outside the compound but its branches straddled the top of the wall and overhung the interior lawn. As she watched she glimpsed, for a split second, a pale face, like the Cheshire cat, among the leaves. Then it twitched and vanished and she was left wondering if it had just been a trick of the light.

It was getting late and the sun was setting. She walked down the gravel path accompanied by Leon's dapper assistant, Neville. Something about his smooth smile and careful tailoring made her wonder idly if he was homosexual. He let her out with a little bow and waved goodbye.

She was outside the gates before she realized that her taxi driver was nowhere to be seen. She had promised him that she would only be five minutes but the time had slipped by while she was talking to Leon and the driver was gone, probably home to his family and supper.

She turned to speak to Neville but the elegant Antiguan was gone and the gates were shut and locked.

It was getting dark and the road was empty. She was stranded.

She was also tired and hungry. She had a phone in her purse; she could use it to call Oliver for a ride home. She expected volleys of criticism when he learned what she had done but the thought of his stable presence was appealing. She tried to think of a suitable excuse. Nothing sprang to mind but finally hunger won out, so she took a deep breath and dialled the hotel.

After talking to Oliver, she sat down on the grass to wait. There was a commotion in the foliage overhead and she looked up to see a substantial figure drop with a thump to the ground beside her.

She had almost forgotten the Cheshire cat face. Now here it was again, this time attached to a dishevelled body atop white legs in baggy khaki shorts. The young man stared at her, mouth open, possibly wondering whether she was friend or foe. He ran a hand through a mop of red hair, dislodging sundry twigs.

'Hi,' she said.

He blinked.

'What's wrong,' she asked tartly. 'Cat got your tongue?'

'Just g-getting my breath back.'

She noticed the stutter. 'What were you doing stuck up that tree?'

'T-taking a look.' He patted the tree trunk with pride. 'Good vantage point, huh?'

'Why were you up there?'

'Reconnaissance.'

'For what?'

He looked suddenly thoughtful, as if he had just remembered he must not say too much.

His appearance was intelligent but oddly naive and, she suspected, without much sense of humour. The word 'nerd' came to mind.

'What's your name?' she asked.

'Ron. Ron Rigby.

'Well, hi, Ron. Do you realize we are stranded here?'

He shook his head. 'No, I'm okay.' He looked at his wristwatch. 'Wait just a minute…'

Moments later she heard the sound of a car and a black Mercedes appeared. The window slid down and the driver looked out.

'Don't hang about,' he grunted at Rigby, 'Get in.'

'Got room for one more?' Kathy asked quickly.

Uncle Norrie frowned at her. She smiled back.

Norrie Flack did not have much time for young American women. Or for women at all, come to that. They had their uses but not in the business world and especially not in Norrie's line of business – shadowy territory on the violent side of town, as befitted his job as the Flacks' enforcer. Besides, he had a lot on his mind. 'Where is it you want to go?'

'The Antigua Star Hotel.'

'We're not going that way.' Who was this woman?

She stared in disbelief. He was apparently driving back to St. John and, if so, her hotel was almost exactly on the way.

'Fine, just take me as far as you can.'

He scowled.

Kathy, despite her undoubted academic skills, was not the world's most dependable person. She had a quick brain but she had a way of occasionally forgetting things, no matter how important. So it completely slipped her mind that Oliver was on his way to fetch her. She nipped round to the other side of the Mercedes and jumped in beside Flack before he could leave without her. In the meanwhile, Rigby had climbed into the back.

As they drove off, she watched Flack out of the corner of her eye. He was solid with a bodybuilder's meaty shoulders. He drove with a frown, his fat rosebud mouth pursed in concentration.

'What are you doing out here?' she asked.

He scowled. 'None of your business.'

'It might be.'

'I doubt it.'

'Look,' she said, 'there's obviously no love lost between Frankie Leon and you people, whoever you are. I happen to feel the same way as you do about Leon.'

She paused for a reaction.

Flack drove on through the dusk. It was Ron Rigby who broke the silence.

'She knows Leon. Maybe she can get us into the computer centre.'

'That's enough,' snapped Flack.

But his rebuke of Rigby confirmed Kathy's suspicions. The cat was out of the bag as far as she was concerned. This pair was up to something.

'Look,' she said, 'My father was screwed pretty badly by Leon's Casino. I intend for him to make it right.'

'In what way screwed?' asked Rigby.

'He was tricked into placing bets he couldn't afford.'

There was an awkward silence in the car. The Flacks were long-time turf accountants to the British gentry and such situations were not uncommon. Gamblers had been getting into trouble since time began. It was an unforgiving business.

'Are you sure your father is not part of the problem?' said Flack curtly.

She frowned, 'I suppose that might sound reasonable if you were a bookie.'

Silence.

Slowly light dawned on Kathy. She whistled.

'Oh, now I get it,' she said. 'That's who you are, you're the competition.'

'We're not *just* the competition.' Rigby was indignant. 'Flack is the fastest-growing, sports-wagering group in Europe.'

She looked at him. 'Where are you from? You sound American.'

'Seal Beach, California.'

'What about him?' She indicated Flack. 'He has to be British.'

Rigby nodded. 'Flack is a British company, or used to be. It's international now.'

'Based in Antigua?'

'No, Gibraltar.'

'So what are you doing here on Antigua?'

Both men clammed up at that point and she got nothing more out of them as they approached the island's capital.

When they reached the exit to her hotel, Flack drove straight past it without turning.

'Would you kindly take me back to my hotel,' she said crossly.

Silence.

'Did you hear what I said?'

'Be quiet,' said Flack coldly.

'Don't talk to me like that.'

'Shut your mouth,' he snapped.

'How dare you!' She was angry and a little scared.

With an unexpected movement, Flack turned and slapped her face hard.

CHAPTER 10

TWO OLD FRIENDS

AFTER DINNER, Carlton Tisch and Kon Feaver sat on the terrace of Carlton's cliff house on Tortola, looking out over the dark ocean, two old friends with some shared history chatting on a warm night.

Tisch offered Feaver a Monte Cristo cigar and poured cognac into two balloon glasses. Once the cigars were drawing, he turned to his guest.

'So what brings you here this fine evening?'

'The pleasure of your company.'

Kon's Slavic face was impassive but Carlton was aware of the peasant shrewdness beneath.

'Bullshit.'

'Can't fool you for a minute,' said Kon.

'How's that 'plane of yours,' Carlton asked. 'Running okay?'

'Very nicely. Stays airborne when it's supposed to, comes down when I tell it.'

Feaver was constantly on the move, flying round the Caribbean in his small amphibious plane, often using its pontoons to land on the ocean. In his Air Force days he had excelled as a pilot, being blessed with fast reflexes and a cool head although down on the ground there were problems and after a year he was kicked out of the service for drunkenness.

He did a brief stint in Africa as a mercenary but eventually came to rest in South Florida. For a while he ran his share of grass out of Miami and made a lot of money, all of which he squandered on fast living. Now he ran errands for Carlton Tisch, which occupied about half his time. As for the other half, nobody knew quite what he did, which was how he liked it. He was apparently sober and seemed content. On paper, at least, he was chronically broke.

Superficially, Feaver and Tisch looked similar – both were in their early fifties and deeply tanned although Feaver was barrel-chested, more robust and several inches taller. In other ways, they differed sharply. Whereas Feaver was impulsive and a man of action, Carlton Tisch was more of a planner and calculator. His thin, birdlike face reflected every nuance of thought the moment it crossed his mind. He made his living by being subtle and creative with a wry humour that sometimes made even his adversaries warm to him. He was also unabashedly self-centred.

'So why *are* you here?'

'What's going on with Oliver Steele?'

'Do you always answer a question with a question?'

'Why shouldn't I? I had a call yesterday from some lawyer on Antigua. He wanted a reference on Oliver. Something about a casino down there.'

'So?'

'I smell a rat. It does not sound like Oliver's style.'

'Why not?'

'It's just not him. He's pretty honest and that industry is a bit marginal quite frankly.'

'Really?'

'Oh please. Anyway, am I somehow involved?'

Tisch shook his head. 'No. You are part of a cover story for Oliver while he looks into something for a friend of mine.'

'Which you forgot to tell me about?'

'Yes.'

'Thanks a lot.'

Feaver feigned annoyance but he was not really concerned and they both knew it. When you worked for Carlton, stuff like that was part of the job.

But he was curious by nature.

'So tell me more. In case I get more calls.'

Between sips of brandy, Carlton related Larry Smith's gambling problem. He explained that Oliver was following the trail, hoping to put pressure on whoever was hounding Smith.

'And the casino is based on Antigua?'

Carlton nodded. 'Fellow called Leon.'

'What's he like?'

'Ruthless, from what I hear.'

'By any chance, are you talking about Frankie Leon?'

'I don't know his first name.'

'There was a Frankie Leon who used to deal coke out of Miami.'

'Could be the guy. Oliver said he was from Florida.'

Feaver drew on his cigar. 'That's not good news.'

'Why?'

'That Frankie Leon is a little nuts.'

'Nuts how?'

'Crazy. Cuckoo.'

'Worse than me?'

'Much worse. You know that I used to be in that business?'

Tisch paused. 'Yeah.'

'I got out fairly early on but for a while, frankly, it was fun. You have to understand how things were in those days. There were fewer hard drugs around than today, and more marijuana. The atmosphere was a little bit like a college campus, crazy as that sounds. A younger population of dealers. Kids spent a lot of time on the road between Miami and New York with a trunk full of weed.'

Feaver grinned. 'They used to say that if you saw a two-year-old white family car on the interstate driving just under the speed limit and looking totally innocent, then it was a dealer for sure.

'Anyway, when the Colombians moved in, that changed. Things got more dangerous.'

'Is that when you quit?'

'Yeah. It wasn't just the danger, it was the insanity. The stakes got higher, with all the hard drugs. The violence got worse. You would arrive at a rendezvous not knowing whether to expect a briefcase full of money or a bullet in the stomach. The Colombian dealers show no mercy. No honour among thieves, no trust, just death and destruction. That is their culture.'

'Most of the clean-cut youngsters who thought it was hip to deal an ounce of weed to their friends had no stomach for the new situation. They had to look around for other work.'

'How very sad,' said Carlton sarcastically.

'It was, in some cases. Late twenties, no job, no credit history. The smart ones might have money tucked away but usually it was just a few thousand dollars. A big house in Coral Gables with a Mercedes in the driveway is very nice but the overhead is a killer. When the property taxes come due and there's no cash flow, reality hits home.'

'What happened to them?'

Feaver grinned. 'Oh, they went and became stockbrokers. Or realtors. Sales jobs, in other words. I know a former millionaire who is still working in a Palm Springs telephone boiler-room today, pitching vinyl siding to homeowners.'

'They didn't adjust too well?'

'Some struggled with depression. One shot himself in a motel room in Tampa. Another contrived a car accident that cost him both legs and then collected the insurance money. He thought that was worthwhile, apparently.'

Carlton frowned. 'Incredible!'

'Of course, these folks were misfits to begin with,' said Feaver, 'Swimmers against the current, not model citizens.'

'Typical business entrepreneurs,' said Carlton. 'Except that entrepreneurs are on the right side of the law.'

'Sometimes,' said Feaver.

'Watch it, now.' Tisch scratched his stubbly chin. 'Where did Leon fit into the picture?'

'He was the exception that proves the rule.'

'How so?'

'He switched to dealing hard drugs without missing a beat. The rougher things got, the rougher he got. His income multiplied many times.'

'He could deal with the violence?'

'He thrived on it. He acquired more weaponry than the opposition and enjoyed using it. People learned not to mess with him.'

'So what's the big deal? He had survival skills.'

'Yeah but he went too far.

'Oh?'

'One incident was notorious. Leon was supplying cocaine to some rich playboy in a luxury penthouse on Naples beach. A Colombian dealer objected. He accused Leon of poaching his customer. He threatened to come to the penthouse and shoot Leon's eyes out. So Leon brought along some muscle of his own and ambushed the Colombian instead.

The guy begged for mercy but Leon gouged his eyes out with a steak knife and threw them in the trash.'

Carlton Tisch winced. 'Did the man die?'

'No. The playboy to his credit loaded him into his Ferrari – blood dripping all over the leather – and got him to the emergency room. Leon intended him to live as an example to others. That's how things work in that world.'

'And you think this is the same Leon?'

'Has to be. I heard he left Florida; the IRS were starting to look at him and he must have decided that butting heads with Uncle Sam could only end up one way. He had plenty of money, I guess he used some of it to start the casino.'

'The timing sounds right,' said Carlton.

'I'm surprised he hasn't been extradited by now,' said Feaver.

'For what?'

'Tax evasion?'

Carlton shook his head.

'Doesn't happen very often,' he said. 'The IRS is not all-powerful. It is reasonably effective in the States but 'abroad' is tougher territory. Foreign banks don't issue 1099 forms telling the

IRS where people's money is and what interest it earned. Nobody uses Social Security numbers. Foreign governments are slow to help out. So the IRS may have difficulty snaring him unless he sets foot on American soil, which he probably has the sense not to do.'

Feaver nodded. He did not possess a social security number himself, not being an American resident and that suited him just fine.

'So do you think Oliver is okay down there in Antigua, nosing around after this guy?'

Tisch stared out to sea thoughtfully.

'Oliver is resourceful. He knows how to stay out of trouble.'

He moved to refill Feaver's glass but the Israeli deftly moved the goblet away. He had hardly drunk anything. Tisch shrugged and replenished his own glass.

They sat there awhile finishing their cigars, then Feaver looked at his watch.

'I must go.'

'You can bunk here if you want.'

'Thanks, but I have stuff to do. You know me, always busy.'

Tisch watched Feaver climb into his rented Toyota and speed away down the hill. Then he turned and walked back to the house.

Feaver drove into Roadtown and returned the car, then took a taxi over the Queen Elizabeth Bridge from Tortola to the small airfield on Ile de Boeuf.

He spent a few minutes in the airport office filing a flight plan. Then he walked out to his plane and strolled round carrying out visual checks before climbing aboard. He spoke briefly by radio with the control tower, then guided the streamlined silver aircraft down the runway, took off and disappeared into the night.

CHAPTER 11

ANTIGUA'S SEAMY SIDE

T HE MERCEDES with Kathy Smith, Ron Rigby and Uncle Norrie
on board was approaching the outskirts of St. John's.

It was definitely not a tourist area, Kathy noticed. The buildings
were poor and run down, made of clapboard with crumbling
frames. Reeking waste flowed in open gutters down both sides of
the street. Warehouses alternated with dimly lit shops and chipped
enamel signs advertised Pepsi Cola and Cherry Blossom boot polish.

There were a few residences with rickety porches, their front
yards strewn with trash. On the porches, some sticks of furniture,
a rocking chair or an old sofa with its stuffing bursting through the
seams, sat forlornly.

The Mercedes purred to a halt at one of the houses. On the
verandah, young men lounged in the dark, drinking. The clink of
bottles mingled with harsh laughter.

Norrie Flack got out of the car. 'Keep an eye on her,' he told
Rigby. He climbed the porch steps and went inside, the young men
parting deferentially to let him through.

Kathy took a quick look around her, taking in the derelict neighbourhood. She considered making a run for it but then had second
thoughts. Visions of her body being discovered in the cold light of
dawn by some curious traveller were enough to change her mind.
She decided instead to pick Ron Rigby's brain.

'What exactly is going on here?'

He looked embarrassed. 'This is management, Norrie style.'

'Is that how the Flacks run their business?

He shook his head. 'Normally Wilf is in charge but he had to fly back to London for a few days – some kind of filing deadline. We took him to the airport this morning. On the way back, Norrie started getting bossy, issuing orders. He drove straight out to Leon's place. He made me climb that tree.'

'What exactly does he want?'

'He's after the Casino's computer programmes. So am I, actually.' He fidgeted uncomfortably.

Kathy gave him a long look.

'I'm in a weird situation,' he said half apologetically.

'Good or bad?'

'Oh, I don't know. A bit of both... Six months ago I was a systems analyst for Lockheed in Los Angeles. It was okay. I lived down at the beach, drove a nice yellow convertible – everything was fine. But the work was kind of dull so I answered an Internet ad. It promised fascinating work and a chance to see the world. A month later I was in Gibraltar, working for Flack.'

'Is the work difficult?'

He shook his head. 'Gaming has been computerized for years – figuring the odds, basic number crunching, that kind of thing. My assistants do most of the day-to-day programming. I work on special projects with Wilf.'

'And this is a special project?'

'Yeah.'

'What is Wilf like?' she prodded.

Ron perked up. 'He's great. Very fair. Knows the business inside out. He can even programme a bit.'

'Not like Norrie?'

'Nope. What a contrast, eh? Talk about tunnel vision. Norrie just barrels ahead with that nasty scowl of his, and if anyone gets in his way, watch out.'

'No kidding.' She fingered her cheek, which was still tingling.

'Take this project, for example. Wilf initiated it but now Norrie wants to muscle in and do things his way.'

'How did the whole idea get started?'

'Wilf has a long-term plan and this is part of it. He wants us to double our business in five years. We all sat down and hammered out scenarios. I designed spreadsheets to compare the options – different levels of business, different markets, growth versus acquisition and so on. Everyone was involved. It took months. It became clear that we needed to be in the on-line casino business. It was an exploding market.

Specifically, we needed the computer programmes that play the games – roulette, poker, blackjack. Since we lacked the expertise, that suggested we needed an acquisition.'

'And you selected Casino Caribbean?'

He nodded. 'We made a list of the leading casinos – no problem identifying them, their web sites are easy to find.'

'Did you approach all of them?'

'Pretty much. Some belonged to our competition so they weren't available but Casino Caribbean was privately owned – by Mr. Leon – and it was well designed.'

'I'm curious about one thing,' said Kathy. 'Are these casinos honest?'

'You mean, does the house cheat?'

'Right.'

He shook his head. 'It doesn't need to, the profit margins are so good. Besides, if the house wins too often, players will switch to a competing web site. It's like being in Las Vegas and walking out of the Mirage if you are losing. A few yards up the Strip are the Bellagio and the MGM Grand. Same principle but, on the Internet, it's even easier.'

'So are you going to buy Casino Caribbean?'

Rigby shrugged. ' I think we were going to, but now Norrie has a different plan.'

'And you are going along with him?'

'He's a hard man to disobey. His orders were to look around, see what went on in there. That's what I was doing when I met you.'

'What happens now?'

Rigby shrugged. 'I don't know. It doesn't sound good. He's got a bunch of toughs in that house that I don't like the look of. I hope he's not planning a war.'

'That's crazy.'

'Norrie may be a bit crazy. He has that reputation. There have been incidents in the past.

'What kind of incidents?'

'Early on, when Flack was just a handful of betting shops. Break-ins. Suspicious fires on rivals' properties. Competitors terrorized. The competitors often ended up selling to the Flacks cheaply.'

'Aren't there laws against that kind of thing in Britain?'

'It's hard to enforce the law if witnesses are too scared to testify.'

Kathy digested all this. It did not sound auspicious. She felt a shiver of fear run through her. Then she thought about her father. She stiffened herself.

'When is Wilf coming back?'

'In a couple of days.'

'Shouldn't you call and tell him what's going on? Right away?'

Rigby looked round doubtfully. 'I don't see a phone anywhere.'

'There must be a pay phone nearby. You can drive me.'

He fidgeted. 'I'm not sure.'

'Come on, what can you lose?'

'You don't know Norrie.'

'Well, we can't just do nothing,' she said stubbornly.

Rigby looked miserable. She realized that doing nothing was exactly what he had in mind. He was just an employee. She wasn't going to let him off the hook so easily, but she saw that she could not expect any heroics. His job was at risk. He was weak.

Uncle Norrie had come out onto the front porch. With him was a surly looking, dark-skinned man in his mid-thirties, powerfully built, with a disfiguring pink scar on his cheek. He seemed to be in charge of the younger men. They stood around waiting for orders while their boss listened to Norrie.

She caught the tail end of Norrie's words. 'Then you bring them up in the boat, Rollo.'

'Got it,' Rollo grunted.

What boat was he talking about? She barely had time to wonder as Norrie approached the car. If he had overheard her conversation with Ron she was in trouble but he seemed to have other things on his mind.

'You drive,' he snapped at Rigby. He bundled Kathy into the back seat and climbed in after her, slamming the door.

As the Mercedes picked up speed, a dusty Land Rover containing Rollo and his men fell in after them, fifty yards behind.

'What's going on?' she asked indignantly. Privately, she had a pretty good idea.

'We're going to pay a call on Mr. Frankie Leon.'

'What kind of call? Who are all those people?'

'A social call,' Norrie smirked.

He leaned forward and spoke to Rigby.

'Open the glove box, son.'

Rigby pushed the catch and the lid fell open. Inside was an automatic pistol.

'Put it in your pocket.'

Nervously Rigby complied, one hand on the steering wheel, the other handling the heavy black weapon gingerly. Norrie turned away from Kathy on the leather seat, reached for his own firearm and counted the bullets in the clip. It held about a dozen rounds, Kathy thought.

He replaced the clip and pushed the weapon inside his waistband. It was out of Kathy's reach even had she wished to grope at his ample midriff, which she did not. A chill in the pit of the stomach, fear mixed with disgust, gripped her as she watched, amazed.

'I can't believe this.'

Norrie shrugged. 'Believe whatever you want. This is the real world. People like Leon only respect force, like some Londoners I've known.'

'Violence breeds more violence.'

'Violence works. My nephew Wilf thinks he can just sit in a conference room and talk but he's wrong. Life isn't like that. It's dirty and it's bloody. Rigby says we need the programmes and they are there for the taking, so I'm going to take them. To hell with Wilf and his nice suits and corporate crap.'

'You are going to take them by force?'

A grim smile flickered on Norrie's saturnine face.

'This isn't Minnesota or wherever you come from. We are offshore. In a way this is the new Wild West; it's frontier country.'

'And that's where you feel comfortable, right?'

Norrie shrugged. 'Yes I do. Wilf wants to pay hundreds of millions of dollars for something we can get this way for pennies. Would Leon pay that kind of money if he was in our shoes? Of course not, it wouldn't be good business.'

'How will you do this?'

'You'll see.'

'Won't he call the police?'

He snorted. 'Leon doesn't do business with the police. Anyhow, we'd be gone before they arrived. In and out. Like I say, a social call.'

With what Rigby had told her, things were depressingly clear to Kathy. Norrie Flack might indeed be crazy but, as she watched him making plans and directing his people, she had to admit he looked well organized.

She felt anxious but also oddly excited. After all, Leon was about to experience a major disruption. That could only distract him from minor matters like terrorizing her father. And she was a captive, not a participant. She would not be wielding a weapon, she was not to blame. But what if she was hit by a stray bullet?

'Why don't you let me get out? I am only in the way,' she said.

Norrie Flack shook his head. 'You're part of the plan.'

'Excuse me?'

'When we reach the plantation, I need you to call Leon from the gatehouse. Just tell him you have to see him. Get him to open the door. You're our calling card, so to speak.'

'You're kidding!'

But privately she told herself, 'wait now.' There could be something for me here. Why am I really here? To get a reprieve for my dumb father. So what if the Flacks get what they want? What is important is that I get what I want. So she fell silent.

She looked at her watch. It was an hour before midnight.

'It's pretty late. I doubt if he'll let me in.'

'Sure he will. You're a good-looking girl, just ask him nicely.'

'And then what?'

'We'll take it from there.'

The small caravan of vehicles, led by the Mercedes, was approaching Conway Hill. Next came the Land Rover and, farther back, an elderly Ford truck, pitted with rust. Several young toughs sat in the open bed.

The Mercedes approached the plantation making no attempt at concealment and parked just outside the wrought iron gates. She looked round. Now the Land Rover, too, had disappeared.

Norrie climbed out, pulling Kathy after him. Keep the motor running, he muttered to Rigby.

He waved the Walther at Kathy.

'Go ahead, press the buzzer. And no tricks.'

Nervously she approached the intercom. Flack pressed himself against the crumbling wall, out of sight of the TV cameras. Holding her breath, she pressed the button.

Frankie Leon was working at the desk in his oak-panelled study. He continued to write but moments later the buzzer sounded again and he put down his pen. Irritated, he hit a key on his phone.

'Answer the buzzer, Neville.'

'Could you do us a favour and get that, boss. We're kind of busy in here.' Neville's tone was servile and at the same time excited.

'What, you're too busy to answer the door?' Frankie grumbled.

'We're having a chat with your visitor, Mr Steele.'

Frankie's lips parted in a smile. He could imagine how that conversation was going.

'Okay.'

He hauled himself out of his leather swivel chair and headed for the door.

At the last minute, he went back to the desk and took a pistol from his desk drawer. Pocketing it, he strolled down to the main gate.

Kathy heard the crunch of his steps on the gravel and the sound of the door to the gatehouse opening.

'Who's there?'

'Hi Frankie, it's me Kathy again.' She stood in the cameras' field of view and smiled. Flack was crouched to one side, out of sight.

'Back again?'

'We have to talk.'

Silence.

'Can I come in?'

'Who's in the car?'

'Just my driver. He'll wait outside.'

Frankie's voice softened slightly. 'I'll get the latch.'

Dead bolts disengaged electronically and the gates swung open. The plump New Yorker stood there, anticipation creasing his face at the sight of the young woman standing there alone. He stood aside, holding the pistol loosely.

He saw her eying the gun.

'Can't be too careful.'

Norrie Flack erupted from the shadows, shoved Kathy aside and jammed the Walther into Frankie's stomach.

Kathy thought fast. How should she portray herself in this drama? Flack was in control at the moment but that could change.

Exaggerating the effect of Flack's shove, she contrived a stumble and fell to the ground with a convincing cry of pain.

Her theatrics were barely noticed by Frankie who had eyes only for Flack. The two men watched each other intently.

'Drop the gun,' grunted Flack.

Frankie let it fall.

But he did not lose his composure. Kathy guessed that being

held at gunpoint was not a new situation for him. He even smiled slightly. Looking at Kathy he shook his head reproachfully.

She shrugged and gestured to Flack's gun as if to say, 'See, I had no choice.'

Frankie's eyes swivelled between Flack and Kathy. Slowly he raised his hands above his head.

'What do you want?'

'A talk,' said Flack.

'Just a talk? So why the gun?'

Flack ignored him 'Let's go to your office.'

Frankie smiled mockingly and waved towards the house.

'Shall I lead the way?'

By way of response, Flack shoved him in the back with the gun. He beckoned to Rigby.

'You too.'

Rigby scrambled to comply, leaving the Mercedes door open.

'Lock the car, dummy,' Flack barked.

Rigby did so, then pocketed the keys and trotted to catch up.

As they marched up the driveway, Flack kept his gun in Frankie's back. Kathy, who had actually twisted her ankle slightly, hobbled along behind them.

The house appeared deserted. As they entered his office, Frankie moved towards his desk and reached for a drawer but Flack grabbed his arm.

'Hang about, son.'

He moved in front of Frankie and peered suspiciously at the mahogany desk.

'Going to press the panic button, were you?'

Frankie rubbed his arm where Flack had gripped it. He tried to look uncomprehending but Kathy thought his expression masked respect.

'As you wish.'

He scowled at Kathy, or so she thought. On that moon-face it was hard to tell.

'What are you doing mixed up in this?'

It was a fair question, one Kathy had asked herself. How did she justify joining Norrie Flack's invasion?

'I just want you to stop harassing my father,' she blurted.

He raised his eyebrows.

'My dad is Larry Smith.'

He looked at her blankly. If she had expected him to recognize the name, she was disappointed.

'He lost a fortune at your casino.'

He shrugged. 'We have thousands of players.'

'You sent one of your goons to his home to collect money.'

'Must be a misunderstanding. Our customers pay by credit card.'

'Most of them do, but you also do business with people who are maxed out on their cards.'

'In a very few cases.'

'Well, my father is one of the few.'

'He frowned. 'Actually we refer those people out.'

'Refer them out? What does that mean?'

'We refer them to a finance company. We're a casino, not a bank. It is the finance company makes the loan, not us. That way we don't have any bad debts. Gambling debts are not legally enforceable.'

She snorted. 'You probably earn a commission.'

'What if we do? We provide the introduction. But the gambler uses the loan to bet with, so we know we'll get the money in the end.'

At that, Kathy's self-control almost gave way.

You piece of trash, she felt like saying, my dad went to hospital after a beating from one of your goons and you pretend you don't even know?

But she bit her tongue. Stay on his good side, she told herself.

Frankie frowned. 'You never mentioned your dad earlier.'

She shrugged. 'It's something to be negotiated. That would be part of our arrangement.'

Flack pricked up his ears. 'What arrangement? What are you two talking about?'

'Personal stuff,' said Kathy.

'Meaning?'

'Nothing that affects this discussion, trust me!'

Flack looked puzzled but only briefly. He had other things on his mind. He looked round the room.

'Where are the computer programmes?'

A look of comprehension began to spread over Frankie's face. In that instant, Kathy realized that Frankie understood everything – what Flack wanted, why he wanted it and how he planned to get it. Despite the age difference and the accents they were two of a kind, Uncle Norrie and Frankie.

Frankie shook his head. 'Those programmes are critical to my business, as you well know. If you think I'm going to give them to you, you must be dumber than you look.'

'Dumb is as dumb does,' said Flack equably. 'Where are they?'

Frankie shook his head.

Flack raised the gun. The atmosphere was tense. Kathy was convinced he was going to shoot Frankie. She was already covering her ears when Rigby spoke.

'Wh-what's in there?' He nodded at a white painted door across the room.

'Nothing,' said Frankie.

'Shall we take a look,' said Flack.

Rigby was already trying the door. It was locked.

'The key,' Flack snapped.

'I don't have it,' said Frankie.

'Who does?'

Frankie shrugged.

Flack raised the gun. Kathy flinched.

Flack put the heavy weapon to the lock and fired. The report was deafening, rattling the windows. The door swung open, its handle twitching like fingers on a dying hand. Inside was a computer workbench on which sat three monitors, screen savers flickering – tropical fish floating amid bright coral.

'Bingo,' said Rigby. He sat down at the nearest monitor and started typing.

Everyone had crowded into the computer room. Rigby typed faster and faster, mouth open, humming tunelessly. 'Damn,' he said. Then, 'Ah… Got it.'

'What's going on,' muttered Flack.

'I'm on the t-t-trail,' said Rigby. 'Give me a minute.' He was tapping his foot excitedly.

Frankie was sweating now. Moisture ran down his forehead into his eyes and he wiped it away. Flack, who was watching the screen, kept his gun pressed firmly in the small of Frankie's back.

Rigby kept typing. Letters and numbers raced across the screen, then finally stopped, displaying the instruction 'Enter Password.'

'It seems we have a problem,' said Flack.

Frankie said nothing.

'Oh, tell him the password,' said Kathy. She was not sure why she said it. She just wanted things to end without bloodshed.

At that point Frankie groaned and sank to the floor. He lay on his back, breathing heavily.

Kathy dropped on one knee, concerned despite herself. 'He's fainted.'

'He's faking,' sneered Flack.

'Looks real to me,' said Kathy.

Flack leaned over Frankie's body, reversed his gun and tapped smartly with it on the knuckles of one pink hand.

Frankie cursed and sat up.

'You might as well give us the password,' said Flack drily.

Frankie just scowled at him.

Flack shrugged. 'Okay, enough games.'

He seized Frankie's left wrist and pushed his hand down on the desktop. Holding his pistol by the barrel he again rapped Frankie's knuckles, harder this time. There was the crunch of metal on bone and Frankie bit back a scream.

Flack released him. You want to tell us the password now?

Frankie rolled his eyes. 'F___ you, he gritted,' barely audibly. He cradled his mangled left knuckles in his good hand. Blood oozed between the fingers.

'Your choice,' said Flack.

He grabbed Frankie's other hand and spread it in the same way as before, knuckles upwards. He raised his pistol again.

He was not expecting the bullet that slammed into his right shoulder just as he was raising his arm. He spun round, dropping the gun, which clattered to the floor.

Neville stood in the doorway, pistol in hand, a half smile on his lips, Judith close behind him.

'You okay, boss?'

'I've been better.'

Frankie was far from okay, but the sudden change in the balance of power clearly improved his mood.

He rounded on Flack and, with his good hand, delivered a vicious punch to Flack's wounded shoulder. Flack drew a sharp breath and the blood drained from his face.

'Shall I kill the jerk?' Neville asked.

'Maybe later.'

Neville looked round the room. Seeing that Flack was incapacitated and reckoning that neither Kathy nor Rigby posed a threat, he lowered his gun.

Kathy glanced covertly at the four men.

Only the suave Neville seemed comfortable. He strolled over to where Flack's gun lay on the floor and picked it up. He removed the clip and slipped it in his pocket.

'That's better,' he said. 'Let's see, where were we?'

Frankie Leon frowned. 'Mr. Flack, you are a real embarrassment. What were you thinking of, breaking in like this? I thought we had a deal where I would sell my casino to your company and I would still like to do that, but now…'

He sighed. 'I should probably ignore you and deal with your brother, but where shall I put you in the meanwhile? If I send you home, you will only come at me again. You are a problem.'

'Let me shoot him,' said Neville.

'Oh, yes,' said Judith involuntarily, her eyes gleaming.

Kathy watched and listened. When she had visited Frankie

earlier that day, she had proposed a deal to him that would change everything. But she could not mention that in front of the others.

She raised a hand. 'Excuse me.'

Frankie looked at her surprised. 'Oh yes, your project.'

'There's no time like the present,' she said.

'Your dad would be part of the package,' said Frankie.

Norrie Flack pricked up his ears. 'What the hell is he talking about,' he scowled.

She smiled nervously. 'Nothing that concerns you.'

He gave her a long, suspicious look but said nothing.

Out in the warehouse, Judith had been getting ready to work on Oliver in earnest when a shot rang out. It seemed to come from the house. She cursed and lowered the bullwhip.

She and Neville looked at each other, then turned and hurried from the warehouse. Oliver was left trussed to the iron grid. He breathed deeply for a few seconds, temporarily relieved but well aware that his situation was still perilous.

A moment later, the door opened and in strolled the reassuring figure of the Israeli, Kon Feaver.

'Need any help?'

Without waiting for an answer, he unfastened Oliver from the rusting iron press. Oliver tottered, barely able to stand. Feaver saw blood seeping through his white cotton shirt.

'What happened?'

'Judith is a bit rough,' said Oliver grimly.

'I'll say.'

'I won't ask what you're doing here,' said Oliver, surveying the stocky figure, 'But I'm quite glad to see you. How did you find me?'

'Educated guesswork. I figured you might be sniffing round Leon's place.'

'Well, you were right.

Feaver nodded. 'I saw the Mercedes parked by the gate but there was no-one around. It looked kind of fishy, so I hopped over the wall and this was the first building I came to.'

Another shot rang out.

'What's going on across the way?'

'Damned if I know,' said Oliver. He brushed himself down gingerly.

Feaver rubbed his chin. 'I saw a woman and three men going into the house. One guy had a gun in the ribs of another guy.'

'What did the woman look like?'

'A blonde in her twenties. Short shorts, nice legs.'

'Sounds like Kathy Smith.'

'Larry Smith's daughter?'

'Yeah. And the fat guy with the gun to his ribs was Frankie Leon.'

'I thought I recognized him. I guess he got ambushed.'

Oliver grinned at Feaver. 'Well, you saved me from some serious pain. Thank you.'

'You're welcome. You think we should stroll over there and take a look?'

'Good idea,' said Oliver. 'Do you have a gun?'

Feaver shook his head. 'Nope. Guess I'll have to improvise.'

'You don't sound too concerned.'

Feaver said nothing but there was a thoughtful look in his eye.

They approached the house from the back. As they crept quietly along the beach and paused outside the French windows, they could hear raised voices from inside.

'You go in first,' said Feaver.

'Oh, thanks.'

'I have my reasons. Trust me.'

Oliver took a deep breath and entered.

'Hi guys!'

Everyone turned and faced him.

'Come in, Mr. Steele' said Neville. 'Judith *will* be glad to see you.'

Judith smiled, showing perfect white teeth.

Frankie scowled at Oliver. 'They were supposed to shoot you in the restaurant.'

Light dawned on Oliver. 'So that was you?'

'Yeah. You got lucky. What a screw-up that was.' Frankie did not seem too concerned about collateral damage in the shape of the dead waiter. Any minimal sympathy Oliver might have felt for the embattled casino owner quickly evaporated.

He looked round the room, wondering who would make the next move.

Neville could see that Oliver was unarmed. He waved his gun, herding him into a corner along with Kathy and the injured Norrie Flack.

For a moment Neville had his back to the window. In that instant, Feaver burst into the room, his strong legs moving fast, making straight for Neville. Neville heard him coming and turned to face Feaver, who karate-chopped Neville's gun arm, numbing his wrist, and the automatic fell on the floor. Feaver kicked it aside.

The two men faced each other.

Neville smiled. He was several inches taller and probably outweighed Feaver by twenty pounds. Assuming a boxer's crouch, he moved towards the Israeli, fists ready.

He threw a lightning left jab. In a blur, Feaver caught the arm and, using the bigger man's momentum, twisted. There was a crunch as the arm broke. Neville's cry was a whimper, part fear and part surprise.

Oliver was impressed and his face showed it. Kon grinned.

'Tel Aviv Judo team,' he explained. He retrieved the gun.

Norrie, who had lost a lot of blood, rolled his eyes and slid slowly to the ground.

For a minute nobody spoke, frozen by the pace of events. For no particular reason, Oliver remembered he still had Kathy's mobile phone. He took it out and looked at it.

Kathy saw him holding it and their eyes met. She gave a nervous, semi-apologetic shrug as if to say, 'I got you into this, I'm sorry.' Watching the forlorn way her shoulders drooped, he felt his irritation at her start to evaporate. He handed her the phone.

'This is yours.'

She took it from him, looking thoughtful, and mouthed the words 'Thank you' silently. Then he saw her lean forward and whisper in Frankie's ear. Oliver tried to hear but he could not make it out. It sounded like, 'This would be a really good time,' or words to that effect.

Then he saw Kathy walk in front of Feaver, passing between Feaver and Frankie, momentarily unsighting the Israeli. Oliver saw what she was doing without understanding why. He reached out to pull her back but it was too late.

Neville Morgan had grown up hard in a world where a back-up plan was a necessity. In his case that took the form of a second weapon, a .22 calibre Beretta Bobcat weighing a mere 12 ounces. Its short, five-inch barrel barely disturbed the hang of his jacket. Taking advantage of the brief cover, he eased it out of his waistband and jammed it in Kon Feaver's back.

'Drop it,' he snarled. He was white with pain from his arm but could deal with it, Oliver noted with grudging respect.

Reluctantly Feaver obeyed.

Frankie Leon was quick to note the reversal of fortune. Recovering his own weapon, he waved it at Oliver.

'Get over here!'

Oliver complied, having little option and Frankie herded Oliver and Kathy towards the door. As they reached the door, almost as an afterthought, Frankie turned and indicated Ron Rigby. The programmer was sitting at his stool in front of the computer.

'Take a shot,' Frankie muttered to Neville.

Neville smiled and took aim. A horrified look spread over Rigby's face. The young man covered his face with his fingers as if his bare hands could ward off bullets.

Neville fired and a black hole blossomed in the wall, inches above Rigby's head. Although he was not hit, Rigby jerked back in terror, then he slumped forward. A damp stain spread on the front of his khaki shorts, accompanied by the warm smell of urine.

Oliver was watching Frankie closely. The plump New Yorker's

face was impassive but there was an air of triumph about his body language that Oliver interpreted as revenge. Ron Rigby had been threatening to steal Frankie's valuable business secrets from under his very eyes – in front of witnesses – and hand them to rivals. Frankie might or might not be able to prevent that from happening but he could at least humiliate the young man for insulting him in public.

'You bastard,' Oliver could not stop himself gritting at Frankie who just smiled coldly.

Oliver was completely baffled by Kathy's attitude. Whose side was she on? The assault on Rigby was a shocking act, yet she seemed completely unmoved.

By now most people were standing with their mouths open but Frankie Leon had made a surprising recovery. Sidling along the wall, he slipped through the open window and was gone before anyone could move.

Kathy followed him, wordlessly.

Oliver and Feaver gave chase. Outside, Frankie was racing for the jetty. Surprisingly agile for his bulk, he leaped into a stream-lined motor launch.

Norrie Flack's hired hands had been stationed there to cut him off and were standing between Frankie and the jetty, but he dodged past them before they saw what was happening. Unfortunately they were in time to get in the way of Oliver and Feaver, who stood and watched helplessly as Frankie sped away.

'Damn,' said Kathy.

'Hush,' said Feaver. 'Listen to the engine. It will tell us which way he's headed.'

'Out to sea, obviously,' grumbled Kathy.

They heard the boat accelerate. The moon was emerging from behind a cloud and they glimpsed the vessel picking up speed. A trail of phosphorescence spread from under its floats. Then to Oliver's amazement it altered course and swung in to the shore. Frankie stood, guiding the boat with one hand on the wheel, the other covering Oliver and the others with his pistol.

'Get in, you.' He motioned to Kathy. He had wrapped a dirty rag round his mangled left hand.

Kathy said, 'We should take Steele too.'

'Okay but not the other guy, I don't trust him.' He motioned at Feaver. Kathy shrugged, 'Whatever.'

With Kathy and Oliver safely aboard and Oliver thoroughly confused, the launch accelerated away from land leaving Feaver helpless on the jetty.

'Where is he taking us?' muttered Oliver.

'We're heading for the Florida Keys,' Kathy said.

Oliver shook his head. 'No way. Leon won't risk setting foot in the States.'

'Trust me,' she said. 'Just keep quiet.'

She turned away and went and sat by herself in the stern of the launch. He saw the blue screen light flicker on her mobile phone – she seemed to be sending a text message.

He was deeply perplexed – when he first met Kathy he had been annoyed that she had turned up on Antigua at all, a sort of wild card; he preferred to work alone, he could plan better that way. But her quirky way of thinking had intrigued him and he even started to believe her off-beat approach might achieve something, help bring Leon to account. Now he was changing his mind. Perhaps she meant well – he would give her credit for that – but he suspected she was far out of her depth and too stubborn or too scared to admit it.

Back on land, Feaver, who had been tracking the path of the motorboat by ear, heard his mobile phone ring. He read the incoming message – it confirmed his own shrewd guess as to where the craft was bound – and headed for his plane.

CHAPTER 12

DOWN IN THE KEYS

A S THE LAUNCH cruised through the night, Oliver watched Kathy carefully. He was no longer sure of her allegiance. He studied her face covertly but could read nothing. She had a series of muttered conversations with Frankie but she never spoke to Oliver while they were at sea.

She was no more forthcoming after they made landfall at a small beach in the Florida Keys just north of Key West. Apparently Frankie maintained a property there. They were met by a dour Hispanic servant, who answered to Luis and seemed to know exactly what Frankie wanted. He had at the ready a fresh dressing for Frankie's mangled hand and a syringe containing a shot of what Oliver assumed was painkiller. The place seemed to be just a modest beach house but there was a gleaming black Jaguar XJR fuelled and waiting in the garage, possibly for just this kind of occasion. Luis brought the car round to the front door and the party climbed in, including Oliver at gunpoint, still very much a prisoner.

'You're going to regret this,' Oliver muttered furiously at Kathy.

She smiled coldly. 'If there is one thing worse than a bean counter, it's a bean counter who pokes his nose into things he doesn't understand.'

His shock was complete. She had changed sides and he could not understand why. Apparently she had some kind of arrangement with Frankie Leon that had nothing to do with what she had discussed with Oliver. Had her loyalty to her father blinded her to all other considerations? He forced himself to endure the rest of the journey in dignified silence.

An hour later, they were speeding north along the narrow two-hundred-mile stretch of US1 that connected the Florida Key, the roadster's powerful headlights eating up the night. Oliver felt pressure in the small of his back as Frankie floored the accelerator, driving crudely with little respect for the car's smooth instincts.

As they passed through Tarpon City, just north of the long ribbon of the Seven Mile Bridge, Kathy muttered something to Frankie and they jolted to a halt in front of a vine-covered, four-storey hotel, unusually tall for the Keys. A huge banyan tree stood in front of the hotel's main entrance.

'This way,' said Kathy.

'Is this where we meet your friend the country broker,' asked Frankie suspiciously.

What was he talking about, Oliver wondered.

Kathy nodded. 'Sure!'

Inside, she led them to a reserved hotel suite. The first person Oliver saw as they entered the room was Kon Feaver. He blinked.

'How the hell did you get here?'

'I flew.'

'Very funny. How did you know where we were?'

Feaver did not exactly smile but a cheek muscle twitched. He produced a small mobile phone and held it up for them to see.

Kathy said, 'I told him. Don't be cross, I promise you will know everything in a few minutes.'

'I certainly hope so,' grumbled Oliver. She had done it again, departed from the script. Or, rather, had written her own script which she chose not to share with Oliver.

A slightly built man came forward to greet them. He was neat and businesslike in white shirt, navy tie and knife-edged dark trousers. His tanned face and John Lennon glasses seemed vaguely familiar to Oliver.

'Here's your country broker,' Kathy said to Frankie with a sudden note of sarcasm.

The man nodded, acknowledging Kathy and Oliver, then turned to Frankie.

'I guess you don't know who I am,' he said pleasantly.

Frankie shook his head. 'Should I?'

'And you're certainly not afraid of me?'

'I don't scare easily,' Frankie growled. 'And not for some smartass who isn't even armed.' But he looked like someone who might have been seriously made a fool of, and was beginning to realize it.

The man pursed his lips. 'Depends what you mean by armed. Guns aren't the only weapons.'

Frankie's eyes narrowed and he looked momentarily uncertain.

Oliver, meanwhile, was searching his memory. There was something familiar about the man, not his physical appearance but his voice and the way he carried himself. Somewhere recently, they had come face to face.

'Have we met?' he asked.

The man smiled. 'Fort Lauderdale, a week ago.'

'Sorry?'

'Lunchtime. You were eating a hamburger that looked seriously overdone.'

Light dawned.

'The guy in the Key West t-shirt!'

'There you go.'

Oliver struggled with his memory. 'You looked different then. I got the idea you were in construction.'

'Oh really?'

'You drove off in a truck. As if you were heading back to the job site.'

He grinned. 'I might have given that impression.'

Mildly irritated, Oliver said, 'You look smarter now – are you an executive of some kind?'

'Sort of.'

'So who are you?'

The man produced a leather wallet and flipped it open, revealing a small brass shield.

'Charlie Green, Field Agent, IRS Compliance Division.'

He waved it for all in the room to see, then turned back to Frankie.

'I guess you could call this a secret weapon.'

Frankie had turned dead white but he said nothing.

Green produced a set of plastic handcuff ties.

'Franklin Leon, under the powers vested in me by the United States Government, I arrest you for narcotics trafficking, suspicion of racketeering and income tax evasion. I understand there may also be a murder charge imminent. Turn around and put your hands behind your back.'

Frankie rounded on Kathy. 'You tricked me, you bitch.'

Kathy looked him in the eye. 'Damn right I did.'

She caught Oliver staring at her intently and looked away.

Oliver sighed. 'I guess you're not just a pretty face,' he said with a mixture of bafflement and relief.

She coloured slightly. 'Thank you.'

Frankie cursed. Breaking away, he lumbered towards the door.

Kon Feaver moved quickly across the room and planted himself in Frankie's path, barring his exit. Frankie had to stop. Moments later he was securely handcuffed.

Charlie Green made a phone call to the Tarpon PD and a few minutes later two uniformed police arrived. Green identified himself and explained the situation to them.

'I'd sure appreciate the use of your jail to house this gentleman overnight.'

The troopers had looked uncertain at first but the mention of big-time tax evasion and drug dealing, let alone murder, soon ensured their cooperation and Frankie was led away scowling.

It was late and nobody felt like driving the 120 miles back to Miami so Kathy spoke to the hotel's front desk and arranged rooms for the night.

Kon Feaver stretched and gave a huge yawn. The Israeli had been quiet for some time.

'Don't know about the rest of you, but I'm bushed.'

He looked really tired and showed every sign of having only sleep on his mind as he headed for his car in the hotel's garage.

As the rest of the group was preparing to disperse, Oliver turned to Green.

'I'm glad we have Mr. Leon under lock and key but one thing puzzles me. How the heck did you get here all of a sudden?'

'Better ask the young lady.' Green nodded towards Kathy.

Oliver looked at her inquiringly.

She blushed. 'Charlie and I have been working together for a while now. Sorry if I seemed to hold out on you.'

'*Seemed* to?'

'Well I couldn't tell you everything. I didn't know when this was going to go down. I did not know how it would happen, or if I could even swing it at all. It was essential to get Frankie back onto US soil so that the IRS would have jurisdiction but I knew the Antiguan authorities wouldn't be much help. As it turned out, Norrie Flack's bizarre guerrilla warfare was a huge stroke of luck. That was something I never anticipated.'

Oliver was still annoyed.

'I'm starting to get it. You've been working with the IRS all along – since before I started talking to Carlton Tisch.'

A thought struck him. 'Do you work for them full-time?'

She shook her head.

'This is strictly a one-off deal. When my father got into trouble I guessed that something illegal was going on, I could smell it. And I knew I needed help. While dad was appealing to Carlton Tisch, I was looking in a different direction. I did some research and came up with Frankie Leon's name.'

'Which you could have told me.'

'I told you at Demon's office anyway.'

'A bit late in the day.'

She waved a hand dismissively. 'I had to keep faith with the IRS. We had ambitions in common.'

Green broke in.

'We've had our eye on Leon for years. There is a joint IRS/DEA task force that tracks major players in the drug world, cross-referenced to other information, banking records and so on. It's not easy. Good records are hard to find – it's a cash business – but the general idea is to nail them for tax evasion.'

'If there's so much cash being generated, it has to be banked somewhere,' Oliver said. 'Those millions we hear about can't all be stashed under the bed.'

Green nodded. 'It does get banked, but offshore. And the real owners hide behind nominee companies in Panama or Aruba, trusts with bank accounts in Cayman or Belize. The whole thing is a tangled mess of dummy corporations and smoke screens.'

'Don't those small countries cooperate with the US?'

'Sometimes, but very reluctantly. Most of them have a reputation for secrecy to protect. It can take the IRS years to gain access to foreign bank accounts if they have to go through all the proper channels. And when they do finally get the information, guess what? The money has gone. The company that owns it has been liquidated and a new entity in a different jurisdiction has taken charge of it. So the IRS is back to square one, with nothing to show for their pains. And if they start all over again, the same thing will happen. The IRS never catches up.'

Oliver scratched his head. 'How do the bad guys know the Feds are on their heels?'

'Sources.'

'Informants?'

Green nodded.

'Are you saying that people in banks, or in governments, are rewarded for tipping off the Frankies of the world?'

'Sure. What's a $10,000 "commission" paid to a local bureaucrat if you have $50 million in the bank? It's just a minor cost of doing business.'

'So were you both looking for a way to snare Frankie Leon?'

Kathy perked up. 'Exactly. I wanted to get my dad out of trouble. Charlie Green and his colleagues wanted Frankie for tax cheating. Our interests coincided.'

Oliver said: 'You're a pretty cool customer.'

She shrugged. 'Whatever. Frankie is toast and that's what matters.'

Green chipped in: 'With the records from Frankie's mansion, there's little doubt we can nail him.'

'Aren't those still in Antigua?' Oliver asked.

Kathy held up her briefcase. 'Guess what I have here?'

'From Leon's office?'

'You got it. While Ron was hacking into Frankie's computer, I was going through his filing cabinets. Everything we need is here.'

'By the way,' said Oliver, 'There was a Gladstone bag on the back seat in Frankie's Jaguar. It's probably still there. And people like Frankie usually carry plenty of cash.'

Kathy's eyes lit up. 'Let's go look.'

Moved by a single thought, they hurried outside.

Sure enough the carpet bag was still in the sleek black car.

Kathy unzipped it and felt inside, frowning. Picking it up she waved it at the assembled group, showing its empty interior.

'Funny that he would travel with an empty bag,' mused Green.

Oliver looked around. 'Has anyone seen Kon?'

The muscular pilot was nowhere to be seen.

In the distance, the rumbling of an aircraft engine was heard. As the moon rose over the Gulf of Mexico, a little white seaplane raced across the bay gathering speed, lifted off and disappeared in the warm South Florida night.

'How much do you think he got?' asked Kathy.

'That's the problem with cash,' sighed Green philosophically. 'You just don't know.'

It might have been Oliver's imagination but he thought he could faintly hear the sound of Feaver's engine mocking them? Maybe, though, it was thunder because just then it began to rain.

Oliver drew Kathy aside. 'What was that expression you used awhile back – something about a "country-broker"?'

'Oh, that was just the story I put together for Frankie. The idea was to tempt him back onto US soil.'

'What kind of story?'

'I told him I could find him a country to buy.'

'A what?'

She looked embarrassed. 'I told him he could own a small independent country, one without an extradition treaty, and that Green was the guy who could arrange it for him.'

Oliver was not sure whether to laugh or cry.

'You must be crazy – or is he the crazy one?'

'It worked, didn't it?'

He shook his head. 'I just can't believe someone as smart as Frankie would fall for that. It's the equivalent of the old Brooklyn Bridge scam.'

She nodded. 'Yes, it is. But you have to understand how Frankie thinks. He has made two fortunes, one large, the other enormous. So far, everything has worked for him. He has kept clear of the law. He is rich. What does a man like that do next? There aren't many new heights to scale.'

'But still, a *country*?'

She grinned. 'Well, there are countries and countries. It all depends what you mean, doesn't it. Countries come in all shapes and sizes. Remember Robert Vesco, the crooked financier? He tried to buy the island of Barbuda from the Antiguan government. And in England a singer called Screaming Lord Sutch took over an old WW2 gun turret in the middle of the Thames estuary. He ran a pirate radio station from it in the 1960s.'

'Vesco was turned down by the Antiguans.'

She shrugged. 'Maybe he didn't offer enough money?'

'That's not what the Antiguans said.'

'Oh, please. Don't you think there were some interesting discussions going on behind the scenes?'

'You're so cynical.'

'Studying tax law makes you that way.'

Oliver took a deep breath. 'Anyway, what details did you trail in front of Frankie? They must have been pretty compelling to get him to take the bait.'

She nodded.

'I told him that there is an island in the Bahamas that is for sale. And that, as part of the deal, the Nassau government is willing to grant it legal independence.'

'There are hundreds of Bahamian islands,' said Oliver doubtfully. 'Most of them have no fresh water and are uninhabitable for that reason.'

'In the past you would have been right. But nowadays that can be fixed. All it takes is money. Ever hear of desalinization plants or reverse osmosis?'

'I think so. Don't they have them in the Persian Gulf states?'

'Right. And on ships, too. A 90,000-ton ocean liner with several thousand passengers has to produce a thousand tons of water a day, for everything from drinking to cooking to cleaning. They use a process where they boil seawater under pressure. It's routine.'

'So how much would it cost to buy an island like that?'

'Altogether? It depends. You would have to start with the published price, factor in various bribes and commissions, then add the costs of construction – a lot of concrete would have to be poured. But that's no problem; the big resort developers do that stuff all the time. A hundred million dollars should get you a fairly decent setup. Then you'd have to write the constitution and the tax laws and so on. The legal fees would be hefty.'

'Is that what you told Frankie?'

'Pretty much.'

'And he bought it?'

'Yup. Didn't bat an eyelid. He said he had the money in his checking account.'

'That's probably true,' said Oliver thoughtfully. 'But do you really think the Bahamian government would go for it?'

She laughed. 'No way, not for a minute. Can you imagine the

heat they would catch from Washington if they started auctioning off tax-sheltered mini-countries right on America's door step? But the point is, Frankie bought the idea, at least to the extent of agreeing to come and meet Green, whom I described as having an inside track to the Prime Minister of the Bahamas. Since Frankie has no ethical standards himself, he had no difficulty in believing the worst of others.'

You might expect that that would be the end of the story. That Frankie Leon would be tried for tax fraud, convicted and locked up for a long time. But that would be underestimating Frankie. He was a man of exceptional energy and initiative, clearly demonstrated in creating not one but two very successful businesses. He was also a ruthless sociopath.

Here's what did happen:

♠

CHAPTER 13

ENTER MAX GUBERMAN

F RANKIE SAT IN THE BACK of the police car, handcuffed uncomfortably. But at least he had some time to think. Next to him was a khaki-uniformed trooper. A plastic card on the man's shirt said 'Pike.' He had a ginger crew cut and solid freckled forearms. With that colouring he would always have a problem with the sun. His partner Chavez was darker, Cuban for sure, thought Frankie.

They rode in silence. Both rear windows were wound down, letting the night air blow straight through the car. Frankie found this uncomfortable but it did not seem to bother the troopers.

Although Frankie was without question taken aback by recent events, his reaction was not to give in. Instead he racked his brain for options. There was always a way out, it was just a matter of finding it.

First get a conversation going, he thought.

He looked around the car's interior. 'This a Crown Vic?' he asked his neighbour companionably.

He got an affirmative grunt.

'What kind of gas mileage these babies get?'

Pike sighed as if Frankie had interrupted an important reverie.

'Depends. Twenty, maybe fifteen in the city.'

'That city would be Tarpon?'

Some city, Frankie was thinking. It had a population of 10,000 and was roughly half way along the Keys, a bit closer to Key West than to Miami.

'I drive a Mercedes. Got a Ferrari too. For the weekends.' He laughed. He wasn't sure how that little crack would play. Risky but it might pique the troopers' interest. It did.

'So how much that Ferrari set you back,' asked Pike after a while.

'Two hundred big ones.'

'That much?'

'Would have been more but I got a discount for cash.'

Pike's silence was eloquent. Frankie sensed that trooper Chavez was listening also. He let the thought mature for a few minutes before speaking.

'This is all a big misunderstanding, you know.'

'That a fact?'

'Sure. Those gentlemen you met were business colleagues of mine. We used to be partners. We had a disagreement.'

'What type business are you in?'

'I own a casino.' He did not mention Antigua; keep things simple. His listeners digested that.

'I heard this was about drugs,' said Chavez.

'No, sir,' said Frankie. 'No way. I am not in that business.'

Conversation was suspended as they rumbled noisily over a bridge. Salt air gusted past their faces. Then more palm trees whizzed by, picked out by the car's headlights.

'Are there any other hotels in Tarpon?' Frankie asked casually.

'You won't be needing no hotel,' said Pike.

Chavez said, 'We'll provide bed *and* breakfast.' He laughed.

'Sure,' said Frankie quickly. 'But, see, I'm going to need my attorney to come down here. You know how attorneys are, they like to be comfortable.'

'There's a Holiday Inn,' said Pike.

'Is that right? That sounds good.'

He allowed a moment of silence, not wanting to dominate the conversation. Then:

'I tell you what, we could clear this all up, real easy.'

'How you plan to do that?'

'Couple of phone calls should do it.

'You got no problem, then.'

'Right. So if we can stop at that Holiday Inn I'll make my calls, get the charges dropped.'

No answer from the troopers.

'I'd appreciate you guys helping me out here,' said Frankie. He held his breath.

'Hear that, Pike?' asked Chavez.

'Sure did,' said Pike. Both troopers were smiling. Pike turned to Frankie.

'You from Miami, boy?'

'Yes.'

'You Jewish'?

'Yes, sir, I am.'

He knew immediately that he was on thin ice.

'Tell you what,' said Chavez. 'We'll make sure you get your phone calls.'

'You will?'

'For free. From the lock-up.' Chavez laughed uproariously.

Well, he had tried. The rest of the journey took place in silence apart from an occasional chuckle from the troopers as they reflected on how they had made the city slicker look foolish.

At the police station he endured the booking and searching process with stoic dignity and then waited in line to use the phone. He finally got through and spoke to his lawyer Max Guberman in Miami, the same lawyer who had kept him out of trouble with the IRS before he left the States.

Max was both a tax attorney and a criminal attorney, with a lot of trial experience. He charged a thousand dollars an hour and not too many people could afford him. He had several major drug dealers as clients. 'Say nothing to anyone,' he told Frankie.

'You gotta get me out of here.'

'Calm down,' said Max, 'I'm coming. There's nothing to be done until tomorrow anyway.'

Max Guberman was in his fifties and looked older, with rimless glasses and a pale complexion that marked him out as the northerner he was. His suit was black silk which, along with his white shirt and dark tie, looked out of place in the Florida Keys, like something that had crawled out of its hole after a long winter and was uneasy in the sunlight.

His manner was that of a lifetime civil servant. This was not surprising; he had spent twenty-five years with the Justice Department, becoming expert on all matters involving extradition from foreign countries. When he finally left, he caused a furore by going straight to work for several wealthy overseas clients. His quick change of direction displeased many in Washington.

The US Secretary of Commerce at the time said 'I am disgusted that Mr. Guberman would ally himself with major drug traffickers. He is profiting personally from inside knowledge of our justice system that he gained while he was on the US government's payroll.'

But Guberman was unmoved. All he would say when interviewed by the news media was: 'The suggestion by some that I have a conflict of interest is a disgraceful slander.'

Max was not the only attorney travelling from Miami to Tarpon the next day.

While he was sitting in the back of his gleaming chauffeur-driven Lexus, cruising down US1, Brenda Nimitz, a career IRS attorney from the Miami office of the Internal Revenue Service was driving her five-year-old Camry down the same stretch of road.

The little town of Tarpon City, the county seat of Tarpon County, sat close to the mid-point of the Florida Keys. In a palm-shaded street stood its court house, a two-storey modern building whose clean lines contrasted oddly with the faded wood porches and clapboard walls of its neighbours.

The morning sun baked all buildings impartially. A yellow dog lay in the road, licking itself. It lurched resentfully away as Max Guberman's Lexus drew up at the courthouse. Guberman got out just as Brenda Nimitz arrived.

The two lawyers shook hands. Brenda knew Guberman by reputation.

Guberman looked at his watch. It still wanted twenty minutes to the time of the hearing. 'Got time for a coffee?'

'Sure,' said Brenda.

They strolled across the street to the corner diner. It was blessedly cool after the rapidly building steamy heat outside.

They sat in a booth. A waitress plonked two white mugs on the Formica table and poured coffee. Brenda added imitation milk from a steel jug and stirred her coffee thoughtfully.

'You still with that big Washington firm,' she asked.

Guberman nodded. 'Sure am.' He did not mention that he would soon be leaving them, not entirely voluntarily. Some of the firm's more respectable clients had protested to his partners about his frequent trips to Bogota and Cali. Still, the move was not a matter that worried Max since his annual income, already in seven figures, would probably be increased by the change.

'Planning any surprises this morning?' asked Brenda.

Guberman just smiled.

'I guess you'll plead not guilty and request bail,' she prompted.

'Something like that.'

'Bail is a dreadful idea.'

'Depends on your point of view,' said Guberman drily.

Brenda had a sinking feeling in her stomach. She was pretty sure that she knew Guberman's game plan. His skills were in the area of extradition or, more precisely, successfully opposing it. If the judge granted Frankie bail and Frankie skipped the country, then with Guberman advising him the IRS might never see him again.

At the arraignment, the two lawyers stood in front of Judge Homer Harris in the Tarpon County Courthouse while Frankie was indicted on a list of charges.

There were charges of tax evasion for several recent years with the promise of more to follow. Also, one count of operating an unlicensed casino. Finally, a charge of murdering the waiter at Johnny's Crab Shack on Antigua. The IRS agent Charlie Green was in court. He sat in the body of the hall among the scattering of spectators observing the proceedings as Frankie, coached by Max Guberman, pleaded not guilty to everything in a respectful tone of voice.

Max Guberman addressed the judge on the subject of bail.

'Your honour, my client has never been arrested let alone convicted of any offence. He is a respectable homeowner in Coconut Grove in Dade County with strong ties to his community.'

Brenda Nimitz cleared her throat, trying hard not to smile.

'Mr. Leon has not set foot in his Coconut Grove house for several years,' she said drily. 'To call him a Florida homeowner is a stretch; he lives on Antigua now. He came here last night in his own power boat and, if you let him, he will be gone again by lunchtime. We were very lucky to have the chance to apprehend him.'

'Fast footwork, eh,' said the judge. 'I take it you are opposed to bail?'

'We are indeed.'

'If released, my client will be happy to surrender his passport,' said Max.

'I assume you're joking,' said Judge Harris. 'The prisoner is remanded in custody.'

So Frankie was sent back to jail. On the way out of court he passed within a few feet of Charlie Green.

'Come and see me,' he said. 'We'll work something out.'

'I doubt that,' said Green, 'But I'll drop by. You never know.'

Two days went by as Frankie sat in jail with no visit from Agent Green. Green was deliberately letting Frankie stew, hoping that prison would soften him up a bit.

Meanwhile, Max Guberman was visiting Frankie for several hours each morning. In the afternoons, Guberman went back to the Holiday Inn and made phone calls.

Several of his calls were to his brother attorney on Antigua, Jasper Demon. Others were to various banks including one in

Belize and one on Grand Cayman. By the second day a plan was starting to form and Frankie Leon was feeling much better.

Max Guberman was feeling better too. Life in Tarpon was no small sacrifice for a man who liked his comforts. True, fresh seafood was abundant in the Keys but Max's taste ran to French cuisine and vintage wines, neither of which were readily available at the Holiday Inn. Still, he stuck it out bravely.

Oliver had telephoned Carlton Tisch to give him the news of Frankie's arrest, and had been ordered to report in person. So next morning, he and Kathy flew to Tortola.

As the taxi from Road Town airport rattled up the goat path that passed for a road to Tisch's cliffside villa, they talked.

The danger to Kathy's father seemed to be over, so Oliver had a certain feeling of accomplishment. That, after all, had been his mission. But, in the back of his mind, was the nagging thought that Larry Smith still owed the money. He found it hard to make excuses for Smith. He had gambled and lost. Collection action was still possible although, given the chaos at Casino Caribbean, it was likely that nothing would happen.

'Any chance he'll stop gambling?' Oliver asked.

She shook her head. 'I doubt it.'

'To stop, you have to want to stop, right?'

'Exactly.'

'I feel sorrier for his wife than for him, to be blunt.'

'I don't,' said Kathy. 'The only thing that will stop my father gambling is a lack of money. He is broke and his credit is shot, so that is now the case. As for my stepmother, I don't know how long she will stick around.'

'Would she leave him?'

'Let's just say she's a survivor.'

'You don't like her much, do you?'

Kathy rolled her eyes and looked out of the window.

♣

CHAPTER 14

ON CARLTON'S TERRACE

C ARLTON TROTTED OUT TO MEET THEM in a old yachting cap and khaki shorts.

'Well, it's the conquering heroes, come on in.'

Clearly delighted, he pumped Oliver's hand and gave Kathy a big hug that might have looked fatherly to the uninformed but, to Oliver's trained eye, lasted a bit longer than necessary.

He led them through to the verandah overlooking the ocean. Mimi Tisch was sunbathing in a lilac bikini, wrestling with the crossword in a week-old New York Times.

'This calls for drinks all round,' said Carlton cheerfully. 'My special Margaritas.' He set about mixing tequila, triple sec and lime juice at the outdoor bar.

Comfortably ensconced in a deck chair with salt-rimmed glass in hand, Oliver gave a detailed account of the last few days. He described his unpleasant encounter with Neville and Judith, Flack's shooting and Frankie's escape and recapture down in the Keys.

Carlton listened carefully.

'But things are under control now, eh?

'Seem to be. There are still a few loose ends.'

'Such as?'

'What's going on in Antigua?'

'Meaning?'

'Who's running the Casino, for one thing.'

'He's right,' said Kathy. 'We left Ron Rigby and a wounded Norrie Flack glaring at Neville and Judith. They may all have killed each other by now.'

'Oh, I doubt it,' said Carlton. 'From what you've told me, those people are all survivors.'

'Anyway, do we really care?' asked Kathy. 'I mean, we got my dad off the hook. They can all go straight to hell now, as far as I'm concerned.' She looked round defiantly.

'Is there not one good guy among the lot of them?' asked Carlton.

She shook her head.

'What about Rigby?' Oliver asked.

'He's nothing. Just a technician.'

'Who is likely to prevail, Leon's people or the Flacks?' asked Tisch. He looked at Oliver. 'What's your take on this?'

'My money's on Leon's lot – Neville and Judith. They've been running that business for several years. They are quite capable of keeping things going indefinitely. They may be low lifes but Judith is the brains on the technical side and Neville is no fool either.'

Mimi Tisch put down her paper.

'It's not our concern is it? I mean, the business still belongs to Leon.'

'For now it does,' said Oliver. 'I imagine the IRS will grab it for taxes pretty soon.'

Carlton looked thoughtful. 'That could take a while,' he said.

'I thought the IRS were pretty good at filing liens.'

'They are but there are steps to be followed, even by the IRS. First they have to make their case in the US.'

'Due process, so to speak?'

'Right. It could be months before they gets a US judgment. Then they have to get co-operation from Antigua by going through channels. Some time after that, they could finally get the Antiguans to move in and take things over.'

'So they could do it?'

'Eventually. But what do you think they will find?'

'An empty office?'

'Exactly. Judith and her chums will have due warning and plenty of time to pick up and move on.'

'Move on to where?'

Carlton shrugged. 'It doesn't matter. That's the beauty of that business. It could be Gibraltar, Vanuatu, the Marshall Islands, Anywhere that welcomes casinos and other offshore businesses.'

Mimi sighed. 'So we just have to watch as he sits in jail getting richer and richer?'

They sipped their Margaritas in silence.

'Maybe not,' said Carlton. He stood up.

'Can you ladies amuse yourselves for a bit? Oliver and I have some work to do.'

He ushered Oliver indoors.

Oliver followed him into a shaded den where blinds kept out the tropical sun. In the corner, a flickering Bloomberg terminal displayed streams of data culled from the world's stock exchanges by satellite.

'Now, 'said Tisch, 'Tell me everything you know about the ownership of Casino Caribbean.' His manner was noticeably sharper when the women were not present.

'There's not much to tell, I'm afraid,' said Oliver. He described his visit to Antigua's Financial Regulatory Commission and the slim file on Casino Caribbean.

Tisch nodded.

'That's normal. I'd have been quite surprised if there was more. If there were, it would probably have been false. Did it say who owned the shares?'

'No.'

'Did it say what type of shares they were?'

'What type?'

Tisch nodded impatiently. 'Ordinary shares? Bearer shares?'

'Hold on!' Oliver reached in his pocket for a sheet of notes he had brought with him. He had anticipated this kind of grilling from Tisch.

'Here. Authorized capital of $50,000 Caribbean – about $18,000 US – in bearer shares.'

'Bingo,' said Tisch.

'Is that good?'

'It's a start.' Tisch jumped up and paced the room. 'I expected something like this. It's what someone like Leon might do, someone who's suspicious, even paranoid.' He grinned. 'I've played similar games myself.'

'Oh?'

Tisch was silent for a moment, lost in thought.

'Sorry. Got distracted there. Yes. It means that the Casino belongs to whoever physically has possession of the share certificates.'

'Which is Frankie.'

'True. But I doubt if he carries them around in his back pocket. And he did leave Antigua in a bit of a hurry.'

'I think I see where you're going with this,' said Oliver.

'Where could the certificates be?'

'Not in his office, as far as I know. Kathy had a look around down there.'

'What about the attorney's office? In his safe?'

'Jasper Demon? I could believe that.'

Tisch looked pleased. 'I'll bet you anything that's where they are. What sort of guy is Demon?'

'You mean, can he be influenced?'

'Exactly.'

'That's a bit far-fetched,' said Oliver. 'Surely there is some kind of governing body for lawyers in Antigua. Wouldn't they suspend his licence if he misbehaved?'

'Only if they found out.'

A bead of cold sweat had formed between Oliver's shoulder blades. He wriggled uncomfortably and it ran down his back.

Carlton laughed and slapped his shoulder. 'Don't look so

worried. I wouldn't ask you to get involved in anything shady.'

Oliver was silent. When Carlton said something like that, he usually meant precisely the opposite.

After the men went indoors, Mimi Tisch and Kathy were left together outside.

'Want another drink?' asked Mimi.

'Love one.'

As Mimi was pouring from the half-full pitcher, Kathy said:

'Doesn't that annoy you?'

'Does what annoy me?'

'When the men shut you out like that.'

Mimi shook her head. 'I'm not sure what you mean.'

'Well, they just went inside and left us out here.'

Mimi shrugged. 'But I'm still working on my tan, I didn't want to go inside.'

Kathy felt like a fool. 'You're right. I'm sorry, I shouldn't have said anything.'

Mimi put down her drink and looked at Kathy.

'May I speak plainly?'

'Why wouldn't you?'

'Because some people can't handle the truth. You may be one of them.'

'That's a bit patronizing,' said Kathy. 'We Americans respect plain speaking.'

'So do we British,' said Mimi, 'But you never know. Okay, here goes. For starters, how much money do you have?'

'Excuse me?'

'Money. How much? In the bank, under your pillow, wherever you keep it?'

'Er...'

'Ten thousand? Twenty thousand?'

Kathy was disconcerted but she had agreed to answer.

'Something like that.'

'Got a job?'

'No. I'm looking around at the moment. What's your point?'

'Well I have a job. It's called being married to Carlton. I enjoy it and I'm pretty good at it. But there is one *really* significant thing about the position.'

'I'll bite, what's so significant? Or can I guess?'

'Maybe you can. It's the salary. I'm very well looked after. For instance, I have a million in the bank at the moment. Not Carlton's bank, my bank.'

Kathy blinked.

Mimi laughed. 'I didn't mean to show off. It's usually only about a hundred grand but I'm in the middle of moving some investments around.'

'Do you do your own investing?' asked Kathy weakly.

Mimi nodded. 'I get the odd suggestion from him of course.'

'Is he okay with that?'

'Why wouldn't he be?'

'Well – forgive me – he's quite an operator. He might not want you buying stock in companies where he's putting a deal together.'

Mimi laughed. 'There are ways of handling that.'

She did not explain. Just then, Oliver and Carlton came out of the house.

Oliver was looking at his watch. 'We have to leave, there are things to do.'

'What sort of things?' Kathy was disappointed. She was enjoying herself.

'Stuff,' said Oliver vaguely.

'You don't have to leave with him,' said Mimi. 'Why not hang out for a bit?'

'Good idea,' said Carlton. 'Mimi gets short of female company.'

Privately, Oliver was relieved. Having Kathy around could be disconcerting, never knowing what she would do next. It was a control thing.

'I always assumed you led a hectic social life,' he said lightly to Mimi.

'In some ways I do. Parties, the yacht club, the tennis club. But this is a small island. Day after day you meet the same old people.'

'Old?' asked Carlton.

She punched him playfully.

'You know what I mean. Besides, they're a bit upper crust.'

'I thought there was no class distinction among Americans,' said Oliver.

'Don't you believe it, chum.' She deliberately broadened her Huddersfield accent.

'You belong to all the right clubs, don't you?' he asked Carlton.

Carlton nodded. 'Sure. But Mimi's right. There may be no titled heads around here but there is a definite aristocracy based on money.'

'You have money.'

'I have new money. I don't have old money. There's a difference.'

'I didn't know the subject bothered you.'

'It just irks me sometimes. I guess my competitive instincts kick in. A lot of the real estate around here is owned by Rockefellers and Du Ponts or the like. I used to compete successfully with people like them all the time on Wall Street, yet here I'm not regarded as being on the same level.'

'I should be pretty satisfied if I were in your shoes,' said Oliver.

He shrugged. 'It just doesn't taste as sweet when your rivals act so damn pleased with themselves.'

'Well, I'm happy,' said Mimi. 'There are more important things than that to worry about.' She turned to Kathy. 'How's your tennis game? A group of us girls play most afternoons.'

'Passable. I don't have any kit with me, though.'

'You and Mimi are about the same size,' said Carlton. He eyed both women with undisguised approval. 'She can fix you up. Stay a few days.'

'That's settled then, 'said Mimi, 'Let's go and find you some clothes.' The women disappeared into the house. After some parting words with Carlton, Oliver got back in his car and headed for the airport.

Later on, at the Coral Island Country Club, Kathy and Mimi sat around the pool sipping sodas – Mimi confessed she drank Margaritas only to please Carlton. They had played several sets of doubles against a pair of sisters from Athens, whose father was in shipping, and were feeling pleasantly exhausted.

'I had a plan to get rich,' said Kathy.

'Attagirl!' said Mimi.

'But it involved Frankie Leon. I don't see how it will fly now that he's behind bars.'

'Want to tell?'

'It involved taking his Internet operation and going public with it – issuing shares on the Stock Exchange.'

'Nice idea. Sounds a bit complicated, though. You might do better to find a rich husband.'

'I don't seem to run into them. Where did you find yours?'

'I was a bunny at the London Playboy club. No problem meeting men there.'

'I bet.'

'I'll mention your project to Carlton, though,' said Mimi.

After dinner that evening, when everyone was feeling mellow, Mimi picked her time and said to Carlton: 'Kathy wants to talk to you about a business proposition.'

'I never said that,' Kathy protested.

Mimi laughed. 'That's how you talk to Carl, it gets his attention.'

'Tell me,' said Carlton.

'Well,' said Kathy, 'Frankie's Casino makes a lot of money – more and more every year.'

'How much?'

'It should take in $400 million this year. Thirty percent of that is profit.'

'Gross profit or net profit?'

'Net.'

Carlton whistled. 'That's comparable with Microsoft's percentage. And Frankie pays no US taxes.'

'Exactly.'

'How do you know all this?'

'You mean, besides having a degree in taxation? Frankie told me so himself. I visited him at his plantation just before the break-in by the Flacks. He had been putting numbers together for the sale to Flack. We talked. I showed him how much better off he would be if he forgot about the Flacks and went public on his own.'

'You were certainly right,' said Carlton. Whatever price the Flacks were going to offer, the price the Casino could command as a hot stock would be much higher.

'He agreed to pay me a finder's fee,' said Kathy. 'One per cent. Depending how the stock performed, my share would have been worth about $30 million.

'Sounds about right.'

'But it's not going to happen now,' she said wryly.

'A couple of thoughts,' said Carlton. 'First, you would never have collected your finder's fee. Frankie would have found a way to stiff you.'

'You think?'

'I know. People like Frankie do that.'

'What's the other thing?'

'I don't think the flotation would have got off the ground.'

'Why not?'

'Internet gambling is illegal in the United States.'

'I thought that was a grey area?'

'But it's illegal *enough*. The Justice Department argues that a home computer used for gambling is an unlicensed gaming establishment and thus illegal. The argument on the other side is that the casino is not in the States, it's wherever the server is located – Antigua, say – and that its customers in the USA are behaving perfectly legally. But not enough cases have gone through the courts to prove Justice wrong.'

'So the investors in Casino Caribbean would be taking a risk,' said Kathy. 'So what? Lots of investors take enormous risks.'

Carlton smiled. 'Unfortunately, some other major players involved would be taking just as big a risk, the risk of being lynched by disgruntled investors. So they would probably pass on the transaction. That goes for the banks, the reporting accountants and anyone else involved.'

'So my deal would never make it?'

'I'm afraid not.'

She sighed. 'It would have been so neat,' she said wistfully.

That evening, Carlton called Kon Feaver.

'I need you to go back to Antigua.'

'Anything special?'

'You might have to open a safe. You can do that, can't you?'

'Do you mean, without the key?'

'Of course.'

'There are a few safes I can't open but not many,' said Kon modestly. 'Where's the job?'

'In the office of an attorney in St. John's.'

'I'll pack my toolkit.'

CHAPTER 15

IN TARPON JAIL

C HARLIE GREEN of the IRS finally paid a call on Frankie Leon in Tarpon Jail.

What he found was not at all what he expected. The plump young man sat in a corner of his cell, his orange prison suit belted tightly round his body, staring at the wall.

He turned and looked blankly at Green when the agent entered but his expression did not change.

'How are you doing?' asked Green.

Frankie stared at him silently.

'They feeding you okay?'

He felt a bit foolish enquiring after Frankie's health, the man was an adversary, after all. But he was conscious of holding the initiative and, not being a malicious person, was inclined to be gracious.

'I'm no lawyer,' he began, 'But I guess we can chat off the record. Frankly we've got you cold on the tax evasion. However, we'd like to avoid a long trial. It would be expensive. And no fun for you, of course, being locked up in here without bail.'

Frankie just stared at him blankly.

Green started to get irritated. It was awkward talking to some-one who did not seem to hear a word you said, but he pressed on.

'I'm thinking that if you plead guilty and pay restitution including interest and penalties we could put a cap on the sentence – say ten years.'

No reaction.

'You could do the time in a decent place. No prison farms.' He laughed but his humour brought no response either.

Just then Max Guberman appeared, dapper in dark suit and club tie, accompanied by a warder.

'They told me you were here. Trying to influence my client?' he asked briskly.

Green wondered who had told him but he let that pass. 'We were just chatting,' he smiled.

Guberman went over to Frankie and put an arm round his shoulder. 'How are you, Franklin?' he asked solicitously. Frankie mumbled something inaudible.

Guberman turned to Green. 'He's taking this very hard.'

'Oh sure,' said Green. He was starting to smell a set up.

'I'm afraid he may not be fit to plead.'

In twenty years as an IRS agent, Charlie had seen every kind of ploy tried by characters who wanted to pay no income tax, so he showed no surprise.

'That's too bad,' he said. He turned to leave. 'I told him we could work out a deal, get paid up and do a maximum of ten years.'

'What about the murder charge?'

Green spread his hands. 'I can't help you there. That is outside my field.'

'No deal without a pass on the so-called shooting,' snapped Guberman. 'It's a bullshit charge. Meanwhile we have to get my client some top-quality medical care.'

Alarm bells went off in Green's head. Frankie wanted to get out of jail. Well, of course he did. No prizes for guessing what would happen after that, though.

'Nice talking to you guys,' he said.

From his car he called his office in Washington.

'Who's handling the Leon prosecution?'

'Someone in Legal I guess.'

'Give me a name.'

'Just a minute.' She shuffled papers.

'Fellow called Harrison Upham.'

'Switch me through.'

Upham answered the phone

'We've got a situation,' said Green. He explained the details:

'Harry, once that jerk sets foot outside jail, we're screwed. He'll be airborne in minutes and out of our jurisdiction in half an hour.'

'Don't worry,' soothed the IRS attorney. 'We'll make sure it doesn't happen.'

'You'd better,' said Charlie. 'This is a big case for me, I don't want anything messing it up.'

CHAPTER 16

MEANWHILE, BACK ON ANTIGUA

KON FEAVER hummed quietly to himself as he piloted the amphibian south-east through clear skies. On the seat beside him was a leather bag with an array of stainless steel instruments that would have made a brain surgeon jealous. Also a lap-top computer with some very unusual software.

But before he tackled Demon's safe he had things to do. First he wanted to visit Frankie's plantation and see what was going on. Specifically, who was running the store? Tisch had given him precise instructions, making it clear that the casino must continue to operate profitably.

Kon had not asked Carlton to explain but it was easy enough to guess. The casino was a massive cash cow. Thousands of gamblers were sending in their money every day. Such situations were rare and to compromise one would be downright indecent. If he knew Carlton, there was a plan to make some of those funds flow Carlton's way.

He landed at Antigua Airport, rented a car and drove out to Conway Hill.

Back at the plantation, after Oliver and his allies had left in pursuit of Frankie, there was an awkward standoff. Three of the four people in the computer room were furiously calculating the strength of their positions.

A nervous Ron Rigby sat at his computer, oblivious to the poisonous atmosphere, methodically trying one option after another to find the password. From the Internet he downloaded a random character generator. This was a programme that generated a series of combinations of letters and numbers at very high speed. If the password were a simple character sequence, it would find it in a few minutes and let him into the computer's secret files.

Judith understood what Rigby was up to, being a programmer herself, but she pretended not to notice. She was not worried that he would break in. The password system was something of her own devising. It was too sophisticated to yield to that kind of attack, since it depended not just on the right sequence of characters but also on the elapsed time between keystrokes, a feature that the random number generator could not deal with.

As far as she was concerned, the onslaught by the Flacks had failed. Rigby was bereft of any ideas that would constitute a threat. Norrie Flack was nursing his wounded shoulder. She could not prevent a smile as she looked at the ashen Britisher slumped in the corner and then at Neville who, gun in hand, seemed in complete control.

Neville himself was thinking more ambitiously. With Frankie absent, he, Neville, was in charge. Judith, his only rival, was ineffective outside the realm of computers. He knew, having worked with Judith, that she did not handle chaos well and the situation was chaotic. In cases like this she would be clinging desperately to her idea of order. To do so, she might even be capable of killing. Better not to involve her in the decision process.

He toyed with the idea of turning Norrie Flack over to the police. Frankie might have broken the laws of the United States but here in Antigua he had kept his nose clean and respected the law. He was also on chatting terms with a couple of Antigua legislators so he might even be able to present himself as the white knight in the situation.

On the other hand, calling the police might not be a smart move. As far as he knew, the Flacks were still candidates to buy the casino. The evening's excitement could still be papered over quietly if both parties to the deal wanted to go ahead. It would be a major transaction – worth hundreds of millions – and with that kind of money at stake you had to be careful.

He decided to eject Flack and Rigby from the compound and let them find their way home on foot. That would be humiliating for them but so what? It would send the wounded Flack a strong message. He would think twice before breaking into the plantation again.

He glanced at Flack, a pathetic figure nursing his injured shoulder. Neville tried not to gloat. He felt very comfortable about what he was about to do.

But Uncle Norrie was not as preoccupied with his injury as he appeared. Pain was not a novelty – he had been there before and there was no school like experience. As soon as Neville looked away, Flack put his good hand to his mouth and, inserting two fingers, emitted a piercing whistle.

Rollo and his gang of toughs had been waiting in the bushes, listening for just this signal, which Flack had prearranged during their war council earlier. They surged across the lawn and burst into the house. Neville barely had time to raise his gun. In minutes he was overpowered and his wrists lashed securely behind his back.

Norrie, much recovered, sauntered over to the scowling Judith and, raising his good arm, slapped her hard in the face.

'That's just for starters,' he said softly.

'Bastard,' she spat. The imprint of his hand was vivid on her cheek.

Without emotion, Norrie motioned Rollo to tie her up too.

'Now,' he said, 'You were going to tell Ron here how to access your programmes.'

'It's just the source code I need,' said Ron helpfully.

'Whatever!' Norrie lit a cigarette and drew on it until the tip glowed orange.

'Here's how this works,' he said pleasantly. 'We've wasted a lot of time and we're not going to waste any more. In the next thirty seconds, one of two things is going to happen. Either you tell Ron the password or I burn a hole in someone's face.'

'You wouldn't dare,' snapped Judith. 'I could have you tossed into an Antigua jail for the rest of your life.' Her voice dripped with contempt.

Flack drew steadily on the cigarette, turned and, in a swift movement, ground the tip into Neville's cheek.

Neville was no coward, but he screamed in a mixture of surprise and pain. He struggled with his bonds but he was completely powerless.

Flack turned back to Judith. 'You next,' he said. 'But this time it goes in your eye.'

Judith perceived that for Flack such an act was no worse than swatting a fly. She even felt reluctant respect – it took one sociopath to know another.

'The password is Royal Flush,' she said quietly. 'It's case sensitive. Between the two words, count out seven seconds on your watch.'

Rigby did as she said and, moment later punched his hand in the air with a broad grin as the screen filled with line after line of flickering machine language.

'Is that it?' asked Flack. The symbols on the screen meant nothing to anyone but Rigby and Judith, the two programmers.

Rigby watched the screen in silence for a minute.

'Sure is,' he grinned

'How long will it take you to copy it?' asked Flack.

'Let me try something here.

A few more keystrokes, then he sat back with a whistle of satisfaction.

'It's g-g-gone,' he said cheerfully.

'What do you mean, gone? Aren't you going to print it out?' asked Flack suspiciously.

But the dismay on Judith's face told him that the damage was already done. Rigby confirmed the fact.

'I just e-mailed most of the files we need to Flack's server in Gibraltar. It may take a few minutes to download all of the data but the first lines of code are already there. The job is essentially finished.'

'Brilliant,' said Flack. 'Let's get out of here.'

He turned to Neville. 'I'm guessing that you would have made us walk home. Just for that we'll take your car.'

He spoke quietly to Rollo. The Antiguan grinned in appreciation and left the room taking his people with him.

Flack nodded at Judith. 'Something tells me you're going to be redundant here very soon. No hard feelings. If you are ever looking for a job, give us a call at Flacks. We pay well and Gibraltar is a decent place to work.'

He indicated Neville. 'You can cut this clown loose once we're gone.'

Outside, one of Rollo's troops drove Flack's Mercedes away. Others were methodically slashing the tyres of the other vehicles in the garage but taking care to leave Neville's sleek navy BMW intact.

Leaning on Rigby for support, Flack walked over to the BMW. Rigby was looking a bit bemused.

'You drive,' said Flack.

From the steps of the house, Neville, his face dark with anger, watched his car describe a circle on the gravel and head for the wrought iron gates.

Behind the passenger window, Norrie Flack's pale face showed his satisfaction at a busy and productive evening's work.

Another quiet morning outside Tarpon Courthouse a few days later:

The same yellow dog still lay in the road. It loped slowly away as, for the second time in a week, IRS attorney Brenda Nimitz's Toyota and Max Guberman's Lexus arrived at the courthouse.

Judge Homer Harris was off playing golf in South Carolina that week, so Judge Leroy Huckleberry, aged 76 and semi-retired, was pinch-hitting for him. The courtroom was almost empty as a hand-cuffed Frankie Leon was led in for a special bail hearing. Judge

Huckleberry was thin and bony. A lifetime in the Florida Keys had sweated every spare ounce of flesh from his desiccated frame, so he looked well suited to the job of trying cases in one of the hottest counties in the United States. That was if you considered the Keys to be part of the United States. Those who recognized the sovereignty of the 'Conch Republic,' the hundred miles or so of small islands connected by causeways and bridges to the southern tip of Florida and acknowledged Jimmy Buffett and Carl Hiaasen as their cultural heroes, would disagree.

Max Guberman had been monitoring the judges' vacation schedule carefully and knew about the substitution several days in advance. He made plans accordingly. He had researched Judge Huckleberry's background and was aware of his reputation over many years as a consistent jurist. Consistent, that is, in his agreement with a low-key fraternity of fellow good ol' boys that any case with the potential to affect their collective well-being would come out the proper way. This had been a guiding principle all Judge Huckleberry's life and he saw nothing wrong with it since he and his friends were decent church-going people.

In this particular case, there had been much telephone activity between them including some discussion of a financial nature and certain conclusions had been reached.

The judge peered out over half-moon glasses at his clerk. 'Three counts of tax fraud and one of murder? Is that a fact?'

'Yes, Your Honour,' said Billy Bob Burriss, the Clerk of the Court, a florid forty year old.

'Don't believe I've seen that combination in all the years I've been sitting here. How many years would that be, Billy Bob?'

'Thirty-five years, Your Honour,' grinned Billy Bob. Judge liked to reminisce, especially at the expense of folks from up north and he had a sympathetic audience in the courtroom staff.

The judge glanced at Frankie who stood contemplating his feet with Max Guberman at his side.

'How do you feel?'

'I have these panic attacks your honour.'

'Hmm.' Judge Huckleberry studied the papers on his desk as if he had only just noticed they were there.

'And are you planning to enjoy our hospitality a while longer?'

'I would prefer not. I believe my mental health is at risk.'

Guberman cleared his throat. 'My client is deeply, deeply depressed at the unjustified charges against him, it has been a traumatic experience. He is in imminent danger of a psychotic breakdown and needs specialized treatment.' He tapped an inch-thick manila file folder. 'We have several expert medical opinions to that effect. Appropriate treatment is available at the Mayo Clinic in Jacksonville. We are prepared to post substantial bail, your honour.'

Judge Huckleberry sniffed. The thought of all that reading did not appeal to him. 'How much do you consider substantial?'

Before either of them could answer, Brenda Nimitz was on her feet.

'Your Honour, with great respect, this is a bad idea. A capital crime is involved. The defendant lives on Antigua where he runs a hugely profitable business. He personifies the term flight risk.'

Guberman smirked. 'Your Honour, my client has a spotless record. When he recovers his health, he will vigorously dispute all the charges, which constitute a vendetta by the IRS. They have also recklessly exaggerated my client's income.'

Judge Huckleberry, who had made up his mind before even entering the courtroom, pretended to give the matter careful thought.

Finally he said, 'Lives on Antigua, eh?'

'Your Honour,' said Brenda Nimitz, 'If bail is granted the prisoner will flee the jurisdiction in minutes.'

'Good point. Defendant will surrender his passport, 'said the judge. 'Prisoner is released on two million dollars bail. Cash only. Next!'

Secretly jubilant, Max Guberman strolled out to the Lincoln and popped the trunk. He mopped his brow, the heat was almost unbearable. In the trunk was a black leather briefcase containing three passports. Each bore a photo of Frankie Leon but each was inscribed in a different name; he selected the one made out in Frankie's real name and slipped it into his pocket. Also in the trunk was a second briefcase containing bundles of hundred dollar bills. Trying not to sweat on the banknotes, he counted out two million dollars and transferred it to his own briefcase which he snapped shut. He returned to the court-house and disappeared into the bailiff's office.

Fifteen minutes later he and Frankie, now sans handcuffs and smiling broadly, emerged from the court-house, climbed into the Lincoln and drove away.

Cruising twelve miles offshore in Frankie's ocean-going motor yacht, Gold Digger, Neville got the call on his satellite phone and set course for Tarpon.

Oliver's phone rang early. His programmable Mr. Coffee had produced its first brew at seven am but he was still trying to muster the energy to stumble into the kitchen and pour it.

It was Carlton Tisch.

'Better get up here,' he said. 'We need to talk.'

'What's up?'

'They let Leon out of jail.'

'Impossible!'

'Apparently not.'

'How the hell could the IRS lawyers let that happen?'

Carlton laughed shortly. 'Max Guberman got him a medical exeat to visit the Mayo Clinic in Jacksonville. He uttered scary warnings about a psychotic episode and claimed that to keep him locked up could lead to suicide, so the judge let him out on two million dollars bail. Guberman produced a suitcase full of cash, and bingo!'

'Where is he now?'

'Gone. Probably out of the country.'

'What about the bail money?'

Carlton laughed. 'What about it? Forfeit, of course, but he'll not miss it. Just the cost of doing business.'

'How could the judge be so gullible?'

'It's a long story. I'll explain over breakfast.'

'Damn,' said Oliver. 'I'm upset.'

'Me too,' said Carlton.

They reviewed the situation over orange juice and scrambled eggs and bacon at Tisch's villa – Carlton had abandoned any faith-based dietary limitations years ago.

Oliver speared his bacon angrily. 'Something about this situation doesn't smell right.'

Carlton shrugged. 'Money had something to do with it, I daresay.'

'You think Leon bribed the judge?'

Carlton poured more coffee. 'Not directly, but money buys influence and influence can reach all the way down to small-town judges.'

'Well, it's wrong.'

Carlton sighed. 'Yes it is. But unfortunately it happens. Does the name Robert Vesco ring a bell?'

'Remind me.'

'Vesco was the mother of all fugitive financiers. He fled the States in 1973 to avoid standing trial for the theft of $200 million which he had allegedly looted from a company called IOS – Investors Overseas Services.'

'Wasn't that the fund started by Bernie Cornfeld?'

'Right. It became the target of a bid. Vesco was a corporate raider specializing in hostile takeovers.'

'A bit like you, Carlton?'

Carlton frowned. 'Not like me. He was completely amoral.'

'Er…'

'Don't be funny, it doesn't suit you. Anyway, shortly before Vesco left town he made an illegal contribution of $200,000 to the Nixon re-election campaign.'

'In cash?'

'Of course. The money, in a suitcase, was handed over to Nixon's campaign treasurer, Maurice Stans. Stans eventually paid a $5,000 fine for "non-wilful violation" of campaign-finance law!'

'What happened to Vesco?'

'He was indicted, but in his absence. Later, he was indicted again for drug smuggling. Another parallel with our friend Frankie.'

'Did he go to Antigua, like Frankie?'

'Yes, but not right away. His first port of call was Costa Rica. He donated a couple of million dollars to a company partly owned by the Costa Rican president, Jose Figueres. Costa Rica passed a law, the "Vesco Law" that guaranteed he would not be extradited. What a coincidence! Unfortunately for him, Figueres was voted out of power a few years later and soon after that the Vesco law was repealed.'

'What did he do about that?'

'Moved to the Bahamas. Then to Antigua. He tried to buy the island of Barbuda from the Antiguans and establish it as a sovereign state.'

Oliver laughed. 'He certainly had chutzpah.'

'Vesco always thought big,' said Carlton. 'When that didn't work, he moved to Nicaragua and from there to Cuba. One attraction was Cuba's excellent medical system. He suffered from urinary tract infections, very painful, and Cuba was somewhere he could find good doctors.'

'So there was a happy ending for him?'

'Not exactly. In 1995, Castro had him thrown into jail. Something about a scheme to defraud Cuba's pharmaceutical industry.'

'Couldn't stay out of trouble, eh?'

'He over-reached himself.'

'Messing with Castro was not smart.'

'Right. He would have had it made there, too. Cuba has no extradition treaty with the US.'

Oliver buttered a croissant and added a dab of honey.

'There's a footnote,' said Tisch. 'Vesco's partner in the Cuban scam, also arrested, was Donald Nixon, nephew of the former US president. Nixon was allowed to return to the US but Vesco was sentenced to thirteen years in prison. He would have been 74 when he finished his sentence but according to reports coming out of Cuba, he died of lung cancer in 2005, aged 70, and presumably still in prison.'

'There's a moral there somewhere.'

Carlton unwrapped a Cuban cigar. 'It shows that throwing money around can work wonders.'

Oliver nodded. 'It makes Frankie's bail tale seem much less surprising.'

Carlton waved a match under his cigar until the tip glowed orange.

'It also gives us an idea of what his overall play book will look like.'

'So what do we do next?' asked Oliver.

'Glad you asked.' Carlton drew smoothly on his cigar. 'Frankie will probably have to cut his ties with Antigua but he may not be mentally ready for that yet. I suspect the first thing he will do is to check up on the casino, his major asset. He'll want to see that the business is being properly run – that the cash is coming in and, just as important, flowing out to his bank account, wherever that may be.'

'So?'

'You presumably agree that we must stop Frankie from causing more grief, either to pretty Kathy's deadbeat father or, for that matter to anyone else,' said Tisch.

Here comes the Tisch plan and some more unpleasantness for me, Oliver thought.

'Makes sense, I suppose.'

'Which means that we must be there to reason with him.'

Tisch was looking at him expectantly.

'So it's back to Antigua, eh?'

'Afraid so.'

After Oliver left, Tisch pottered round the terrace finishing his cigar. His wife hated tobacco smoke in the house, even from a good Havana, and he was wise enough not to make an issue of it.

He had not told Oliver that Kon Feaver was busy on Antigua also. He had a separate plan for each man. He saw nothing to be gained by letting the right hand know what the left hand was doing so, true to form, he did not.

Glancing at his steel wristwatch he saw that it was 10am. Where did the time go? There was someone in England that he wanted to telephone so he did a quick calculation involving Greenwich Mean Time. In the City of London it was 3pm. He went indoors to make the call.

CHAPTER 17

A WELL-FED BANKER

*I*N LONDON, the Honourable Quentin Teague saw from the screen on his Blackberry that Carlton Tisch was calling. He was intrigued. He had done business with Carlton before and had made a lot of money as a result.

The well-fed young banker in the Savile Row suit had just left Sweetings restaurant near London Bridge when the call came. He had enjoyed a *Sole Veronique*, with a glass of Sancerre, and was strolling up Broad Street on the way back to his office. He ducked into a nearby pub to get away from the roar of traffic. The streets of the financial district were still a noisy place to take a phone call, although the 'congestion charge' introduced by the previous London mayor Ken Livingstone had thinned private traffic considerably, limiting it to those willing to pay eight pounds a day for a permit.

The saloon bar of the Golden Fleece, a dark, panelled room with leather booths and a strong smell of beer, was deserted; city workers were all back at their desks. Things would not get busy again until 5.30pm when they would pour in, eager to fortify themselves with a quick one before catching their trains or buses home. At this hour people like Teague, independent enough to set their own hours, had places like the 'Fleece' to themselves.

He ordered a small glass of Cockburn's port and answered the phone.

'Carlton, young man, how the heck are you?'

Tisch was actually his elder by thirty years but the relationship was one of equals. Despite their contrasting backgrounds, the two men were oddly similar.

Some might have called them gamblers. Tisch preferred the word 'entrepreneur,' which on Wall Street was a term more or less of respect. Teague preferred the phrase 'tough but fair risk taker' which his PR people had been instructed to work into his press releases whenever possible.

'Just trying to eke out an honest buck,' said Carlton.

'Splendid. What's up?'

'Got something that might amuse you.'

Tisch outlined briefly what he had in mind. He had judged Teague well – the Britisher was interested, and fired off several questions with a sharpness at odds with his plump face and bland appearance.

Tisch did his best to answer but finally he said:

'Why not hop over to Tortola? We can sit and work on the details.'

Teague hesitated. 'I'd love to. The only thing is, there's a lot of stuff going on here.'

'Like what? This is a fast-moving situation.'

'Yeah, but the timing is not good. Ascot week is coming up.'

'Ascot?'

'Racing. Starts Monday. Biggest meeting of the year.'

'So?'

'I'm taking a party.'

'You're going to the track? How is that important? Send someone else!'

'No can do. I'm taking some Arabs, big racing fans. Don't want to disappoint them.'

Tisch's steel edge broke through the surface. He did not like having his plans thwarted.

'If you're not interested, I can get someone from the States.'

'Oh, I'm interested.'

Silence on the line, both men calculating.

Teague was thinking, if he could use someone in the States, then why did he call me? He must need someone offshore.

Tisch was wondering, I should have developed some alternatives to this guy. Who else in the UK can I use? Maybe it's not too late.

'These particular Arabs are the Arabs that tell the other Arabs where to invest their money,' said Teague, 'I'm not about to put them off.'

To Tisch that logic was compelling; he did not like it but he understood it.

'Look,' said Teague, 'Why not pop over here? You can come to the races with us. There is stuff to be done here anyway, people you would have to meet if we go ahead on this.'

'I suppose I could get away,' Tisch grumbled.

So that's settled, said Teague to himself. The Yanks were like that. There had been an edge to their verbal sparring but now they were friends again – sort of. Friendship was nice but, below the surface, business was business.

'Bring Mimi, it will be fun,' he said cheerfully.

Once Carlton had mentioned the trip to Mimi, he was a dead duck, there was no turning back. Two days later they were in first class on a British Airways Boeing to London.

After a tolerable transatlantic flight and a limousine ride through drab West London, they checked into the Berkeley Hotel. Carlton had wanted to stay at the Savoy but Mimi insisted on the Berkeley. Her reasoning seemed convoluted to Carlton. 'What day are we going to Ascot?' had been her first question. It turned out that it was the opening day and in the Royal Enclosure. Which, as Mimi pointed out, necessitated shopping.

'I always stay at the best hotel in town,' Carlton explained patiently. 'In London that is the Savoy.'

'Who says?'

'People I talk to.'

'You talk to the wrong people. The real best hotel is the Berkeley.'

'Who says?'

'People I talk to. Also, it is within walking distance of Harrods and I need a new hat.'

He gave way reluctantly. 'Must I pack a suit?'

'If you want. Not for the races, though.'

'What should I wear for that? Something with an equestrian motif?'

'Don't worry. I've got plans for you.'

Carlton had to admit the Berkeley was very pleasant. The staff in the quietly elegant lobby were welcoming and as he glanced at some of the other guests, few of whom appeared to be businessmen, he started to get a tingling sensation that he might be in the presence of that elusive 'old money.' Their suite overlooked Hyde Park.

So he was already feeling mellower when Mimi said, 'Don't get comfortable, we have a call to make.'

Their taxi rumbled around Hyde Park Corner, along Piccadilly and past Leicester Square.

This town could be a bit cleaner, thought Carlton, looking out of the window. But so could most big cities. Manhattan was on the grubby side, even post-Giuliani. That was why he felt more at home on his Caribbean island. In the tropics, a little dirt was okay.

The cab ground to a halt. He fumbled with some notes, then turned and surveyed the store, a men's tailor. The clothes in the windows looked smart but he was a bit confused. He knew the best tailoring was made to measure and with the races starting next day there was no time for that. The sign over the door said Moss Bros. Mimi saw him looking puzzled. She grinned. 'Follow me.'

The elevator took them up to the second floor where she approached the floor manager, a Mr. Gupta. Carlton hovered in her wake.

'We're here to pick up an outfit for my husband, Carlton Tisch. I called from Tortola a few days ago.'

Mr. Gupta was immaculate in black jacket and striped trousers. He smiled, showing very white teeth.

'Ah yes, Mrs. Tisch. I am glad you called ahead. We always have a run on morning dress for Royal Ascot. We're ready for you, come this way please.'

He ushered Carlton into a fitting room. A few minutes later the small New Yorker emerged in full morning dress – tail coat, striped trousers and pale grey formal waistcoat.

He received judicious approval from Mr. Gupta. 'A good fit, I think,' said the young manager. 'One last thing.' He produced a grey silk top hat and fitted it gently but firmly onto Carlton's head.

'I feel a complete fool,' muttered Carlton.

'But you're my fool,' grinned Mimi. 'And you look pretty hot.'

'How much will this cost?'

'Not much, it's only rented. And they'll all be wearing this gear, trust me. The fools will be the ones *not* dressed like that.'

Armed with their spoils, they taxied back to the hotel.

They were sipping sherry in the lounge when a uniformed page appeared at Carlton's elbow.

'There is a delivery for you outside, sir.'

Mimi looked inquiringly at Carlton.

'You're not the only one who can pull surprises,' said Carlton. 'Come with me.'

In the hotel forecourt, gleaming in the sun, stood a pale blue Rolls Royce. A grey uniformed chauffeur held the door open for them.

Carlton ushered Mimi into the back seat.

'Take us for a spin, James,' he said. 'It is James, isn't it?'

'It's whatever you wish it to be, sir,' said the chauffeur gravely. 'Shall we drive up Park Lane, round Marble Arch and home across the park?'

'Perfect.'

Mimi stroked the soft leather upholstery. 'This is also rented, I hope.'

'Of course.'

CHAPTER 18

OFF TO THE RACES

MIMI BOUGHT A DRESS at Harvey Nichols and a hat at Harrods, so they were all set when James called for them next morning and drove them in silent luxury along the Cromwell Road.

Teague lived near Windsor, the pleasant Thames-side town dominated by Windsor Castle some thirty miles west of London. He had explained to Carlton that he and his father shared the family home which struck Carlton as odd – he envisaged cramped accommodation and wondered if Teague was less affluent than he had assumed.

In fact, the Teague estate turned out to be 500 acres of the richest farmland in England. As the Rolls passed through the outer gates it clattered over a rusty cattle grid and proceeded in a sweeping arc of gravel drive up to a huge grey stone house. The place appeared to Carlton to have at least a hundred rooms, its stonework mellow and weathered by several centuries of English wind and rain. That morning, bright sunshine showed the façade to advantage but a blustery wind bent the treetops nearby. So much for flaming June, thought Carlton.

A long-wheelbase Land Rover stood in the drive. It had a dented fender and looked as if it hadn't been washed for months, earning a disapproving frown from chauffeur James.

A ruddy-faced man with a grey moustache appeared at the front door and trotted down the steps to meet them. An older version of

Teague, he looked like a farm labourer in a shapeless wool sweater, old flannel trousers and muddy green Wellingtons.

'I'm Bill Teague, Quentin's dad.'

He beamed cheerfully but did not shake hands.

'You coming with us today, Mr. Teague?' asked Carlton.

'Of course. Got a nag running actually.'

'Am I going to be overdressed?' asked Carlton. He had been worrying all morning, despite Mimi's assurances.

Teague noticed Carlton eying his mud-smeared boots.

'Don't worry, I'm not going like this. I'm hopelessly late as usual. Here, come in and relax.'

He showed them into a high-ceilinged sitting room with full-length windows looking out over rolling fields that disappeared over the horizon. A log fire burned in the huge fireplace, acknowledging the chill outside.

A pale young man in his twenties, formally dressed like Carlton, sat shivering by the fire, warming his hands at the blaze. He jumped up as they entered. 'Meet Al, he's coming with us,' Bill Teague explained.

Al nodded shyly and shook hands.

'And this is Fatty.' Teague indicated a dark-haired girl of about seventeen, anything but fat, in a frock that emphasized her youthful figure and flawless skin, and with a smile that lit up the room.

Fatty saw Mimi's surprised look and laughed.

'It's an old nursery nickname. Can't get rid of it.' Her upper class English accent was redolent of gymkhanas and English boarding schools.

'It doesn't match the reality,' said Mimi. 'You look gorgeous.'

She blushed. 'Thanks.'

Nobody said much.

'Do much racing?' Carlton asked Al conversationally.

'A bit.'

'I'm the same way,' said Carlton, trying to put the young man at ease. 'What do you do for a living?'

'I'm an accountant.'

That figures, thought Carlton. It goes with the lack of personality.

'A friend of Quentin's from the City?'

'Something like that. We were articled clerks together.'

'Articled clerks?'

Al smiled. 'That means we trained at the same accounting firm.'

Quentin Teague appeared, faultlessly dressed as usual. He explained that the rest of the party would meet them at the track. Everyone got ready to leave.

'Looks like we'll need two cars with the six of us,' said Quentin.

'We could take my Rolls,' said Carlton hopefully – he rather liked the idea of rolling up at Ascot in his new toy.

'Oh, we can all squeeze in the Land Rover' said Bill Teague cheerfully. 'It's not far.'

He turned out to be a haphazard driver with a disconcerting habit of cutting in front of other cars and then glaring indignantly as if they had tried to tailgate him. That explains the dent in the fender, thought Carlton. But they arrived at Ascot High Street without incident. At the racecourse entrance round the corner they climbed out of the Land Rover, which was driven away by a valet.

To get into the Royal Enclosure, they had to present their bar-coded tickets to be scanned at a well-controlled gate presided over by a man with a steward's badge.

Bill Teague, now looking as smart as the rest of the party, took charge and greeted the steward briskly.

'Morning, Rogers.'

'Morning, my Lord.'

And I called him Mr. Teague, thought Carlton. Damn!

The steward handed out little white and gold lapel badges that guaranteed admission to the enclosure for the rest of the day.

Shortly they were esconced in a reserved box where, to Carlton's relief, all the men were wearing morning dress. He had seriously considered leaving his top hat, which still felt uncomfortable, behind in the car but he noticed that the other men seemed to have brought theirs along – some black, some light grey.

Bill Teague looked at his watch. 'The Queen should be turning up soon.' He went off to talk to his trainer and Mimi went with Al and Fatty to place a bet on the first race.

There were several empty seats beside them, which Quentin Teague explained were for the rest of their group when they arrived.

'Those would be the Arabs?'

'No, just some other clients of the bank.'

'I thought you said there were some Arabs coming?' Carlton tried not to sound plaintive but he had been nursing his resentment at having to leave Tortola and the Arabs were the excuse Teague had used to pry him loose.

'There are. You already met them.'

'You mean?'

'Al'

'But…'

'Sheikh Ali bin Anwar al Khalifa.'

'He said he was an accountant.'

'He is. His uncle is the ruler of Ras Al Doha, one of the Trucial States in the Persian Gulf or, as they prefer to call it, the Arabian Gulf. Al is being groomed to keep the state's books in order.'

Light started to dawn.

'So Fatty…'

'Fatima. She is his sister.'

'But she is British.'

Teague laughed. 'No, she just sounds that way. It's the boarding school education.'

'I thought they had to wear veils.'

'They do when they are at home. That's why they like to spend so much time over here.'

'Well, she sure fooled me 'said Carlton.

Teague grinned. 'Nothing over here is what it seems. You might not think I had a Harvard MBA.'

'Do you?'

'Absolutely. Hang on – here come the royals.'

There was a pause while they took in the racing scene. The sun had come out and lines were forming at the Tote windows in an atmosphere of mounting expectation. Elegant women in thin dresses and outrageous hats sipped champagne and nibbled on smoked salmon. Men in morning dress strolled round the raised balcony above the paddock, binoculars at the ready, checking out the horses.

Then all heads turned towards the track. There was a ripple of polite applause as a procession of open coaches flanked by uniformed outriders approached along the straight mile in front of the grandstand. In the leading carriage sat a small female figure in a turquoise coat and large hat, waving graciously to the crowd. Beside her the somewhat gaunt figure of a man in a brown topcoat also waved but less often.

Mimi jabbed Carlton in the ribs. 'Look!'

'I'm looking.'

'It's the Queen.'

'Well, whoopee!' he grunted. 'Who's the guy with her?'

'That's the Duke of Edinburgh. He's her husband.'

'Edinburgh, eh? Is he Scottish?'

'No, Greek. Well, English really.'

Carlton shook his head. 'Whatever you say.'

Carlton was drinking everything in and enjoying the parade but his mind never strayed far from his main mission.

'Talking of surprises,' he asked Teague, 'How would you propose to handle my casino situation?'

'I've been thinking,' said Teague. 'It would make a wonderful new issue.'

'What in the States we call an IPO?' asked Tisch..

'An Initial Public Offering? Very similar.'

Carlton thought for a minute. 'On-line betting is to all intents and purposes illegal in the United States. How would you deal with that?'

'Ignore it. Who cares?'

'What about British law?'

'I don't think the subject is addressed in UK law. But just to be safe, I'm getting us some high-powered legal advice from a top law firm.'

'I hope that will work.'

'Of course it will.'

Teague had the bit between his teeth now. The younger man's enthusiasm was almost scary, thought Carlton. He wondered if he would soon be getting too old for this kind of thing.

'We leave the casino offshore, obviously,' said Teague. 'The Feds might put pressure on Antigua to ban Internet casinos some day, but that is way down the road. We can always move shop to Gibraltar if things get tricky. And we shall need to be damn sure there are no assets in the United States for the Feds to attach.'

Carlton nodded. 'You will also have to discourage the firm's executives from setting foot in the States. They would risk being arrested as soon as they got off the plane.'

'Is that a problem for you personally? You have a home in the USA, don't you?'

'I have several. But I don't plan to become an executive, so that wouldn't matter.'

'You want to be a stockholder, don't you?'

Carlton looked evasive. 'I have ways of arranging that side of things.'

'Using your buddy, Kon Feaver?'

Carlton was startled. 'What do you know about Feaver?'

'I've met him, with you, remember? We were all at that seminar in Palm Beach last year.'

'Why would you think that I work with him?'

Teague chuckled. 'Takes one to know one, old bean. Everyone needs a Kon Feaver. I have one, too, he just has a different name.'

Carlton relaxed. 'You had me worried.'

'Your secret is safe with me.'

'I hope so,' said Carlton tartly.

The horses were approaching the starting gate, the jockeys' silks making dazzling splashes of colour against the green turf. Over at the Tote, Al was placing a bet.

'So what do you think about an IPO,' Teague asked Carlton.

'For the casino? I hoped you would suggest it. I'd say we are on the same page.'

'Good,' said Teague, 'Because I have another suggestion. A successful IPO requires a strong group of underwriters, right?'

'Of course.'

'Well, I know the first place I would look.'

'Where?'

'There is a young man here today who likes a bet now and then, even though his religion frowns on it. It's one reason he likes to live here.'

'I've run into a few Arabs in Las Vegas,' said Carlton, 'and I don't think they were there for the cheap buffet dinners.'

Teague nodded. 'It's a grey area. Some of the world's great horse owners are Muslims – the Aga Khan, the Maktoum family from Dubai. The temptation for some more westernized racegoers to back horses from those stables must be great.'

Carlton said nothing but he was beginning to see a link.

'I see him coming now.' Teague beckoned to the young man. 'Al, can we have a word.'

Al was brandishing a betting ticket. He looked pleased.

'I found an interesting situation. Lover Girl at 6 to 1 with Dettori up.'

Quentin Teague sucked his teeth.

'Maybe. But her trainer has been unlucky at Ascot lately, I'd call that a risky proposition.'

Al grinned. 'We'll see.'

'Enough of that,' said Teague. 'Here's something that really is a winner.'

He turned to Tisch. 'Tell Al about the Casino while I go and get a bet down.'

'Sure,' said Carlton. 'Do you like to gamble, Al?'

Al rolled his eyes. 'Now and then.'

'As do millions of other people around the world,' said Carlton. 'Though not in posh surroundings like this.'

'That's exactly right. But on the Internet, that's another matter.'

Al nodded. 'Myself, I do both.'

'What do you play?'

'Blackjack. And some poker. I use Casino Caribbean.'

'Do you now?'

'Sure. They are fun, very realistic. It's almost like being there.'

Carlton held his breath. 'How would you like to own a piece of that company?'

'I would love to. They must make millions.'

'Yes, they do,' said Carlton. 'And we may be able to arrange that.'

He proceeded to tell the story of the renegade drug dealer's casino, omitting only a few of the more hair-raising details that he thought might diminish its appeal as an investment.

'Of course, for legal reasons any public offering would have to be arranged outside the United States, possibly in London,' he said.

As he spoke, he was mentally commending Quentin Teague for providing the perfect environment for a pitch – here at the races, surrounded by the trappings of grace and affluence, it was as good a start as he could have wished for.

Al listened carefully.

'How much business are they doing at present?'

'It's hard to say. They are growing so fast, what with poker on TV and the recent technological advances like virtual reality…'

'Take a guess.'

'Last year they grossed 170 million. Which was 70 per cent better than the year before. This year, they should do 400 million.'

'Dollars or pounds?'

'Dollars.'

'What do you think the business is worth?'

Carlton was wily enough not to name a figure. What usually worked for him was to let the buyer be the first to mention a price and Al was the buyer.

'It depends what price-earnings ratio you use,' he said. 'Internet businesses have been fetching some pretty high multiples.'

He paused.

'Higher in the United States than here,' said Al quickly.

Carlton sensed that he might already be in a negotiation but just then the public address system crackled to life as the next race was announced.

'They are about to go off,' he smiled.

Al turned. 'We can continue this later.' He hurried down to the rail to watch the race.

Carlton sipped his champagne. He considered betting on horses to be a mug's game. He enjoyed racing for the atmosphere and the spectacle but it was not a good way to put money at risk. He only liked to bet when he understood the motivation of the parties. He had never met a horse that understood the value of money.

The horses charged down the home stretch and the crowd noise swelled to a roar. After trailing all the way, Lover Girl mounted a last minute challenge on the outside and just got her nose in front to win. Al came back grinning self-consciously and holding a wad of banknotes. Judging by its thickness, Carlton estimated the young man had bet at least a thousand pounds. Not a lot of money for a rich sheikh but Carlton was slightly disapproving, never having been that rich that young.

But Al was clearly delighted.

'It's an omen,' he said. 'Perhaps I should buy the whole casino.'

'Are you serious?'

'By me, I mean my country's Investment Office, of course.'

'That's an interesting offer,' said Carlton, 'But I can see complications.'

'You think we can't afford it?' asked Al sharply.

'That's not what I meant,' Carton said slowly. Privately he was telling himself that this young man's enthusiasm should be encouraged but when the British bankers who staffed the Ras al Doha Investment Office got wind of the deal they might be less keen. They were probably paid to stop young princes from making costly mistakes and if Carlton knew anything about employees they would relish shooting down an idea not originated by themselves.

Still, it could not hurt to discuss strategy with Al, who was clearly not stupid.

'About the price-earnings ratio…'

Al interrupted him. 'Well let's do some estimating. You said sales were approaching 400 million dollars. How much of that is profit, about fifteen percent?'

Carlton smiled. 'Higher.'

'Twenty?'

'Try thirty percent. And a price-earnings ratio of, I don't know, say twenty five.'

For the first time, Al hesitated. Carlton could see him doing the arithmetic in his head. Thirty percent of four hundred million was one hundred and twenty million dollars a year. Multiply that by 25 and you had three billion. Al was secretly amazed. Three billion was a lot of money, even for a sheikh.

But he was not going to be intimidated. Especially by some scrawny American who looked a bit down-at-heel even in his formal clothes which, unlike Al's, were probably rented.

'Three billion? No problem.' He tried to look nonchalant.

'My people might want cash,' said Carlton mischievously.

'That's about the value of the oil pumped by my country's wells in a week,' said Al drily.

Carlton nodded politely, having no idea if that was true. 'One more thing.'

'What's that?' Al fidgeted. The start of the next race was imminent and the Tote would be closing.

'We don't want to sell the whole company.'

'Why not?'

'It's just too good.'

'Meaning?'

'We think this is just the beginning. There are six billion people in the world. A significant percentage of them gamble. And more of them acquire computers every day.'

'So?'

'So Casino Caribbean will continue to grow. That valuation may sound high today but the business will be worth far more in five years time.'

He could see Al was intrigued. Don't behave as though you were desperate for his money, he warned himself. He made a pretence of studying his programme. 'Well, this is fascinating but I need to go and place a bet.'

It wasn't true but it was time to break off. He had given Al something to think about.

On the way to the Tote, he met Teague coming back. 'Just had a piece of luck,' he said excitedly.

'Oh?'

'I think your young friend Al wants in.'

'Well, good.'

'I mentioned a value of three billion dollars and he hardly blinked.'

'Uh huh.' Teague glanced at his watch. 'Better hurry if you want to be in time for the next race.'

'You don't sound very excited.'

Teague stared at the American without blinking. His expression was impassive but the corner of his lip twitched upwards in the trace of a smile.

The truth dawned on Carlton. 'You set this up!'

'Me?'

'Well you didn't bring me all the way down here in these ridiculous clothes just to help you pick the winner of the three o'clock.'

Quietly, Teague said: 'As you know, there are several elements to a successful public offering. I'm sure it's the same in New York. We need a merchant bank – a firm with a history of success. We need an audit report from a good accounting firm. But few things are more important than lining up some serious money early on.

Money attracts money and when the institutions hear that Al's people are in they'll want a piece too.'

'What institutions did you have in mind?'

'Pension funds, unit trusts, the outfits that invest other people's money for a living.'

'What are Unit trusts?'

'What you call mutual funds.'

'How long will all this take?'

'My guess? We'll have things blocked out in a week. Letters of intent. The investigations will take longer, say a couple of months.'

Carlton began to realize that he might have a problem. Given the speed at which things were moving, he could soon be in an embarrassing position. He would shortly be asked to show that he could assemble the deal. He would have to prove that he could deliver title to the casino and right now he could not.

He had counted on having plenty of time to set things up but now he would have to hustle. He needed to call Kon Feaver, and soon.

Portly Quentin Teague was eying him.

'You *are* ready to move, there's no problem there, right?'

'None whatever.'

In the Land Rover on the way home, Lord Teague, driving with one hand, took a swig at a silver brandy flask and passed it to Carlton. 'Enjoy yourself?'

'Very much.'

'Good day financially, eh?'

'Oh, I think so,' said Carlton.

CHAPTER 19

GOING THE ROUNDS IN THE CITY

NEXT MORNING, the phone rang in Carlton's hotel room. It was Quentin Teague. As usual he came straight to the point: 'We need an investment bank to manage the offering.'

Carlton was cradling the telephone between chin and shoulder while trying to butter a roll. He took a bite of the roll and asked, 'Got any ideas?'

'Several. I'll pick you up in an hour and we'll go the rounds.'

'Should I wear my top hat?'

Teague sniggered. 'That's up to you.'

The Rolls into which Carlton stepped an hour later was a black clone of his own sky-blue model.

'Morning,' said Teague cheerfully.

'Didn't know you had one of these.'

'It's the firm's. Bit of an old boat but appearances count in the City.'

'Aren't London bankers past that? I thought it was just us colonials who had to put the best face on everything?'

'That may be true of the Brits, but the financial district is very international. We have American stockbrokers, Swiss insurance companies, Japanese banks. One of the biggest building societies belongs to Banco Santander, a Spanish outfit. Then there are the Arabs, like Ali.'

'All of whom, unlike the Brits, rely on appearances?' asked Carlton.

'No,' said Teague, slightly irritated. 'But it's like chicken soup, it can't hurt.'

'Anyway, where are we going this morning?'

'I've lined up a couple of banks. First we'll visit Hill and Dale. A bit traditional but one of the biggest in terms of new issues.'

'Traditional, eh? Would it bother them to be in bed with Arab money?'

Teague shook his head. 'No way. In the City, *pecunia non olet* – money has no smell.'

'No need to translate,' Carlton grinned. 'Even in linguistically challenged New York we understand that phrase.'

They drove past Nelson's Column in Trafalgar Square, then down the Strand past St. Clement Dane's church. Carlton gazed out of the window, enjoying the free tour. Reaching the City, they turned right at Bank underground station. He noticed a classical pillared building that reminded him of the New York Stock Exchange.

'Is that the Bank of England?'

'No, that's the Corn Exchange, but the Bank of England is just a few blocks away. London Bridge is coming up ahead.'

They drew up at an imposing stone building just short of the bridge. A uniformed porter sprang forward to open the car door. As they walked up the steps to the entrance Carlton noticed a tall obelisk on his left with a round top like a gilded cabbage.

'That's the Monument,' said Teague.

'Monument to what?'

'The Great Fire of London, 1666. The cabbage-like thing represents flames.'

'This bank looks almost that old,' sniffed Carlton.

The façade, which had once been white, was now a sooty grey. Inside, they found themselves in a foyer bigger than the lobby of the US Senate, with a pink marble floor and Corinthian columns on all sides. Morning sunshine filtered down from stained glass windows high above.

There was nobody much around. It reminded Carlton of a museum on a quiet morning.

'*Hello*, sir,' said a male receptionist with a briskly cheerful, drill-sergeant manner. He either recognized Teague or was doing a skilled imitation thereof.

'We're here to see Tim Carrington.'

'Certainly. Sir Tim will be right down, he's expecting you.'

Moments later a young man in a well-cut grey suit came down the marble stairs.

'Morning, Q.'

'Tim, meet Carlton Tisch.' They all shook hands.

'Come on up.' They followed Carrington. He was a fast walker.

'He looks too young to be a knight,' Carlton said, under his breath.

'He's a baronet,' Teague muttered. Carlton stayed silent; he had no idea what that meant.

Carrington showed them into a conference room as big as the main foyer.

'Tea or coffee?' he asked brightly.

'Coffee,' said Carlton.

'Tea,' said Teague.

Carrington picked up the phone. 'One of each, please, Phyllis.'

'Hector Thomas, our new issue wizard, will be joining us. He'll be here in two ticks.'

'If you are not in that department, why are you here?' asked Carlton.

Carrington blinked.

Teague said, 'Tim and I were at school together.'

'Eton or Harrow?' asked Carlton. He was getting mildly irritated without knowing why.

'Rugby.'

They made small talk for five minutes. Finally Teague looked at his watch.

'Tim, we've got some other calls to make this morning.'

'So sorry. Hector was in Zurich all day yesterday, he must be running behind. Let's get going. What's the story?'

Carlton took a deep breath and got started but a couple of minutes later the door opened. In came a florid individual in a Burberry raincoat carrying a briefcase, rolled umbrella and pink newspaper.

'Sorry,' he boomed. 'Bloody train was late. Quentin, how are you?' And, turning to Carlton, 'Don't think we've met.' He turned away almost before Carlton had a chance to shake his hand. 'Let's get started.'

Carlton began again but, almost immediately, Thomas held up a meaty hand.

'Better get one of the young 'uns in here. Take notes, what?' He picked up the phone.

Someone called Toby turned up. A pink-faced youth in his twenties, Toby's role seemed to be to blink politely through gold-rimmed glasses and make copious notes on a yellow pad.

By this time, Carlton was starting to tell the story for the third time, which he did not appreciate, but he soldiered on for ten minutes, then paused for questions.

Hector Thomas seemed distracted, as if his mind was still in Zurich. Toby asked Carlton if he ever gambled on the Internet himself, which he did not. Tim Carrington asked how big a share of the Casino Carlton and his group were willing to give up.

'Twenty five percent,' Carlton replied. In his mind, the remaining seventy five percent was enough for himself, Feaver, Oliver and Kathy plus a bit left over for contingencies.

Thomas finally cleared his throat noisily. 'That's not enough,' he said.

'I beg your pardon?'

'Forty percent is the least we'd go. We would want ten percent ourselves and there has to be enough free stock to make an active market.'

Carlton's argumentative gene kicked in. 'It's twenty five or nothing,' he said sharply.

Carrington looked embarrassed. Quentin Teague smiled, sphinx-like, and glanced at his watch. 'Tim, we really have to be

moving along. Let's leave things there while we go away and think
it over.'

Hector Thomas looked a bit startled but he stood up and
shook hands.

'We'll let you know' he said gruffly.

'No,' said Carlton, 'We'll let *you* know.'

Back in the Rolls, they looked at each other.

'That went well,' said Teague drily.

'No kidding,' said Carlton. 'Where next?'

'Some other chums of mine. The next people are nicer,' he
added slightly defensively.

They drove back past the Bank and up Moorgate for a few blocks
before turning down a side street. Down a steep ramp and well
below street level, they were confronted by gleaming stainless steel
doors. Above their heads, the infrared eye of a scanner winked at
them. Not a human being in sight. A loudspeaker purred into life.

'May we help you?'

'Here to see Nicco Stressman.'

'Your name?'

'Quentin Teague.

A pause. 'What is your date of birth, Mr. Teague?'

Teague gave it, grinning. Apparently he was believed, because
the gates slid smoothly aside and they were able to drive forward
into a spacious parking area.

'What was all that about?' asked Carlton.

'They are a bit security conscious here.'

'I can see that. Why?'

As they walked towards the elevators, Teague pointed to a small
plaque on the wall. It showed a heraldic symbol, crossed swords
above a wheat sheaf. Carlton recognized the arms of a distinguished banking family dating back to the 18th century. Their
name was associated with some of the world's great engineering
projects as well as several wars. Citizens of the world and highly
regarded on Wall Street, he recalled that they were even more
firmly established in London.

'Sorry about the security,' said Nicco Stressman, a few minutes later. He shook hands politely. He was a studious young man, prematurely balding, wearing sober pinstripes. He looked about the same age as Teague.

'We have to be careful, it's the terrorism. Our name makes us an attractive target so there are a few militants who would love to blow themselves up in our lobby.'

'It can get a bit tedious,' grumbled Teague.

'Can't be too careful,' said Stressman lightly.

'I agree,' said Carlton, looking at Stressman. Their eyes met. They were co-religionists but came from different worlds. Carlton was the son of poor immigrants from New York's lower east side whereas the Stressmans had been settled in England for over two hundred years and numbered a couple of peers of the realm in their family tree.

Quentin Teague was sometimes crude but seldom stupid. He saw the look that passed between Carlton and Stressman.

'Mr. Tisch understands,' said Stressman cheerfully.

'Speaking of which,' said Carlton, 'How do you feel about the Ras al Doha Investment Office?'

'Depends which people you mean. The Arabs are okay. Some of the Brits walk around as if they had a poker up their ass.'

'What about Al Khalifa?'

'Ali? He's a good kid.'

'But an Arab?'

Stressman shook his head. 'Doesn't matter. That bunch are good investors. They like to take a position and hold it, not duck in and out like some.'

'Are you okay about doing business with them?'

'Of course.'

'Wasn't Ali at Clifton?' interrupted Teague.

'Shrewsbury, I think,' said Stressman.

Carlton was losing the thread. 'How do you two know each other? No, wait, you were at school together.'

Stressman shook his head. 'Cambridge. We were both Ganders.'

'Both what?'

'Doesn't matter,' Teague broke in. 'We may have a live one for you, Nicky.'

'I'm listening.'

Tisch told his story.

Nicco Stressman heard Carlton's pitch, his face pensive. Then he broke into a smile.

'Sounds like fun!'

Tisch raised an eyebrow. 'Is that a yes?'

'It's a conditional yes.'

'Don't you have to talk to your partners?'

'Oh, I might run it by my brother next time I see him,' Stressman said lightly. 'But he likes that kind of stuff.'

Tisch lit a cigarette. He was feeling a rush of blood to the head, which he tried not to show. His euphoria was checked when Stressman raised a hand.

'Subject to the usual conditions.'

Damn, thought Tisch. 'What are those?' he queried.

'Any deal with us is subject to audit. We'll need a good look at the company's finances.'

Tisch relaxed. 'No problem. I'll send our auditors to go over the books as soon as possible.'

Stressman smiled.

'Okay. But not your auditors, our auditors.'

Tisch shrugged. 'We use _____.' He named one of the three biggest audit firms in the world. 'I know the New York partners pretty well.'

Stressman nodded. 'So do our Wall Street people. But what we find here is that the big firms don't always do the best job for us.'

'How so?'

'They don't produce the kind of report we need. They tend to work for themselves rather than for their client – us.'

'Not sure what you mean.'

Stressman shrugged. 'Some of them are over-concerned with protecting themselves from lawsuits.'

Tisch actually understood quite well what he meant. In recent years the big accounting firms had moved more and more towards avoiding legal liability. As a result, traditional auditing – looking for errors and evaluating how a business was run – had been de-emphasized. Under competitive pressure to keep fees low, audit personnel spent less time in fields where, with additional testing, mistakes might be found. More than once Tisch had seen significant areas completely ignored by an audit partner obsessed with self-preservation and coming in under budget.

'Who are your auditors?' he asked Stressman.

'Calder, Irwin. They do a pretty good job for us.'

'Never heard of them,' Tisch growled. Dealing with unfamiliar advisors made him nervous, it was a control thing.

'If you worked in London, you would know them. They are not one of the big three but they are in the top ten. They certify many of our new issues and their work is impeccable.'

'Can they move fast?'

'When necessary.'

Teague, who looked as if he had been dozing, awoke with a start. His appetite for accounting detail was strictly limited.

'Who is your contact over there?' he asked.

'Angus Mackie.'

'Ah, the Mackie of Mackie. Good man. Bump into him at Whites now and then.'

'At the bar?' asked Stressman.

Teague wagged a finger. 'Naughty! Anyway, we must talk to him.'

Stressman nodded. 'He's doing a job for us at the moment. A new issue, due out next month.'

'Where can we reach him?' asked Tisch.

Stressman leaned forward and pushed a button on his phone console.

Moments later:

'Mackie.' The Scottish burr was noticeable. There was a babble of voices in the background.

'Angus, it's Nicco Stressman.'

'Morning, Nicco. Are you chasing me for the financials?'

Stressman laughed. 'This is something different. It could be your next assignment.'

'Have a heart, man. I'm up to my Scottish arse in the present one.'

'Where are you?'

'I'm in Newcastle on Tyne.'

'Why, for goodness sake?'

'Counting inventory. Which is in warehouses in Whitley Bay. Had to pop up and see for myself.'

'Does that mean we have a problem?'

'I don't think so. But I'll be able to let you know in a couple of days.'

'I'd like you to meet our newest client.'

A pause.

'I'm a bit pinned down up here. First things first, you know?'

'I understand,' said Stressman. 'When will you be back in London?'

'Middle of next week.'

Stressman looked over at Tisch and shrugged as if to say 'Sorry.'

'We can go and see him,' said Tisch.

'They want to come and meet you,' said Stressman into the phone.

'No problem. Give them my mobile number.'

'Will do.' Stressman rang off. With a gold propelling pencil, he scribbled a number on a notepad, tore off the page and pushed it across the leather desktop.

'There you are, gentlemen. The way is clear.'

Downstairs in the car, Tisch asked, 'How far is Newcastle on Tyne?'

'Quite a way.'

'Will we get there before lunch?'

Teague laughed and shook his head. 'Afraid not. It's in the North of England.'

'This is a small country,' said Tisch. 'We'll take the Rolls.'

'I hate to disappoint you,' said Teague, 'But with London traffic the way it is, it would be dark before we reached the edge of town. No, this requires a train journey. If you've never been on a British train, you're in for a treat.'

'Why do I think you're being sarcastic?' muttered Tisch.

CHAPTER 20

NORTH TO NEWCASTLE

T HE ROLLS CRUISED THROUGH GREY STREETS to the bleak
portals of King's Cross station. As he stepped out of the
cleanliness of the Rolls, Tisch's nostrils were hit by essence of
British Rail, a tart amalgam of soot, dirt and disinfectant.

But the train left on time. For the first quarter of an hour, it
rattled through miles of grimy house backs and industrial blight.
Finally a patchwork of green hedges and soft brown fields
appeared and Tisch's spirits began to lift. They were further raised
by the prospect of lunch as a steward brought silverware and white
table linen.

Teague saw him reading the wine list.

'Stick to the house red,' he said quickly.

'It sounds as though you've done this before.'

'Yes, I have. And avoid the fish; the steak is passable.'

Forewarned, Tisch enjoyed his lunch. Over coffee, he said:

'I must be honest. This old-boy network thing that you Brits
operate is very amateurish.'

'Oh, there are a few people doing honest work down in the boiler
room while we lounge about drinking tea,' said Teague lightly.

Tisch shook his head.

'That's all very well, but I just think it leaves too much to
chance. Investment decisions should be based on analysis. These
friends of yours may be adequate but how do I know we are

not missing out on someone even better, who would make us more money?'

Teague thought for a minute.

'You don't.'

Long pause.

'So?' pressed Carlton.

Teague laughed. 'Let me ask you a question, my aggressive friend.'

'Fire away.'

'Think about the last big deal you did in the States.'

'Okay, I'm thinking about it.'

'Who brought it to you?'

'The seller's attorneys.'

'And who are they?'

'A New York firm, called Gerson, Lennox, Xavier, Irwin, Venables, Neff and Niemeyer. They heard we were looking for an acquisition.'

'Well bully for Gerson and company,' Teague said drily. 'And why did they call you rather than someone else?'

'Barry Irwin is someone I've done business with in the past. Actually we were both junior bond salesmen at Goldman, Sachs about a hundred years ago.'

'Really?' said Teague. 'Sounds as if the old pals network works pretty much the same way on Wall Street as it does in the City of London.'

'Not true,' argued Tisch. 'My relationship with Barry is based on working together in the financial trenches for five years.'

'It took that long? Then you should concede the superiority of the British system. I started using my old school and college contacts as soon as I went into banking.'

'But that's my point. You did not really know you could trust them. I knew I could trust Barry because we had worked together.'

'No, that's *my* point. I could trust Nicco Stressman without having to go through a long probationary period.'

'How?'

Teague had to think for a minute. 'His background.'

Tisch almost spat with derision.

'That and fifty pence would not buy a cup of what the British mistakenly call coffee.'

'Yes, it would.'

'What if he lets you down badly?'

'He wouldn't. His family wouldn't let him. If he did, he'd be finished in the City.'

Tisch thought about that.

'Might work I suppose,' he said grudgingly.

'Trust me, it does.' Teague went back to reading the sports pages.

Half an hour later they drew into Newcastle Station.

Teague hailed a taxi. 'Whitley Bay, please, driver – the Royal Albert Hotel.'

'Yes Sir.'

'Nice place, Newcastle,' said Teague companionably, looking out of the window.

'It's all right,' grunted the cab driver.

Carlton laughed. 'You don't sound too sure.'

'I'm from Gearts Hid myself,' he said shortly.

'What did he say?' Tisch asked Teague.

'He said he was from Gateshead. It's across the river.'

'Oh.'

By then it was five o'clock in the evening and shadows were lengthening as the taxi headed east towards the North Sea and the windswept seaside resort of Whitley Bay.

The Royal Albert Hotel was a gaunt Victorian edifice, vast enough to accommodate eight rugby teams at once in the season. In the dim lobby, a string trio was strangling Schubert. The lead violinist, a faded lady in lavender tulle, smiled bravely at them as she sawed away.

In the third floor suite occupied by Calder, Irwin and Company, Chartered Accountants, the air was thick with cigarette smoke. Owlish Angus Mackie, a giant of a man, was peering at a spreadsheet on a laptop computer. Tisch was struck by the gauntness of his profile as he stared at the flickering screen. He ignored Teague and Tisch as they entered the room.

Most of the smoke was generated by Angus, with a pile of butts to prove it in the ashtray at his elbow. The colourful brocade braces keeping his pinstripe trousers up contrasted oddly with his plain white face and plain white shirt. Heaps of manila file folders obscured the dresser behind him. Across the room, two younger accountants were stabbing at a thick wad of computer paper, making marks in red ink.

The visitors waited in front of Mackie. Finally Teague tapped him on the shoulder and he straightened with a start and stared at them.

'How are you, my boy?' boomed Teague.

Mackie pushed a key and the computer screen went dark. He stood up and towered over them.

'Carlton, meet Angus Mackie, ace auditor, sometime point guard for St. Andrews University basketball team and all-around useful man. Angus, meet Carlton Tisch, a pirate from the Caribbean.'

Mackie stuck out a hand.

'You look busy,' said Carlton.

The tall Scot gave him a quick glance. Carlton felt neither liked nor disliked, just analyzed. It was a disconcerting feeling even for Tisch, who had suffered more than his share of boardroom barbs, ranging from subtle insult to all-out abuse.

But the grin that lit up Mackie's face for a moment dispelled his discomfort, making him wonder if he had misread the Scot's previous expression.

'Sorry you had to travel so far but, as you see, I'm in the thick of things.' Mackie pointed to the sofa. 'Sit ye down.'

'What kind of business is this?' Tisch asked.

'Ach, it's a couple of young men who sell drill pipe to the oil companies in the North Sea.'

'How's it going' asked Teague? 'Should I apply for a few shares?'

Mackie wagged a bony finger.

'You know if I told you that I'd have to kill you.'

'Just asking.' Teague was unabashed.

'I heard you might have a job for me,' said Angus. 'Something to do with gambling in the sunshine?'

Tisch nodded. 'Does that bother you, the gambling aspect?'

Angus laughed. 'I don't make moral judgments when I'm working, it's strictly about the numbers. Besides, sunny weather is always a plus,' he nodded at the window. Leaden clouds were swirling across the evening sky, buffeted by the growing wind.

'An accountant without morals?' Tisch spoke playfully. 'That's interesting.'

The Scot frowned. 'In auditing, what we look for is legality. I consider the legality of every transaction because its absence might invalidate the numbers. As for ethical questions, those are normally addressed by others'

'Just kidding,' said Tisch, 'Sorry if I seemed rude.'

'What's rude about it?'

Tisch privately classified Mackie as pleasant but literally minded and not overburdened with a sense of humour.

Later, Teague and Tisch went down to dinner in the hotel restaurant leaving Mackie and his team to their work. They sat in a booth overlooking the seafront. It started to rain. Sheeting gusts thudded against the plate glass windows, punctuated with flashes of lightning.

'Typical English summer?' asked Carlton. Teague shrugged.

'I think he'll do,' said Carlton, referring to Mackie.

Next morning they left the Royal Albert Hotel early and headed back to London. As the train pulled out of Newcastle station, Teague said:

'Well, you are all fixed up, I think. Took about two days.'

'A fast start,' Tisch conceded 'Now let's keep our fingers crossed.'

When he got back to the Berkeley he found a note from Mimi saying, 'Gone shopping.'

He went downstairs to the bar overlooking Hyde Park and waited until 2 pm – breakfast time in the Caribbean – before calling Kon Feaver on his satellite phone.

'How's it going?'

'Okay. Good actually.'

'Where are you?'

'St. John's. I just got through talking to Jasper Demon. Looks like I shan't be needing my safe-cracking tools.'

'Will he go along?'

'Sure. I explained to him how he could make a lot of money from the IPO. He's motivated. If he wasn't before, he is now.'

'Does he have the legal capacity?'

'Yes. The power of attorney that Frankie gave him, plus the fact that Casino Caribbean's stock is in bearer shares, means that he can deliver the company regardless of what Frankie may or may not want.'

'What about Frankie's people – Neville and Judith?'

'They are cooperating, for the moment.'

'Only for the moment?'

'That's what I said.'

'Keep an eye on that pair,' said Tisch.

A week later the Virgin Atlantic flight carrying Angus Mackie of Calder, Irwin approached Antigua after nine hours in the air.

Angus stood up and stretched his legs. A man of simple tastes, he nevertheless insisted on flying first class. When you were six foot eight inches tall, enduring cattle class for anything more than a short hop was torture, akin to being trussed at the knees and ankles and stuffed in a crate.

He strolled back to the tiny bathroom, splashed water on his face and straightened his tie. Returning to his place, he retrieved his jacket from the overhead locker. He was wearing a lightweight suit tailored for his lanky frame by Airey and Wheeler of Savile Row but he was still unprepared for the blast of hot air in his face as he emerged from the plane and strolled across the tarmac with a cluster of other passengers. By the time he reached the small terminal, he was drenched in sweat.

The customs formalities were minimal. He wheeled his single bag out to the street and looked around uncertainly for a taxi.

'All by yourself, Mr. Mackie?'

Judith was wearing a white linen dress, its hemline well above her shapely knees. It was simply cut, showing off her tanned shoulders.

'And you are?' he asked courteously.

'Judith Barcat, your hostess while you are visiting Casino Caribbean.' She shook hands gracefully, letting her cool fingers linger for a moment.

'Make him feel good,' Neville had told her. 'Remember, the better we make this business appear to his eyes, the better it will be for us.' Their understanding with Tisch, relayed by Kon Feaver, was that they would each receive restricted options on 100,000 shares. The recipients could not exercise them until a year after the stock began to trade. If the business continued to flourish, so would they. Neville's broken arm was in a cast and there was a large patch on his cheek covering the cigarette burn but, in spite of physical insults that might have traumatized a weaker character, he had not lost the ability to assess his situation.

Neither of them had much faith in verbal agreements, which, as Neville observed, were worth only the paper they were written on, but it was the only offer on the table. So for Judith, being nice to Angus Mackie was a no-brainer.

CHAPTER 21

THE CATO TWINS

F RANKIE LEON'S FIRST THOUGHT, once Neville had rescued him in the Gold Digger and the ocean-going vessel was safely in international waters, was how to assemble troops for what he fully intended would be a ruthless and bloody campaign.

For his needs, he decided, the best solution was the Colombians and he thought immediately of the Cato twins, Diego and Navidad. They suited his purpose exactly – two young thugs in their twenties who killed without conscience and were known to relish their work to an unhealthy degree. They were thin and muscular, sour-faced, with close-set brown eyes that betrayed little beyond a pervasive dislike of mankind. It was not clear which twin was the more malevolent. Even if you knew, it wasn't much help because they were physically identical.

Frankie had crossed swords with them in the past. He recalled what happened when one of his own men fell into their hands several years ago. He had sent his associate, a crude fellow from Brooklyn called Shelley, to pick up a consignment of cocaine from the Catos. Shelley had just bought a brand new Cadillac SUV and he drove the shiny black vehicle to his meeting with some pride.

There had been no disagreement about money but, as they were all parting, Shelley made an off-colour remark about people who spoke Spanish. By Shelley's standards it was not racist, merely insensitive, but it annoyed the Catos. They tied Shelley to the steering wheel of the Cadillac. Using a bolt cutter capable of shearing through half-inch steel, they cut off both his thumbs and left them on the dashboard, inches from the groaning man's face.

It was not life-threatening although it brought about a career change for the stricken Shelley. In the violent world of drug commerce, worse things had happened. Frankie had been angry rather than intimidated. He was no coward, whatever else might be levelled at him. He made a note to be extra careful with the Catos. If the opportunity arose, he would get even with them one day. But he gave up dealing drugs not long afterwards and the affair receded in his memory

A year later the Catos were involved in another incident. This time, it was so gross that it finally caused them to be ostracized by their peers. Another buy was involved – several kilos of pure cocaine –and the Catos were there for the exchange. There was some kind of price disagreement; however, the brothers appeared to accept that. But, later that night, apparently feeling that they had been disrespected, they followed the seller back to his house where they raped his wife and teenage daughter. They then shot the parents. The girl survived to tell her story to police.

Even in a brutal industry, this crossed a line. The gratuitous violence was bad enough but violating the girl seriously affronted decent Catholic values. Most of the Catos' associates, realizing this was not good for business, ceased to deal with them. The story spread and even reached Frankie, who was still in touch through the grapevine with people in that community.

The Catos, now too hot to handle, retreated to their mansion in Cocoplum, an expensive development in the Coral Gables district of Miami. They did not go out but spent their time playing fussball for a thousand dollars a goal and drugging round the clock with a small circle of loutish friends.

Frankie had destroyed any incriminating records from those days but he knew where to put the word out, so he did so with a view to making his former enemies into allies.

A day later his satellite phone rang.

'Allo, Mr. Frankie!'

'Let me guess, this is Navidad!'

'No, is Diego.'

'How you doing, Diego?'

'No bad, Mr. Frankie. 'Ow 'bout ju?'

'Pretty good. Say, you interested in a few days work, you and your brother?'

'What kind of work?'

'The kind you used to do for the Cali people.'

A pause.

'Where we gotta go?'

'Antigua.'

'Antigua, eh?'

'Yes.'

'We prefer Miami.'

'Yeah, but the job is in Antigua. It pays well.'

'Ow much?'

'Twenty thousand.'

'Each?'

Frankie swallowed. 'Yeah.'

'Ju pay up front?'

'Of course.'

'Well, hokay.' Diego sounded more cheerful. 'We be there tomorrow. Eh, where you stay now, Mr. Frankie?'

Frankie hesitated. It was a good question. Where *did* he live now?

He could not risk going back to Antigua, he suspected he was *persona non grata* after the brouhaha at the plantation. His face was well known there and word would soon get back to the police. Until the recent trouble he had been, if not a model citizen, at least a contributor to the local economy – and to a few carefully selected civic leaders. But things had changed now, he was a person of interest in a shooting and some other stuff; it was a problem.

So Antigua was out for a while. Maybe permanently, he realized with a shock. He needed a new base.

Over the years he had bought homes and banked money in several parts of the Caribbean in case of situations like this. What about Puerto Rico? He liked San Juan, the capital. He owned a house there and knew some senior government officials personally.

As a 'self-governing commonwealth in association with the United States,' Puerto Rico had its own taxation system and was exempt from the U.S. Internal Revenue Code. That was good but it did not make San Juan a safe place for his money or for his body, now that he was a fugitive from US justice. Uncle Sam had too many fingers in the pie there, controlling interstate trade, foreign relations and most other areas generally administered by federal government in the United States.

No, with things as they were, Puerto Rico was not the answer.

'Give me a minute,' he told Diego.

'Sure boss.'

After a moment's thought, he had a better idea. Belize.

Belize, the former British Honduras, might do nicely. Sandwiched between Mexico and Guatemala, Belize had a long 180-mile coastline overlooking the Caribbean and was accessible by boat from where he was now. It was a poor country with a modest economy based on sugar and bananas plus a growing tourist trade but it was not slavishly beholden to the United States so that, provided he was discreet, he need not fear informers. Besides the mainland, it also included two thousand offshore islands with some of the best scuba diving in the world.

It was still a kind of frontier place even by Caribbean standards. Tales were told of remote airstrips where a small plane tranship-ping a cargo of heroin or cocaine could land unobserved, refuel and leave again for Florida. Frankie felt at home there. He knew his way around.

Things were slowly changing of course. Oil had been found in San Pedro, supposedly in commercial quantities. The cruise lines were stopping in Belize City. One day the whole country would be respectable. But for now things were pretty loose. Just about anything went in Belize.

He could hole up for a while at the five-star Fort Victoria Hotel in Belize City. The upscale American-run hotel was a popular rendezvous for well-heeled high life and low life. Its grounds were surrounded by a high wall to keep the riffraff out; the compound within was an enclave of luxury in the run down ex-colonial capital. You met colourful people in the cocktail bar there – entrepreneurs, he thought to himself, though some might have a less charitable description for them.

Belize had celebrated its independence from Britain by hiring a couple of London barristers to draft laws setting up trusts and international business corporations. These could be used by tax-savvy businessmen from richer countries to shelter income and assets from their own governments. Banking secrecy was respected and, not long ago, Frankie had stashed a sizeable nest egg there.

So he agreed to meet Diego and his brother in Belize City the next day.

But something was still bothering the Colombian.

'Ju pay airfare?'

'You'll have to buy your own tickets. But I'll reimburse you, don't worry.'

'Ju had better,' said Diego coldly.

'God bless you too,' thought Frankie.

He looked at his watch. It was mid afternoon – Brenda Nimitz's prediction that Frankie would have fled by nightfall had been spot on.

Leaving Neville at the wheel, he went below to the oak-panelled cabin that doubled as dining room and lounge and spread out his charts of the Caribbean.

Belize was five hundred miles to the south-west. The nearest bad weather was a tropical storm near the Azores, so it should be plain sailing. The Gold Digger could cruise at thirty knots in fair weather and was fitted with capacious fuel tanks so no stop would be necessary. They should be cruising into Belize waters by dawn the next day.

After giving Neville his orders, Frankie repaired to one of the four comfortable staterooms, rolled a joint and, after a few puffs, fell asleep.

Next morning early he brewed coffee in the small but lavishly equipped galley and took a mug up to the bridge for Neville. The sea was as calm as glass and eerily silent. By the pale light he could see land approaching.

He had told Neville to make landfall on the tiny island known as Caye Caulker rather than cruise openly into Belize. He did not want to publicize his movements – with luck, his departure from the States might still not have been noticed and, if so, he wanted to keep it that way.

Caulker was a tiny sand key about 20 miles offshore in crystal-clear water, a favourite of the scuba-diving crowd. Barely a mile long and half a mile wide, it was inhabited by a few fishermen and boasted a handful of cafes and dive shops. People walked barefoot along the strip of warm sand that was the main road, with no auto-mobiles to be seen.

Frankie disembarked unnoticed, wearing jeans and T-shirt and carrying a canvas dive bag. Neville waved goodbye and guided the Gold Digger smoothly away on its return journey to Antigua.

The small jetty was almost deserted. Frankie strolled over to the tiny kiosk and bought a ticket for the next shuttle to the mainland. He merged easily with the assembling passengers, mostly returning divers, baseball caps shading their eyes from the sun. They clambered onto the boat, an open skiff with an outboard motor, and sat on wooden benches along each side, their dive bags stowed under the seats. Frankie kept a careful eye on his bag – inside were his satellite phone, a loaded automatic and several pass-ports. He had thoughtfully hung a dive mask and fins on the outside, as protective colouring.

With a couple of dozen passengers on board, the boat was fully loaded and rode low in the water, its bow smacking against the light swell. Sometimes a bigger wave would spray the occupants but nobody seemed concerned. The atmosphere was cheerful. Conversations sprang up – besides English, he heard Spanish and German as well as some unrecognizable East European tongues. He himself kept quiet for fear of being asked what he was doing on Caulker and possibly being caught in a lie. He just smiled and watched his bag carefully.

Suddenly the sky clouded over and rain bucketed down. Grinning, the crew broke out a large tarpaulin that the passengers had to utilise as best they could. There was some good-natured screaming from the girls as some were soaked to the skin before the squall passed and the sun dried everyone out.

They were never completely out of sight of land. Just as Caye Caulker disappeared below the horizon behind them, the mainland became visible ahead. After 45 minutes at sea, they approached the Municipal Ferry Terminal of Belize City, a noisy, cavernous structure teeming with the next shift of tanned, bleach-blond divers waiting to take their place. Frankie was part of the crowd that streamed out onto the street. It had been easy to penetrate the borders of this small country by keeping it simple, never mind the rhetoric of politicians who talked in terms of 'sealing' borders using high walls or electronics.

It was only 10am but Belize City was already hot and sweaty, lacking the ocean breezes that cleansed the air on Caulker. He did not have far to walk to his first destination, which was in the banking district.

He crossed the iron-girdered Swing Bridge and walked two blocks south. As he passed a news stand he glimpsed some headlines – in a local beauty contest the judge was being sued for taking bribes; a banana farmer had been jailed for hiding smuggled Toyotas on his plantation; the football team had lost two-nil to Guatemala. So far, Belize remained blithely unconcerned with the arrival of one small murder suspect from Florida.

Arriving at Goldson Street, main artery of the financial district, he walked straight past the large offices of the Consolidated Bank of Canada and stopped at a more modest establishment. It announced itself by a small brass plate as the 'Bank of P. J. Hesketh.' He climbed the stairs to a plain reception area with leather sofas and identified himself, showing the receptionist his Leon passport. He was asked to wait.

Moments later he was shown into the office of Ravi 'Roger' Patel, the manager.

'Been a while, Mr. Leon,' said the smart young Indian, shaking hands. In the corner of the room, a computer flickered. He had just pulled up Frankie's history on his screen.

'Here for long?'

'Don't know yet.'

'How's business?'

'Good, good. How's the wife? Ritu isn't it? And your little boy? I forget his name.'

'There is a second son now, my wife gave birth just six weeks ago.'

'Wonderful, wonderful.' Frankie looked thoughtful. 'Mr. Patel, I need a favour.'

Patel was about thirty, dressed like a banker, no concession to the tropics. Before joining Hesketh, he had worked for the Consolidated Bank of Canada, a major bank with offices throughout the Caribbean. CBC's traditional business was financing trade and shipping but Patel had worked in the private banking division, setting up trusts for affluent Americans and others who liked to tread the thin line between tax avoidance and tax evasion. When a head-hunter approached him, Patel willingly jumped to a smaller, faster growing bank. The Bank of Hesketh was a CBC in miniature, once the offshoot of a British meat importer, now controlled by a consortium rumoured to be Dutch, but who really knew?

'Roger, please call me Roger.'

'Roger, I need $100,000.' After Judge Huckleberry's hefty bail demand, Frankie was temporarily short of cash.

'No problem, you have plenty in your account.'

'The thing is, I need it now.'

Patel smiled. 'Also no problem.'

He looked at the American thoughtfully. He had worked for several years in New York and the type was familiar. He felt no affection for Frankie despite the small talk. He was not required to like his customers. He was mildly curious as to why Frankie wanted money so quickly but it was not his business.

'Hundreds okay?'

'Fine.'

Taking a pad of forms from a drawer, he added some hand-written details and pushed it over to Frankie to sign. Then he picked up the phone and gave an instruction. Minutes later, another young Indian brought in a manila envelope. Patel gave it to Frankie.

'Better count it.'

'I'm sure it's okay,' said Frankie.

'Please count it anyway, it's a good policy.'

Frankie raised his eyebrows. He tipped out several bundles of bills, each secured by a rubber band. All was correct. In five minutes he was out of the door and on his way, the envelope stuffed in his dive bag.

A few minutes walk took him to the luxurious Fort Victoria Hotel.

By now his polo shirt was damp with sweat under the armpits. That and the salt on his face from the boat made him look, he realized, like a bum.

'I need a suite.'

The desk clerk looked at him patronizingly.

'Our suites are two thousand dollars a night.'

Frankie threw the man a look. He dug in his duffle bag and counted out four thousand dollars.

'For the first two nights, okay?'

The man nodded, respectful now.

'And send up half a case of Dom Perignon, chilled.'

'Yes, sir.'

As Frankie was signing in, the clerk was checking his records.

'There are two visitors here for you, Mr. Leon.'

'Oh?'

'Two gentlemen from Miami. They are in the cocktail bar.

Frankie scratched his scalp. He needed time to clean up.

'Wait half an hour, then send them up.'

'Yes, sir.'

He went upstairs to the suite on the top floor. It was light and elegant, with sliding glass doors opened onto a wide balcony with a view of the bay.

After he had showered and shaved, he felt much better. He needed space to think after the hue and cry. A lot had happened, none of it good, and his business, previously rock-solid, was slipping from his grasp. He was not broke or even close to it – he had a great deal of money stashed away. It had been a practice of his to squirrel funds away in a number of different banks, using as many names as he had passports. The bad news was that as far as his cash cow, the casino, was concerned, the flow of money was coming to an end.

He had no illusions about that. Even though the business was still legally his, the US Government would find a way of preventing him – a proven bail jumper – from enjoying it. RICO law, the Racketeer Influenced and Corrupt Organizations Act, would see to that, with its broad confiscatory powers. He had studied RICO over the years. Now he reviewed it bitterly in his mind:

'Violators should forfeit to the United States any property constituting, or derived from, any proceeds which the person obtained, directly or indirectly, from racketeering activity. Property subject to criminal forfeiture under this section shall include real property, tangible and intangible personal property.'

That covered just about anything, including an on-line casino. The government had also included language to prevent violators from transferring their assets to another party, so the business was as good as gone. He was down to whatever he had in various banks.

True, there was plenty of money there. But there was another problem: he was now a fugitive from justice, a man on the run.

Even Belize, with its relaxed fiscal laws, was unlikely to want him as a legal resident. Respectability was important to them. They aspired to be a parliamentary democracy on the British model. And Frankie, despite all his efforts over the last few years, was still not respectable.

Maybe his best hope was to do a Vesco and keep moving, he thought. But Robert Vesco had fallen from grace and landed in a Cuban prison. Just thinking about it made the normally resilient Frankie depressed. He was also angry. Well, he knew what to do about that. In business, when you were ill treated, it was important to get even. It made you feel better and the word got round. People knew not to mess with you next time. He had been damaged, sure, but now he would hurt the people who had hurt him, and hurt them badly.

But first, he must first find out what was going on. He picked up his satellite phone and called Judith Barcat in Antigua.

'Hey kid, what's up?'

'A lot,' she said sourly.

She had been expecting him to call and had been considering her position.

Frankie was still her boss and she knew he could afford to look after her. But she felt no loyalty to him, never had. If anything, she felt resentment. She thought of herself as the true creator of Casino Caribbean. The look and feel *were* the programme and her imagination had inspired both. She gave Frankie little credit for his entrepreneurial skill in starting the business. She just knew that, compared to her, he had made a huge amount of money.

Well, things were different now. A changing of the guard was taking place.

She had confided in Neville who was the closest thing she had to a friend on Antigua.

'So what do you think?'

'About what?'

'About what's going down. How will it affect me?'

He smiled sourly. 'Well, you're in a stronger position than I am, that's for sure. You have all the technical knowledge. You wrote the programmes that are at the heart of the business.'

'I know that.'

'You have to ensure that the new people know it too.'

'Don't they understand that I created the software?'

'Maybe, but you still have to sell yourself, show them that you are unique. Then you can name your price.'

So when Frankie telephoned Judith, wanting information, she was guarded in her replies.

She did not realize that Frankie could read her mind perfectly. He might not inspire much loyalty but he did understand people, at least their less noble sides. She was clever, but not as clever as she thought she was. He was well aware that she would be looking out for herself and that she would shade whatever she told him to suit her own purposes.

'How's business?' he asked.

'Great. The gross take last week was $8.3 million. That is up thirty percent over the same week last year.'

'Sounds about right.' Frankie did a quick calculation. The figure corresponded to an annual gross of 430 million dollars of which about 130 million would be clear profit. He multiplied that by 25 to get a rough idea of the value of the business. So the Casino was worth a bit over three billion dollars. It would have shaken him to learn that Sheikh Ali and Carlton Tisch had been making similar calculations in the Royal Enclosure at Ascot and had reached a similar conclusion.

Anyway, his billionaire status did not feel nearly as reassuring as it had a week ago. Being a fugitive had a way of taking the edge off things.

'Where are you putting the money?'

'It will sweep to one of the Swiss accounts as usual.'

He had accounts with two Swiss banks that had been happy to accept his assurances that the money was not drug money, which of course was true. One was in Zurich and the other was in Basel.

'Anything else?'

'They've sent an accountant to examine the books,' she said.

'And are you helping him?'

'As little as possible.' She made a joke of it but he heard the nervousness in her voice.

'Don't tell him anything you don't have to,' he said shortly.

'Of course not. When are you coming back?'

'It may be a while.'

'Okay.'

Frankie hung up and called Neville.

Neville's position was different from Judith's. He had no special skills. His value to Frankie was different – he was a fixer. He was also an accomplished brown-noser, loyal to whoever was paying him at the time, suspicious of his peers and ruthlessly inconsiderate of those beneath him. This unsavoury mix of attributes came packaged in a bland exterior, the smile on his dusky face ready to morph at the drop of a hat into either fawning adulation or a vicious sneer.

He had realized immediately that, with the changing of the guard, his position was very weak. Coming from a background of poverty as he did, raised in a shanty town where regular beatings from a drunken father had sharpened his reactions, he was quick to sense trouble. And, unlike Judith who had valuable secrets in her sleek head, he was replaceable.

He did not buy for a moment the rosy picture painted by Kon Feaver, self-styled 'interim chief executive' of Casino Caribbean. He had been on the losing side before. He knew that if he put a foot wrong, he would be lucky to get a cheque for his last week's pay as he left the building.

So when the call came from Frankie, his reaction was very different from Judith's. Faced with two poor options, an uncertain future with Tisch/Feaver/Steele or a perilous walk on the dark side with Frankie Leon, he had already decided to throw in his lot with Frankie, at least for now. He had been bag- man and gofer to Frankie for several years, through thick and thin. It established a certain rapport.

'What the hell is happening over there?' growled Frankie.

'Plenty,' said Neville drily. He proceeded to lay out the situation with names, dates and figures. He explained how Judith was in the process of revealing to Angus Mackie the entire financial anatomy of the business.

'Thanks, Neville,' said Frankie. 'I'll remember you helped me out.'

'Not a problem.'

Frankie just had time before the Catos arrived to take his money out of the manila envelope and count out forty thousand dollars. He hid the other sixty thousand in the bed, smoothing the covers so that they looked undisturbed. He returned the forty thousand to the envelope, which he put on the dresser in full view.

There was a knock at the door. In walked the Cato twins.

'Ow are ju, Mr. Frankie,' said Diego. He grinned crookedly and shook hands. Frankie suspected he had sipped generously down in the bar, which was not a good sign. His brother Navidad was steadier but he walked with a bit of a swagger and there was a cocaine gleam in his eye. They both wore cream linen suits over pastel T-shirts and could easily have been mistaken for extras in a Miami Vice episode. Small timers, thought Frankie with contempt. But they were perfect for what he had in mind.

The twin brothers were skinny but well muscled, like grey-hounds. They were in their late twenties, slender, with pale complexions and sour, down-turned mouths set in a permanent leer. Frankie recalled a story about how they had treated a pair of drug mules who had got out of line. Diego had tied one man's wrists behind his back, choking him with an arm, while Navidad pulled off the man's shoes and burned his initials on the soles of his feet with a lighted cigarette. The victim's companion reported that the only signs of emotion by the twins were the smirk on the face of Diego and a frown of concentration by Navidad as he carried out his work.

'How you boys doing?' smiled Frankie.

'Good! What ju want?'

'First things first.'

He reached for the manila envelope. Handing over forty thousand dollars was the work of a minute; he watched as each twin counted his share and stowed it in his hip pocket. He sensed from the way they handled the money that their financial reserves might be starting to run low – not surprising if they had been shunned by the dealing community.

'There's more where that came from,' he said gently. He was playing with fire but he had thought out his strategy in advance.

He waited until he had their attention again.

'Here's what I want you to do…'

CHAPTER 22

ANGUS GETS TO WORK

♦

'How's your steak?' asked Judith.

Angus nodded appreciatively.

He was being treated by Judith to a good dinner and a bottle of claret at one of Antigua's finest restaurants. The atmosphere was pleasant although the two diners had widely differing agendas. Judith was shamelessly trying to charm the auditor into a friendly frame of mind so that he would issue a glowingly favourable report. The Scottish accountant, on the other hand, wanted to use the evening to find out all he could about the on-line gambling business.

Not that he was not enjoying himself. He was as susceptible as the next unattached bachelor to Judith's feminine charms. But for Angus, the job always came first.

'Tell me how this industry works,' he suggested.

'Where should I start?'

'Why not follow the money trail? Start at the point where the gambler decides to fire up his PC and play a few hands of poker.'

She nodded. 'Well, first he has to commit to wagering a certain amount of money. He authorizes that on his credit card.'

He interrupted her.

'Does the house need a big cash reserve to begin with?'

She shook her head.

'Not really, that's the beauty of it from our point of view. The only money the player wins is the money lost by other players. It's not the house's money.'

'How does the house make its profit?'

'On the rake.'

'The rake?'

'The term we use for the percentage the house charges on every pot.'

'How much is the rake?'

'About four percent of the sums wagered.'

'Is that enough for the house to make a profit?'

She laughed. 'Oh, sure.'

'So, over time, the money available to the players is being depleted by 4 percent at each round of betting?'

'That's true.'

'So, at 4 percent each time it would take twenty five pots to consume his stake completely?'

She hesitated. 'I guess so.'

'But if that's true, he'll lose all his money and go away. Game over. Then the Casino will be out of business.'

'No.'

'Why not? There must be something I did not understand.'

She laid a hand on his arm.

'You're very smart. I think you understand everything.'

He was not taken in by the flattery. 'Since you are still in business, obviously there is a flaw in my logic. Help me out.'

She took a sip of wine.

'Well for one thing, you used the term "average gambler". There is no such thing, except as a statistical concept. But there are winners and losers. And, believe me, there are far more losers than winners. About one player in ten knows how to win as consistently as the odds allow, over time.'

'He must win fast enough to cover the percentage he has to pay the house,' Angus observed.

'He or she. Women gamble too.'

He laughed. 'Okay.'

'But you're right,' she said, 'It's usually men. Women have more sense.'

'Anyway,' he said, 'I think I understand. You need a steady stream of new players because the ones that lose will quit and not come back.'

She noticed a tightening of his lips. Apparently something about the thought was distasteful to him and she wondered how much of the Puritan there was in his nature.

'So the casino's viability requires that it continues to attract new losers?'

'You're half right. Although many of the old ones do come back. There are the addicts who can't stop, who always believe that they will do better next time. And there are some really hopeless losers. We call them fish, the people who just don't understand the odds. Take the game of poker. One of the addictive things about poker is that it's not just a game of chance. Skill is involved. And most losers genuinely believe they are skilful.'

'But they may go to other web sites. There is competition.'

'Well, of course. We have to keep attracting new players every day.'

'How do you do that?'

'We advertise. We use print media, television, any method we can.'

'Are you allowed to advertise in the United States? I thought on-line gambling was illegal there.'

'It is. But we encourage journalists to write articles and editorial material, generally get the word out. Also, we keep a close eye on our competitors. We have programmes that can track where our players go when they leave us. So we know what other sites they are using.'

'Spyware?'

'Exactly. Then we sneak little pop-up advertisements onto their screens to remind them that they can win big if they come back to us.'

'So that's where much of your money goes, on advertising?'

'Oh, sure. If you stop advertising, you are dead.'

They spent another hour over dessert, coffee and liqueurs discussing the minutiae of running an Internet gaming operation. By the time Judith dropped him off at his hotel with a smile and a warm handshake, Angus was surprised how much he had enjoyed the evening.

Next morning Angus awoke early, he was still on London time.

Judith called for him at 7.00am and they drove out to the plantation.

'You work a long day,' he said.

She nodded. 'It's quiet at this hour, it's a good time to work.'

One end of the old house had been adapted for office use with a general area and half a dozen smaller rooms. In Judith's office, they sat side by side at the computer while she guided him through the process whereby bettors registered and gave their credit card number or bank account information. Angus took notes.

Around 9am Oliver arrived. He was not an early riser. Seeing the two working hard, he left them to it and went and found an empty office where he got on line and set about balancing his bank accounts in England, Florida and Tortola. Internet banking made the process relatively easy.

When Angus thought he had got the hang of things from Judith, he said, 'That's good. Now I'd like to see a profit and loss account for the business.'

Judith hesitated. 'Sure.'

With a few keystrokes, she brought up a screen that requested a password. She typed it quickly, too fast for him to read. Angus smiled to himself. If she thought she could keep him out of the computer's secure areas, she was mistaken. But he did not make an issue of it; there would be time for that later.

She printed out two pages and handed them to him.

He read the first page and whistled. 'The casino earned fifty million dollars in five months?'

Page 1

Summary Income Statement:

Five months ended May 31st (Thousands of US $)

Sales	170,692
Less: Cost of Sales	34,884

Equals: Gross Profit	135,808
Less: Selling & Admin. Expenses	85,346

Equals: Net Profit	50,462
	=======

Page 2

Summary Balance Sheet:

As at May 31st (Thousands of US $)

Assets

Cash in Bank Accounts	11,319
Accounts Receivable	2,197

Total Current Assets	13,516
Fixed Assets	5,332

Total Assets	18,848

Less: Liabilities

Accounts Payable	1,963

Equals: Shareholders' Equity	16,885
	=======

'Yes.'

'Do you have a balance sheet?'

She handed him the other page. 'Is this what you mean?'

Angus read it. 'It's a start. So where is all the money?'

'Excuse me?'

'The money. Where is it?'

'Don't these statements tell you?' she asked innocently.

'No they don't. What they show is that Frankie Leon's interest in the business is only worth about sixteen million dollars, but you told me there were fifty million dollars of profit in the last five months. So where did it all go?'

'The money has certainly gone,' she said casually, treating the question as rhetorical.

His tone sharpened. 'Where did it go?'

'It was paid out.'

'To whom?'

She hesitated. 'It was drawn by Frankie Leon.'

'I see.'

She shrugged. 'Nothing improper about that, he owns the business. And by the way, I agreed to give you information about the business, not about his personal affairs.'

'Okay,' said Angus. 'Let's do it this way: How much was transferred out of the business's bank account in the last five months?'

'A lot.'

'Show me a list.'

Somewhat reluctantly she pressed more keys and another table of words and numbers showed on screen. He scanned it line by line. It appeared to be the business check register.

'There's an outward transfer of funds just about every day.'

'Yes,' she said. 'The available cash sweeps to one or other of Frankie's personal accounts at the close of each business day.'

'All of it?'

'All but a core balance, which stays in the account to provide working capital.'

He considered.

'See, I need to know where the money is now. I am not really doing my job if I don't know that.'

'And I am not doing my job if I tell you.'

Their eyes met.

'So we have a standoff,' he said.

She smiled sweetly.

Angus got up and walked down the hall looking in the other offices until he found Oliver.

'Have you looked at the Casino's financial statements?' he asked.

'Not yet.'

'The business is very profitable.'

'I told you so.'

'And it should continue that way, at least for a while.'

'Even if the owner is absent?'

'Sure, why not? The gamblers don't know that the owner has just been indicted for murder. If they did know, I suppose it might make them nervous. They might think that a man who is capable of such behaviour would also cheerfully manipulate the odds so as to shave some extra profit for the house. But they don't know.'

'You're probably right,' said Oliver. 'By the way, what did happen to all the money?'

'I think it's in Frankie Leon's bank accounts but I can't be sure. I'm encountering some resistance with Judith. He may have moved it out by now.'

'I doubt it,' said Oliver. 'Why would he? Unless he's bought an awful lot of real estate recently.'

'Maybe he has a gambling habit himself?'

Oliver laughed. 'I think it's more likely to be just sitting there.'

'I suppose so,' said Angus. 'But the elegant Judith won't tell me where Leon's bank accounts are.'

'Does she know herself?'

'Oh yes.'

'So what is her problem?'

'I don't know. Perhaps she is still not sure which team to join.'

'I'm surprised,' said Oliver. 'She must see that Frankie is finished.'

'Probably. But she may not know whether her own job is safe.'

'I can understand that,' said Oliver, thinking of his narrow escape at Judith's hands in the barn.

'Well,' said Angus, 'What am I supposed to do? I would really like to know where all that money is. It would give me a much better feeling if I could report that I had located the funds.'

'Why?'

'Well, it would eliminate the possibility of some kind of circular scam with Leon taking cash out of the business with one hand and then putting it back in with the other, creating an illusion of huge profits where there really were none.'

'You mean, the same dollars could be circulating in a never-ending loop?'

'It wouldn't be the first time. It is the sort of thing that happens when a business is being put up for sale.'

'I see your point,' said Oliver. 'Let me think about it.' After duly giving it some thought he called Carlton Tisch in Tortola and they spoke for a while.

A few minutes later the phone on Angus's desk rang. It was Carlton Tisch. He got straight down to business.

'How does it look?'

'It looks good,' said Angus.

'Make a nice IPO?'

'I'd say yes, very much so. The earnings are spectacular, if they're real.'

'Why wouldn't they be?'

Angus explained about the problem with verifying the cash paid out to Franklin Leon.

Tisch listened without comment. Then:

'Is she there with you?'

'She's in the office next door.'

'Put her on the line.'

Angus walked next door. 'Pick up,' he said. 'Carlton wants to talk to you.'

She shot him a questioning glance and picked up the phone.

'Now, young lady, what's the problem,' asked Tisch pleasantly.

'None that I know of,' she said curtly.

'Good. Then listen carefully. I want you to get yourself a pencil and a notepad and write down the numbers and passwords of every bank and brokerage account that Frankie Leon has anywhere in the world. Then give the list to my friend Angus.'

'As I explained to Angus, I would need Mr. Leon's permission for that.'

'And where is Mr. Leon at present?'

'I don't know.'

'Nor do I. And I don't care. I can promise you one thing, though.'

'What's that, Mr. Tisch?' She was getting a bit tired of this old codger.

'You can refuse to help us. But if you do, you will never see another penny from Mr. Leon or any source connected with him. And we shall throw the book at you concerning recent events at the plantation. Antigua's jail is not a nice place to spend time in from what I hear, quite different from the Antigua the tourists see.'

'Is that a threat?'

'You're very perceptive. Yes.'

She laughed. 'I've been threatened by some pretty intimidating people, Mr. Tisch. But they usually find that it is difficult to follow through on that kind of threat, especially from a distance. We live on different islands; it would take more time than you are prepared to spend.'

'I'm sure. That is why I have put my best man on it.'

'If you're talking about your young auditor, don't make me laugh. That straight arrow? He would have to watch me like a hawk and he can't do that from London. I'm a difficult girl to pin down.'

'However, the party I am thinking of wouldn't mind watching you one bit. Check your office door.'

Her door swung open and in strolled burly Kon Feaver. He sat down opposite her and grinned.

'Hi, Judith.' He eased the shoulder harness of his Ruger automatic.

The phone crackled in her ear. 'Are you there, Judith?'

'Still here.'

'Is Kon there?'

'He just walked in. Do you want to talk to him?'

'No, we have already spoken. I just want you to understand how serious we are. So he's going to give you a demonstration.'

She wasn't sure if Kon heard Tisch's words. It didn't seem to matter. Kon withdrew his gun from its holster and raised it to his eye. Then, he took aim at her face, aiming squarely between her ears.

She flinched. But the thought of all the money in Leon's bank accounts lent her strength.

'You don't scare me,' she said shakily.

'Step two,' said Tisch on the telephone.

Kon Feaver swung the gun barrel slightly away from Judith's face and aimed it at the digital clock on her desk. It was one of those electronic toys for the executive who has everything, with an LCD readout that announced the time, the temperature and the latest value of the Dow Jones Index. He fired. The noise was deafening. The gadget disintegrated into a thousand plastic splinters and the windows rattled.

Judith pulled a yellow notepad towards her, picked up a pen and started to write, her hand shaking slightly.

'What on earth is going on?' Angus was at the door, 'It sounded like a bomb going off.'

'Probably a car backfiring outside the gates,' said Kon, who had returned his weapon to its holster. He smiled amiably. Angus's nostrils twitched but he said nothing.

'Judith has something for you,' said Kon.

She pushed the pad at Angus, who read it quickly.

'That is excellent, just what I need,' he said politely.

She scowled. She looked skinnier when she was angry, Angus noticed. Less attractive.

Well, he had work to do. He had no wish to get involved in what looked like a messy argument. He took the list and quickly left the room.

Judith watched him go, looking sour.

'Sensible girl,' said Kon cheerfully.

Judith remained tight lipped for a minute, then finally said: 'You don't really think you'll be able to touch that money, do you?'

'I don't think anything,' said Kon, 'It's above my pay grade.'

'Leon will never authorize its release.'

'I wouldn't either, in his shoes.'

'Besides, those accounts are in five different countries. You would have to take legal action in each jurisdiction where there is a bank account. That would take years.'

'Is that so?'

She nodded. 'Even then, you would be second in line behind Uncle Sam and he pulls a lot of weight with small nations. Even the ones with banking secrecy tend to favour the US government when it puts serious pressure on them.'

Kon smiled. 'There's more than one way to skin a cat.'

'What's that supposed to mean?'

'Aha,' said Kon.

Actually he had no idea what he meant, he just wanted to sound cryptic. He looked at his watch.

'Almost time for lunch. Want to grab a swordfish sandwich somewhere?' She shook her head angrily.

'Please yourself.' Kon hauled himself upright and strolled out of the room.

He looked in on Oliver who was sitting reading *Newsweek*. Oliver was more amenable than Judith to the idea of lunch and put his magazine aside. Minutes later the two men were seated at a wooden table outside Virgil's Seafood Diner on St. John's Beach.

Kon ordered his swordfish sandwich.

'What's in the *fritto misto*?' Oliver quizzed the waiter.

'Calamari, shrimp, clams. Fresh snapper.'

'That's for me!'

The food arrived. A young Antiguan upended the bucket of golden morsels and spilled them onto the paper tablecloth in front of Kon. He also slapped down fried onion rings, a shaker of sea salt and some sauce tartare. Oliver selected a large shrimp and dunked it in the sauce.

'How did things go with Judith?'

'No problem,' said Kon.

'Did you find the money?'

'She gave up the account numbers. So we know where it is, or at least where it was sent.'

'Will that satisfy Angus?'

'I'm not sure. He's one of those po-faced Scots, you never know what they're thinking.'

'A bit like the Swiss,' said Oliver thoughtfully.

'At least the Swiss smile occasionally,' said Kon.

'Not Swiss auditors. They don't smile.'

'I haven't come across many of those.'

'Trust me.'

Kon frowned. 'Angus thinks the money might be part of a circular scam with Leon recycling it into the company to look like revenue.'

'That's possible.'

'Seems a bit pointless.'

'Not if he was planning to sell the company. We know he was talking to the Flacks about selling, so he might have been trying to dress it up for sale. It happens. Remember Robert Maxwell?'

Kon's brow creased. 'The guy who owned the New York Daily News? Drowned under suspicious circumstances?'

'Right. Mysteriously disappeared from his luxury yacht off the Canary Islands. After his death, they discovered that he had raided the pension funds of his newspapers. Siphoned off millions. Many employees were left penniless.'

'I remember. What does that have to do with pumping up profits?'

Oliver chewed an onion ring.

'People have forgotten now, but Maxwell raised profit rigging to a fine art. He owned a company called Pergamon Press. It had become very successful publishing scientific text books. The time came – it was in the late sixties – when he wanted to sell the company. He found a buyer, Leasco. A price was agreed. Everyone was happy until Leasco started boring into the financials. They discovered that a lot of Pergamon's sales were to offshore companies controlled ultimately by Maxwell himself. Turned out the inventory was still sitting there, piled up to the ceiling in a remote warehouse somewhere.'

'The sales weren't real?'

'Exactly.'

'What happened?'

'The deal collapsed. Leasco weren't stupid. They saw that the business had peaked and was going downhill and they wanted no part of it.'

'Are you suggesting that Casino Caribbean is going downhill?'

'I just don't know. That's why we want to make sure that its profits are real. Angus wants to be sure too, it will be his signature on the Prospectus. If he reports that things are fine when they are not, he's in a heap of trouble. The investors would sue his firm up, down and sideways.'

'So we need to be sure the money is still there?'

'Yes. But I'm guessing we won't get Leon's cooperation.'

'Looks that way.'

Oliver ate the last piece of calamari and licked his fingers.

'Maybe we should go and take a look in that big desk of his.'

CHAPTER 23

AT THE PLANTATION

*B*ACK AT THE PLANTATION, they headed for Leon's oak-panelled study. The many drawers in his leather-topped desk had remained shut and locked since its owner's hurried departure three days earlier.

Oliver had collected a tyre iron from the trunk of his car. He handed it to Feaver.

'Want to do the honours?'

'Sure.'

The Israeli inserted the lever between the top drawer and its housing, and slid it sideways. It stopped, hindered by an unseen latch. He jiggled it to left and right, trying to prise the lock aside but it refused to budge.

'Let me try,' said Oliver.

Taking the tool from Feaver he re-inserted the tip and gave it a sharp twist. The polished oak creaked, then split. The broken front panel of the drawer came away and fell to the floor, badly splintered.

'Didn't know you could be so rough,' said Feaver drily.

Oliver shrugged. 'When all else fails...'

The other drawers yielded without a struggle. The two men sifted through files, loose papers and assorted office clutter. In the top drawer, among the Sellotape and pencils, Kon found a transparent sandwich bag bulging with sprigs of what might have been dried herbs.

'Aha!'

He opened it and took a good long sniff.

'Very nice.' He handed it to Oliver 'Smell that.'

'Must I?'

'Go on. It's good.'

The scent was sweet and pervasive.

'It smells like good quality marijuana, not that I would know.'

'Of course not.' Kon retrieved the bag from Oliver and put it in his pocket. He grinned. 'Spoils of war.'

'Isn't that evidence?'

Feaver snorted. 'Evidence of what? That Frankie Leon, ex-drug dealer, keeps pot in his desk? As the kids say, Duh…'

Oliver was hunting through papers in a lower drawer. He found real estate leases, some handwritten letters from Leon's mother, a research study by a New York consulting firm assessing the gaming market in Eastern Europe. Then, tucked away at the back of the drawer, in an unmarked folder, he came across a bundle of bank passbooks held together by a rubber band.

'Bingo!'

He opened one at random. The last entry, a month ago, was a deposit of $14 million. There was a little over $30 million in the account. He counted the zeros again just to be sure before handing it to Feaver.

Feaver whistled. 'Even Tisch doesn't have that kind of money lying around.'

'That's not all. Check these.'

Oliver showed him the other passbooks. One showed $37 million and change, the other just over $24 million. The remaining two, from banks in the Cayman Islands, accounted for $10 million between them.

Feaver totted them up. 'Over $100 million. That's a chunk of change.'

Oliver nodded. 'And notice the dates.'

All the deposits had been made within the last eighteen months. There were no withdrawals. The money was apparently still there, with nothing to indicate a circular cash scam. Casino Caribbean was genuinely, outrageously, profitable.

'You know what's ironic,' said Oliver. 'In most parts of the world, this money is perfectly kosher. Everywhere except in the USA. Compare that with Leon's previous business – drugs – where everything he earned was illegal in most civilized countries.'

'What's your point?'

'Just that if Leon had resisted the temptation to send his goons over to Florida to squeeze Larry Smith, he would still be sitting pretty. If he hadn't got greedy, arousing the wrath of Kathy Smith, the US government and ourselves, he'd be enjoying his wealth today and none of us would ever have heard of him. But instead, he caused a bloody shoot out and is at war with America, Antigua and good folks everywhere.'

Kon sighed, 'Yeah, but you know, people are what they are. Folks like Leon are paranoid, it's part of their personality. They think someone is trying to screw them, so they want to crush him. That's what Leon was trying to do to Larry Smith. He wasn't just collecting money, he was getting even. He couldn't bear to be disrespected by a small timer.'

'Well,' said Oliver, 'I think I'll go and call Carlton, bring him up to date.'

Carlton Tisch answered the satellite phone on the sixth ring. He sounded out of breath.

'You okay?' asked Oliver.

'Just got off the tennis court.'

'Singles?'

'Doubles.'

'Is that all? That's not exercise. Five sets should be a stroll in the park for a fit old gent like you.'

'My wife and her friends are half my age,' growled Tisch. 'You should try it yourself before you criticize.'

'Try what? A woman half my age? That might be risky, she'd be below the age of consent.'

'Your time will come, you won't be young for ever. Anyway, what's going on?'

Oliver explained about the bank books. Tisch listened in silence.

'So what do you think?'

Tisch grunted. 'About what I expected.'

'You don't sound very excited. That's a huge amount of money.'

'But Judith was right,' said Tisch. 'We'll never get our hands on it. It will be tied up forever.'

'So nobody wins?'

'Except the lawyers.'

'That's awful.'

Tisch laughed. 'Deal with it. We'll make our money some other way.'

'On the IPO, you mean?'

'Sure.'

'So what should we do next?'

'Just help Alastair finish his work. Then he can go home.'

'Back to London?'

'Yes.'

The Cato twins were unknown in Antigua, despite their murderous reputation in Florida. They therefore had no problem gaining access to the island.

Before they left Belize, Leon had rented a villa for them on Antigua's north shore, paying the agency a month's rent in advance. They had enough self-awareness not to arrive in their Miami Vice suits, opting instead for polo shirts and slacks. Two attractive young Cuban women, Consuela and Lourdes, completed their party.

The foursome did not rate a second glance from the immigration officer. He put them down as just another holiday group. The men's gold wristbands and white loafers were a bit flashy, not to his personal taste but what was he, the fashion police?

'Welcome to Antigua!' He stamped their passports. By the time they passed through to the baggage area he had forgotten them.

The brothers travelled light compared to the girls, each of whom had several suitcases. The customs agent made Consuela open her big valise – it contained a quantity of exotic lingerie but no drugs or firearms. The men carried tennis racquets – a nice touch, thought Diego Cato. He dodged to one side as his brother waved his racquet experimentally. Neither of them played tennis but the equipment lent just the right image. The agent waved them through and they walked over to the Acme rent-a-car desk.

They had reserved a white Lincoln Town Car, the largest vehicle Acme had to offer.

'Ju drive, Consuela,' said Diego.

That was okay with Consuela. She had been warned that there might be some administrative chores, along with the obvious duties expected of her on a mixed foursome. The girls had been invited along at short notice but they knew the Catos could be fun, if a bit wild, and they were looking forward to the holiday. Diego was a pig but, in the crowd they hung out with, that was not unusual. You just put up with it.

The villa came with daily maid service but Diego had specifically declined it. He told Consuela that the villa would be closed to outsiders, which she could understand. The brothers' fondness for recreational drugs was no secret and she and Lourdes enjoyed a toot themselves now and then. If that was a problem in Antigua, it made sense to do without local help.

She drove carefully. The Lincoln was almost too wide for some of the island roads but the big vehicle's power steering was smooth and efficient, requiring minimal physical strength.

By the time they got to the villa it was late afternoon. The property belonged to a British rock musician who used it for three months a year and rented it out the rest of the time. It was secluded and pleasant with a sparkling pool. A shady terrace led down to a jetty by the ocean. There were four bedrooms and a gleaming kitchen with stainless steel appliances, including a big American refrigerator and freezer.

Consuela made a shopping list and set out with Lourdes on a trip to the little market they had passed a few miles back. When the girls had left, Diego got on the phone.

'We here, Señor Frankie. What the fuck we do now, my fren'?'

'Calm down,' said Leon. 'Everything is on schedule, things are looking good.'

'When the boat arrive?'

'After dark, I told you that. The skipper will call you. His name is Wayne.'

'I wan' my coke, man.'

'It's coming, along with the equipment.'

'How much ju send?'

'Enough,' said Leon curtly.

He was not happy about the Catos' cocaine habit. They had definitely gone downhill in that regard since the last time he had dealings with them. But it was too late to make a change – they would have to do. He was still confident that their experience and natural taste for violence would see them through.

Later on, when it had been dark about an hour, Diego's phone warbled.

'Is this Diego?'

'Yeah.'

'Hey, buddy, this' Wayne, how ya doin?'

'Where ju at?'

'Five miles south of you. I'd say, oh, ten minutes away.'

'I go look for you.'

'You won't see much. No lights, we're not advertising our presence, know what I mean?'

'How I see ju?'

'You won't. Just get down to that jetty with a flashlight and we'll find you.'

'Okay, I do that.'

'There you go, partner.'

Diego nodded at Navidad. Together they hurried down to the dock. The night was calm, with little noise apart from the relentless clicking of crickets. The moon had not risen but they could see faint luminescence as small waves slapped at the wooden jetty. Diego waved his flashlight, its beam disappearing into the blackness.

Suddenly a patch of darker black took shape, accompanied by the throb of a marine engine as forty feet of motor launch slid alongside them. A shadow vaulted off the bow and secured a painter, then ran back along the jetty and did the same with a second line that came snaking out from the stern.

The engine coughed and died. A dim light came on in the cabin and a second figure clambered ashore, broad shouldered in jeans and white T-shirt, and wearing a Yankees cap. He bumped fists with Diego.

'Got some merchandise for you.'

'Guns?'

'Hey, don't ask, don't tell!'

Diego shrugged.

Wayne turned and called over his shoulder. 'Paulie, get the cases up.'

'I need a hand,' Paulie grumbled. 'This shit is heavy.'

'Help him,' Diego motioned to Navidad, who clambered aboard and helped manoeuvre two heavy wooden boxes ashore and up the stone steps to the house.

Captain Wayne followed them but wouldn't come indoors. He lit a cigarette and smoked it outside while Diego and Navidad attacked the crates and pulled out the contents.

The first crate contained four AK47s – Kalashnikov gas-operated assault rifles capable of delivering a continuous stream of destruction. A pair of .45 Ruger pistols followed. Each weapon was separately wrapped in plastic sheeting against the sea air, with bags of drying crystals to absorb humidity.

Another crate contained six large cardboard boxes of ammunition, taped shut. In the same crate was a plastic freezer bag filled with cocaine and an expensive leather briefcase containing more money.

Diego estimated there was about $20 thousand. It was additional working capital – 'expenses' that he had negotiated with Frankie Leon, to be applied as needed but with no refund required if it was not used.

He sighed in satisfaction. He felt better. Before, he just had a plan; now he had the hardware to carry it out. Tomorrow was going to be interesting.

Oliver was talking to Carlton Tisch again:

Tisch, gruffly: 'What is it now?'

'Where are you this time, on the tennis court or your boat?'

'None of your business. What do you want?'

'Angus is at the hotel writing his report. I'm bored. There must be something useful I can do here?'

Tisch cleared his throat. 'The most important thing is to work on Demon.'

'The attorney? Isn't he co-operating? I thought that was settled.'

'Nothing is ever settled with an attorney.'

'Not until it's in writing, you mean?'

'Not even then. As soon as things are written down, they start arguing about what the words mean. That's when they really rack up the billable hours.'

'So should I drop in and see him?'

'Yeah. Stroke him nicely.'

'That's a bit vague. He might not agree to see me, of course.'

Tisch laughed. 'He'll see you, I guarantee. I'll call him.'

The sun beat down on the whitewashed front of Demon's building, but the frangipani around the door was fresh and cheerful. Inside, Demon's secretary smiled as if expecting him and waved him through.

Demon stood and pumped his hand enthusiastically

Oliver returned the grip, more cautiously. 'Just looked in to say Hi!'

'Of course, great to see you.'

They sat. Demon lit a cigarette. 'Well, this is a heck of a situation.'

His voice was firm but Oliver thought he saw his hand tremble slightly.

Oliver grinned. 'You could say that.'

'How do things look?'

'Good! Carlton asked me to bring you up to date. The due diligence is going well. Our accountant seems happy.'

'He should be.' Demon showed a hint of asperity. 'That business is the nearest thing to a money machine I've ever seen.'

'Has Angus Mackie been to see you?'

The swarthy lawyer nodded.

'He wanted to see the stock certificates, to verify ownership.'

'The bearer shares?'

'Right. He made photocopies.'

Oliver nodded, then dived in head first.

'How do you feel about the whole thing?'

'About the IPO? Conflicted, frankly.'

'How come?'

'I have a responsibility to Frankie Leon. He is my client.'

'Your client is a crook.'

'He's no worse than many,' said Demon drily.

Oliver sat up. 'Do you mean that?'

'Oh, I'm not saying that my clients routinely break the law. Ninety-nine percent of them have never been sued by Uncle Sam or anyone else. Let's just say that they take rather a lot of business risks.'

'Risks as in illegal?'

Demon held up a hand. 'That's often unclear. Illegal according to which country's law? Should I drop them as clients while their activity on Antigua is perfectly legal? I don't think so. Besides, everyone is entitled to representation.'

His brown eyes twinkled and he smiled at Oliver as if butter wouldn't melt in his thin little mouth.

Oliver said: 'I respect your feelings, I really do. But this is not a normal case.'

'Go ahead, convince me.'

'Let me try and distinguish this. How long have you known Frankie Leon?'

'Six years.'

' I am sure you know that he made his money dealing drugs.'

'Well…', Demon was protesting. Oliver interrupted.

'Don't pretend you didn't know.'

'What has that to do with Casino Caribbean?'

'Nothing, directly. But it disposes of the argument that your client is a moral person.'

Demon's smile maintained itself by an effort of will but the eyes flashed serious dislike. Oliver pressed on.

'Leon is going to go down, and soon. Then where will you be?'

'Providing the legal advice to which my client has a right,' said Demon virtuously.

'Free of charge?'

'Of course not. He can easily afford to pay for my services.'

Oliver nodded. 'We know. We have a list of his bank accounts.'

For the first time, Demon looked shaken. 'Where did you get that?'

'From Judith.'

'She had no right to give you that without his permission.'

Oliver spread his hands. 'We made her an offer she couldn't refuse.'

He could hear the cogs turning in Demon's brain. He smiled gently.

'You're right that it's very difficult to get governments to release funds held in their jurisdiction.'

'Absolutely,' nodded Demon.

'But we can get them frozen.'

Demon frowned. 'But then you couldn't get your hands on them either.'

Oliver shook his head. 'We don't care.'

'What do you mean, you don't care? Hundreds of millions of dollars are involved.'

'But nobody's going to be able to touch them for a long time. Except the banks.'

Demon was silent – he knew this was true. A few years ago he had done some work for associates of the Marcos family, relatives of the late President of the Philippines. When Ferdinand Marcos died, there had been an unseemly scramble for his enormous fortune, said to be worth billions of dollars. The banks were bombarded with conflicting claims by his widow Imelda, and others, so they politely declined to release the money to anyone. They argued that if they did so and were later ruled to have acted in error, they would be held liable; the chances of clawing back any funds they had already disbursed would not be good, so they would be left looking extremely foolish. It was hard to fault their bankerly logic.

'Now,' said Oliver, 'There is only one way you can benefit personally from this sorry mess. Come in with us. We're going to take the company public in London. New management will be hired, figureheads of course, but squeaky clean. It will be the hottest new issue of the year and if you play ball you can be part of it.'

He paused. 'But if you don't, we shall bury you.'

'Is that a threat?'

'Yup.'

After thinking about it for about five seconds, Demon shrugged. 'What do you want from me?'

'The stock certificates.'

'How do you know I haven't given them back to Frankie Leon?'

'Have you?'

'No, but I could.'

'That would be a really dumb move. When you formed the corporation, what did you promise Leon about the shares?'

Demon smiled. 'Nothing.'

'Did you agree to hold them in trust for him?'

'Yes. He even gave me his power of attorney.'

'That's hard to believe.'

'At the time his primary concern was to avoid liability, rather than to claim ownership.'

'Good,' grinned Oliver. 'So let's get to work. We shall need you to assign those shares to a new corporation to be formed by us.'

'How about an exclusive licence to use the technology as well, just to be safe?'

'Now you're talking.'

Demon looked thoughtful. 'I want at least fifty million out of this.'

'Dollars or pounds?'

'Dollars.'

'We'll do you even better. How does fifty million pounds sterling sound? That's about eighty million bucks at today's rate.'

Demon blinked. Then he drew a pad towards him and started to write.

CHAPTER 24

WHAT THE HELL'S GOING ON?

AFTER MANY ATTEMPTS, Leon finally caught up with Judith again by telephone. Since their last conversation, she had been screening her calls, not wanting to talk to him.

'You've been avoiding me.' He sounded suspicious.

'Not true,' she lied. 'I left my phone at home in my other purse.'

'What the hell's going on over there?'

'I've been busy with the auditor.'

'What auditor? I've never had an auditor. Can't stand them.'

Judith had to explain about the planned new issue. It was the first Leon had heard of it. He listened appalled as she described how Oliver and Tisch planned to steal his business – his creation that he had legally – *legally*, goddamn it – built from nothing.

He saw immediately that their plan absolutely depended on getting control of the bearer shares. Years ago, he had deliberately allowed Demon to set the shares up that way, thinking that he might need to take flight some day and that it would be handy to have title to the business in portable form. But he had never anticipated this scenario, even in his worst dreams. A chill started in the pit of his stomach.

Demon was the key. Leon had no illusions. The little lawyer would cheerfully knife his grandmother – maybe not for a dollar but assuredly for a few million. At first, that quality had endeared the attorney to Leon but now it threatened to be a fatal liability.

Simple greed was Demon's core principle – it would tempt him away and there was very little Leon could do about it.

His frustration was supreme. There was no easy answer because he was at the mercy of people he could not control. The chill in his stomach was working its way up his spine.

Born of desperation, a different plan started to germinate in his mind. He thought of the Al Pacino character in the remake of the movie, *Scarface*, one of his favourites. The little drug dealer played by Pacino had progressed from being ruthless to just plumb crazy, finally perishing in a hail of bullets. Now Leon was starting to relate to Pacino's characterization; it was the nuclear option, the Doomsday scenario. He just wanted to inflict the maximum pain on his tormentors and damn the consequences. But he must do it in a planned way.

'Listen, I need to know what these people are up to hour by hour, so keep me informed, okay?'

'You mean Oliver Steele?'

'Steele, Feaver, all of them. You can do that, can't you?'

'I guess so.'

'You'd better,' he said grimly.

'Where are you now?' she asked.

'You don't need to know.'

'Are you all right for money?'

She sounded concerned for him but actually she was probing. She was not going to tell him that she had given away the information on his bank accounts – the ones she knew about – but she was intensely curious whether there were any others.

He did not bite. The account in Belize was something private – it was not on the list Judith had given Mackie.

'I'll get by.'

He rang off.

Alone in his rented villa, Diego Cato tipped a fat line of cocaine onto the glass coffee table, chopped it methodically with a clean razor blade and inhaled it through a rolled Eastern Caribbean dollar bill, the official currency of Antigua. It felt really good.

On the big flat screen television, a golf tournament was in progress. Enhanced by cocaine, the brilliant images imprinted themselves even brighter on his brain.

He leaned back luxuriantly on the leather sofa. Life was good all round. He had just finished a late breakfast. Consuela and Lourdes were sunbathing topless out by the pool and he considered calling them indoors to come and amuse him.

With an effort, he remembered he was here for a purpose. He must make plans.

Planning was Diego's responsibility. He was more of a thinker than his brother, who mostly just provided muscle. The pair looked identical – both brothers had the same cold-fish expression and wiry bodies – but Navidad had faster reflexes and was a better marksman.

Diego was saved from thinking too hard when the telephone rang. It was Frankie Leon.

'You were supposed to call last night,' snapped Leon.

Diego cursed silently. It was true, he had promised. But between the coke and the women, things had kind of gotten away from him.

He improvised effortlessly.

'We drove out to the plantation, scoped it out. I wanted to get a line on their routine. Nobody came in or out, though.'

Frankie grunted. He could tell Diego was lying, never kid a kidder and he was a master of the art himself.

'I just spoke to my programmer, Judith. The auditor from London has finished his work and is going home but he has scheduled a session with all the people involved at 4pm today. So you need to move fast.'

'They gonna be all together in one room?'

'Yeah, and probably for the last time. You have to seize this chance or it'll be gone.'

Diego was finally alert. 'Don' worry, we take care of everything.'

'How will you do that?'

Diego waved the receiver impatiently and looked up at the ceiling. How could anyone work for this jerk? But the thought of the money he had been paid, with more to come, mollified him.

'Don' microscope me, hokay?'

Frankie assumed Diego meant 'micro-manage.'

'Just be sure you take care of business.'

The white Lincoln drew away from the villa shortly after three o'clock, a nervous Consuela at the wheel. Lourdes was still out by the pool – they did not need her apparently. Consuela had not liked the idea of accompanying the men when she saw them loading firearms into the back of the car. But when Diego beckoned her, she did not dare to ignore a direct order from the cold-eyed Colombian.

She watched uncomfortably as Navidad arranged the weaponry on the leather seat. He put the boxes of ammunition on the carpeted floor for greater stability. Sitting in the front passenger seat, he strapped a machine pistol under his linen jacket. He put a smaller automatic in the glove box.

As a last thought, he swept a few crumbs of cocaine into a sandwich bag and stuffed it in his pocket.

Frankie was talking to Judith. His next phone bill would be astronomical.

'Where are they now?'

'Still at the plantation. But they've changed the place for the meeting. They want Demon to be there but he had a conflict with some other appointment.'

'So?'

'So shortly we shall all drive into town to meet at Demon's place.'

'His office?'

'Yeah. We'll be leaving any minute now. Mackie is copying extra copies of his report.'

Frankie lowered his voice, 'Here's what I need you to do.'

She listened, gazing thoughtfully out of the window while Frankie issued his instructions.

She was still holding the telephone when Oliver walked into her office. She replaced the receiver.

'Hi,' she said brightly.

'Hi, Judith,' said Oliver. He did not trust her an inch, even though she had been cooperating with their investigation. But he had to admit she was high-energy and interesting to have around.

Angus Mackie appeared, stuffing papers into his bulging accountant's briefcase.

'Weel, I think I'm ready.'

Outside, they milled around. Who would ride with whom? Angus had a rented Peugeot. Kon Feaver did not have a car; how he had been getting around was unclear. Like a lot of things about Kon, it was a mystery.

'Kon, you can come with me,' said Oliver. 'Hop in.'

Kon hopped in.

'I'll ride with Angus,' said Judith flirtatiously.

The cars started up.

At the last minute Judith said, 'Oh, wait. If we're not coming back to the office afterwards, I'd better take my own car.'

'I can drive you home,' said Angus. 'And bring you back in the morning,' he added hopefully.

She batted her eyelashes. 'Naughty! Thanks, but it's easier if I drive myself.'

She leaped quickly out of Angus' Peugeot. Oliver and Kon had already driven away. So, before anyone really knew it, the group was travelling in a convoy of three cars – Oliver and Kon in front, Angus in the middle and Judith bringing up the rear.

Once they were driving along the main road, Judith phoned Frankie again.

'We're on the road.'

'Good. Will you be taking the road through Commercetown?'

'Probably.'

In his suite at the Belize Fort Victoria, Frankie calculated how long it would take them to get to Demon's office. He rang off and speed-dialled Diego Cato.

'Where are you?'

'Driving into town.'

'I want you to head for Commercetown. Stop on St. John's Road and wait.'

'Ju the boss.'

Diego consulted the little road map provided by Acme. He nudged Consuela. 'Take the next turning left.'

Frankie knew that Commercetown was a down-at-heel industrial district with few, if any, residents. Oliver's party would only be going that way because it lay on the direct route to Demon's office. Frankie knew that and planned to take full advantage.

From his room in Belize, he was now operating two phones at once, his mobile and the hotel handset. On the mobile he was listening to Judith, while on the hotel phone he was talking to Diego in the white Lincoln.

'Wait up, Diego,' Frankie said, 'I gotta talk to Judith.'

He changed phones.

'Judith, where are you?'

'Approaching the industrial area.'

'Are you at the rear of the convoy?'

'Yes, by a hundred yards.'

'Stay that way,' said Franklin. 'And don't lose touch with them.'

To Cato he said, 'Keep heading for St. John's Road.'

'Then what?'

'The first car to come in sight will have Steele and Feaver in it. The second will have the accountant.'

'Which car ju wan' we hit?'

'Both of them. But don't touch the third car,' he added hurriedly. Judith was valuable. Later on she might be dispensable but not yet.

'Hokay.'

'I don't have a good feeling about this,' said Kon.

'Why not?'

Oliver negotiated a tight left bend. They were travelling between drab warehouses that restricted visibility. As they rounded the curve, they temporarily lost sight of the other cars, Mackie's Peugeot and Judith's Toyota.

Kon ignored him, but reached over and wrenched the wheel to the right. The Ford careened off the main road and bumped up onto the kerb, coming to rest in the alley between two buildings, with the engine stopped in eerie silence.

'What the hell are you doing?' said Oliver angrily.

'You'll see,' said Feaver. 'Stay calm.'

Moments later Mackie's car sped by, followed by Judith in the Corolla.

'Now get back on the road,' snapped Kon. Oliver obeyed and fell into line behind Judith.

'Is that better? We're at the back of the pack instead of the front,' said Oliver sarcastically.

'Much better,' grinned Kon.

'Mind if I ask why?'

'Because we've got Judith confused.'

'Oh.'

In the car ahead they could see Judith talking on her cell phone. She looked back over her shoulder at them. Kon Feaver waved cheerfully to her. She looks nervous, Oliver thought.

It was starting to get dark. Oliver switched on the Ford's headlights.

Judith tried to get Frankie's attention using her mobile phone but could not. She could hear him talking to Diego on the other line.

The white Lincoln driven by Consuela drew to a halt on St. John's Road. Diego had the mobile pressed hard to his ear, the volume came and went.

'What do you see,' asked Frankie.

'Not much,' Diego sounded bored.

Frankie finally heard Judith's voice on the other phone and broke off to speak to her. 'Where the heck are you?'

'Approaching St. John's Road, that's what you wanted, right?'

'Yeah, that's good. Fall back though, let the other cars draw farther ahead.'

She tried to tell him that she was in the middle of the convoy now, not at the rear. But he was back talking to Cato, not listening to her.

'Diego, pull your car across the road so that they have to stop. They'll be there in moments.'

Diego made Consuela move the Lincoln so that it blocked the road in both directions. If any traffic came the other way it would be held up too, but so what?

Hundreds of miles away in Belize, Frankie became aware that Judith was yelling at him.

'Say again?'

'I said, there's a change in the order. The first car pulled over.'

'Why?' he said sharply.

'How should I know? But they're at the back now.'

'Keep them in sight,' he said automatically. Then her meaning dawned on him fully.

'So are you in the middle now?'

'That's what I said. But that's okay, I can watch them both now.'

Frankie never had time to reply. The first two cars roared round the bend in Frontage Road. He heard tyres squeal. It was the lead car driven by Angus Mackie, braking violently to avoid hitting the Lincoln.

The Catos had got out on the far side of the Lincoln and were crouching behind the car's hood, AK47s held loosely in their hands. It took them a second to bring their weapons to bear on Mackie's Peugeot and in that time Mackie saw them. He could not make out what was going on but clearly it was bad. He spun the steering wheel and braked hard. The car skidded and turned completely round, facing back the way it had come, away from the Lincoln.

The Catos unleashed a hail of bullets but they were too late, except for one slug that punctured the Peugeot's rear fender. Nothing else hit the vehicle and Mackie was round the corner and out of harm's way before they knew it.

Judith was less lucky. She arrived just in time to drive straight into the Catos' field of fire. A curtain of hot lead streamed from the brothers' machine guns. Rows of bullet holes stitched linear patterns in the Toyota's side.

Judith's head was almost detached from her body by the gunfire. Inside the car, blood pumped from her wounds drenching the seats and smearing the windows. Driverless, her car skidded broadside across the road. It avoided a direct hit on the Lincoln but grazed its rear wing with a nerve-jarring screech, leaving a long dent in the white metal.

Consuela was still sitting in the Lincoln. She screamed but her cries were lost in the din as Judith's Toyota scraped past the bigger car and smacked into a tubular metal lamp post, which buckled but did not collapse.

But her mobile phone, which had flown from her hand and come to rest on the car's back seat, was still active. Listening in Belize, Frankie could hear, as if he was in the Toyota himself, gunfire followed by assorted thuds and crashes, then silence. He knew something catastrophic had happened. After shouting a couple of times at Judith, he broke the connection in disgust and turned to his other phone.

'What the fuck is happening, Diego?'

'We got the second car.'

Diego was exultant. The first car was long gone but the second lay in a heap on the sidewalk, so much scrap metal. One out of two was not bad. He approached it and tried to peer inside but could not make out much – the windscreen, shattered into a thousand crystals, was still in place and the side windows were so smeared with blood as to be opaque. He assumed anyone inside was either dead or dying.

'Those guys won't cause you no more trouble,' he told Frankie reassuringly.

'Wrong car, asshole,' snarled Frankie.

But he knew as he spoke that Diego did not understand what had gone wrong. It was not the Catos' fault – they had been told to fire on two cars and they had done so; it would only alienate the Colombians if he dumped the blame on them. With an effort, he tried to speak calmly.

'What happened to the first car?'

'He was here before we could get a good shot. You ditn' give us enough warning.' Diego sounded resentful.

Frankie's anger level rose from red to orange. All he had achieved was to kill Judith. Not that he felt any particular grief at her passing – she was an ear inside the enemy camp, nothing more – just pique at the loss of an asset. But he would need a new programmer if he was going to stay in the business, so her death was an inconvenience.

Worse still, the people he wanted the Catos to eliminate were still at large – all of them. And now they would be alert to the danger of fresh attacks. He slammed down the phone in disgust, breaking off his last contact with Antigua. Alone and depressed in his luxury suite in the Hotel Fort Victoria, he went down to the bar and ordered the first of several large scotches.

When Diego realized that Frankie had rung off, he shrugged and holstered his mobile phone. Frankie was a gringo pig. But he paid well, so Diego did not take offence. The man would get over it. The Catos were still his main resource on the island.

Diego took in the empty street – things were eerily silent; the locals were no doubt allergic to the sound of gunfire. He wondered what had happened to the third car. He decided it must have left the area by now.

In fact, Oliver in the third car, had slowed right down when he heard the commotion up ahead. He stopped just south of the corner. Out of sight of the Catos, he never saw the demise of Judith and her car.

He did see Angus Mackie's Peugeot reappear going, he noted, like the proverbial bat out of hell. Mackie's white face, hunched over the steering wheel, looked like Banquo's ghost. When he saw Oliver and Feaver, he skidded to a halt, winding down his window.

Oliver raised his eyebrows. 'What's up, Angus?'

'Ye gods, man, don't go round that corner!'

'Wasn't planning to. It sounded like shooting.'

'It was.'

'Where's Judith?'

'I think they killed her.'

'Who is they?'

'God knows. Men with machine guns.'

A thoughtful silence.

Finally Kon Feaver spoke.

'Oliver, why don't you and Angus go on to the meeting? But don't take the main highway. If you backtrack a couple of miles and turn right you can take the inland road, it's almost as quick.'

'We shouldn't just leave Judith.'

'I know, but this is a mess. Leave it to me, messes are what I do. We don't want this episode sullying your clean character, if you people are going to be involved in a major IPO.'

'To heck with the IPO.'

Feaver smiled and shrugged as if to say, 'it's not up to me.'

Oliver caught a glimpse behind the Israeli's good-natured mask. There was a different dynamic at work, something cold and calculating. He remembered that Feaver worked for Tisch and that Tisch's motivation was money; nothing else must get in the way of that.

Then he remembered that he, too, worked for Carlton Tisch. Not joined at the hip like Feaver, of course.

And yet…

'Look,' said Feaver gently, 'I'll take care of things. The girl was not on our side. And she is already dead. Go on into town.'

Suddenly weary, Oliver did as he was asked. The last he saw of Feaver, the Israeli had locked the Peugeot and vanished into the shadows on foot.

Alone in the darkness, Feaver slipped behind the warehouses so that he could cut off the corner and emerge unseen behind the wreck of Judith's bullet-riddled Toyota. He crouched behind the little car and observed the scene.

The Cato twins were getting ready to leave. They were sitting in the Lincoln with the doors open, taking their time, chatting in Spanish, guns loose at their sides. Feaver carefully memorized the car's number on the car's licence plate. He thought about killing both men – they were within range, unsuspecting, and the window of opportunity was closing. In twenty seconds, the chance would be gone.

He wanted to shoot them. He was a hunter and they were game, dangerous and challenging. Instead he took aim at the rear tyres of the Lincoln and, with two quick shots, punctured both of them.

The rear end of the Lincoln collapsed with a sigh until it was resting on the rims of its back wheels, dignified but crippled.

The Catos reaction was electric. They scattered, machine guns at the ready and peered into the darkness, unsure where the shots had come from.

But Feaver was already gone, fifty yards away, padding quietly with his powerful bow-legged run, arms pumping like an athlete. He could cover long distances like this, jogging all day if necessary. The three miles to Demon's office would be just a light workout.

After half a mile, safely out of earshot, he stopped and took out his mobile phone. He called the operator and was connected to the main St. Johns police station.

'St Johns Police, can I help you?'

The young woman's island lilt was one of the more attractive police voices he had dealt with and he had dealt with a few. He had once spent a week in a Cairo jail. That was the worst. It had been a phoney embezzlement charge – all Carlton Tisch's fault for trying to be too clever. Kon had exacted a healthy bonus from his boss after that episode. All water under the bridge now.

'I want to report an incident. A car crash out on St. John's Road, a couple of miles west of Cable Street, a Peugeot and a Lincoln.'

'On St. John's Road, eh?' She sounded amused, maybe it was his Israeli gutturals.

'Yes, ma'am, two shooters, armed with machine weapons. A woman is dead.'

Her tone changed. 'Who is this speaking?'

'That's not important. But you really need to send someone. The cross street is Arbor Close.'

'What I need is to know who you are?'

He told her the licence number of the Lincoln. Then he broke the connection. She would not ignore the call; someone would be sent out. They would find Judith's body and the cars, the bloody Toyota and perhaps the crippled Lincoln sitting on its rims. They would trace the Lincoln to the rental agency and from there, wherever the paper trail led.

The shooters were clearly professionals and, Feaver surmised, shared some history with Frankie Leon. For the sake of the police at the scene, he hoped they heeded his warning about the guns.

He started running again.

CHAPTER 25

THE INSPECTOR GETS A CALL

WHEN FEAVER'S PHONE CALL CAME IN, Inspector Tom Truro was just leaving for the day. The telephonist waved him down on his way out of the building. She admired as usual the agent's well-cut jacket and the rolled collar of his New and Lingwood shirt.

Damn, he thought – he had been on his way to meet a girlfriend for a daiquiri at the Pink Lobster, followed by dinner and whatever might ensue.

He beckoned a colleague.

'Rory, drive with me. Some kind of altercation out at St. John's and Arbor.'

He used the car radio to summon more help and in minutes half the police force of St. Johns arrived at the scene, armed and wary.

In Belize, Frankie was beside himself with anxiety. Things had obviously gone very wrong. He had tried to call Diego back every twenty seconds but after five minutes of engaged tones he gave up. In the hotel bar he switched from Scotch to rum. One drink led to another and by the time he staggered back to his suite to try calling again, he had put away most of a bottle. His mood was somewhat maudlin.

Diego answered on the first ring.

'Yeah?'

'You screwed up,' said Frankie furiously.

Diego was whiny. 'It was hard, man. They shot up the Lincoln. There was a whole bunch of those mothafuckers you dit'n tell us about.'

'How many?'

'Six, at least.'

Frankie doubted that but he just grunted. 'Where are you now?'

'At the villa.' Diego did not mention that he, too, had been drinking. The villa's liquor cabinet, initially well stocked, was now empty.

'Were you followed?'

'No.'

'You will be.' Frankie knew how Feaver's mind worked.

'So what we do now? We in trouble here.'

'I've got your back, don't worry.'

He was thinking, 'What a mess. The Catos are dead meat. I can save myself but they'll have to go.'

'The Israeli will come after you,' he said thoughtfully

Diego said: 'We not scared of that mothafucker.'

'Of course you're not. In fact it's good that he's following you, it means we can find him. But you need to get out of there.'

'Don' got no car.'

The trauma suffered by the Lincoln from being driven back to the villa on its rims had been terminal. From drive train to half shafts, the whole rear end was a mass of fused metal. The car had just got them home but it would probably never move under its own power again.

'There's a launch in the villa boathouse.'

'So where we go?'

'I have a place on Guadeloupe. You can get there in three hours. I'll meet you there in a day or two.' That would give him time to plan their disposal, he thought.

'What about the girls?' asked Diego.

'Leave them behind. They've served their purpose.'

When Kon Feaver reached Demon's office the meeting was still in progress. The group was seated round the big table in Demon's office. Mackie was standing at the chalkboard.

Demon handed Feaver a summary the accountant had prepared and waved him to a seat. He listened to the Scot's closing remarks.

'In short, gentlemen, the results for the last few years have been spectacular.'

'What about the future?' asked Demon.

'I'm a bean counter not a prophet, so I can't give you a guarantee. But based on the number of gamblers who are registered with the site and the company's experience of what a typical player spends over time, things look very good.'

Kathy asked, 'If it is so easy to make money at this, why aren't more casino operators piling into the business?'

'Count on it, they will,' said Oliver. 'Although nothing lasts forever. Sooner or later the rate of growth will level off, it always does. But Casino Caribbean has two strengths: first, they pioneered the market so they have a lead of about a year over the competition. Also, they are well run; they do what they do very effectively.'

'So the good times should continue?'

'For a while.'

Despite this positive assessment, there did not seem to be much optimism among Mackie's audience. Their thoughts were elsewhere.

Demon, who appeared to be leading the meeting, looked at Feaver.

'So what's going on out there in the real world?'

Feaver shrugged. 'I called the police. They're on their way to the scene.'

'You think they can handle the situation?'

'In what sense?'

'Well, those gunmen might outmatch a small island police force.'

Kon laughed. 'Are you kidding? Do you know how much drug crime there is around here? It will be no problem, it's what they do.'

There was silence, broken by Oliver.

'Judith was smart, say what you like. I enjoyed working with her.'

Muttered agreement round the table.

'Me, too,' said Feaver. 'But we have to focus on essentials now.'

Everyone knew what he meant.

Angus Mackie was conscious of his particular status, alone of those present, as an advisor and not a principal. He started putting his papers away.

'Well, as I said, everything about the Casino's finances looks good, in fact it looks great. Is there anything else you need from me?'

Oliver looked round the table. Nobody spoke.

'In that case,' said Mackie, with ill-disguised relief, 'I'll be on my way.'

'Back to London?' Kathy asked.

Mackie nodded. 'Fewer murders there.'

'Nice job, Angus. Thank you,' said Oliver.

'You're welcome,' the Scot nodded dryly. 'It's been an interesting trip.'

They all left the room in sober mood.

For Oliver the thrill of high finance was fading fast. He was much more concerned with the fact that Frankie's gunmen were still at large.

He and Kathy stopped by the police station and asked to see Captain Tom Truro. The slim Antiguan came out to meet them. He did not look pleased.

'What do you two know about this mess?'

'We've only heard rumours,' said Oliver.

'Did you see the shooting?'

'What shooting?'

'Come on,' Truro snapped. 'Two shot-up cars and a dead woman?'

'I might know someone who did see it,' said Kathy casually.

Truro whirled to face her.

'Who?'

'Fellow called Kon Feaver.' She tossed the little Israeli to the wolves without a qualm.

'Where can we find him?'

'Don't know. He moves around.'

'And what is Mr. Feaver to you?'

'He is a business associate.'

'Does he have an accent?' Truro was thinking about the phone call.

She nodded. 'From somewhere east of the Mediterranean.'

The policeman processed that. 'What about you? Why exactly are you here?'

'It's simple. We need protection. If you can catch those killers, you'll help save our skins and clean up your island at the same time.'

Truro looked as if he wanted to arrest both of them.

'Look,' said Oliver, 'You have an unusual opportunity here to solve a messy problem. Frankie Leon's whole operation is as sleazy as hell. There may be some reputable gaming companies around but this is not one of them. I know Antigua encourages gambling and it's a great source of revenue but you would be better off without them.'

Truro shrugged. 'Maybe.'

Oliver nodded. 'We, on the other hand, are planning a house-cleaning – new owners and new management. Your government will be much happier with us, believe me.'

The Antiguan shrugged again. 'Maybe.'

Oliver asked: 'Have you found the Lincoln yet?'

'Not yet.'

'Did you go out there?'

'Yes, but all we found was a dead woman in a wrecked Toyota. No Lincoln.'

'Did you check the Lincoln's registration?'

'Of course. We're looking for it, believe me,' said Truro. 'It was rented and we're trying to locate the manager of the rental office. He's probably in a bar somewhere. Once we find out where the renters are staying, we'll be all over them. Leave it to us.'

'Thank you so much.' Kathy gave him her best smile.

He ushered them out. 'And don't take the law into your own hands.'

'Absolutely not,' said Kathy.

They left, not greatly reassured.

Kon Feaver called Carlton Tisch on his global mobile. 'The auditor did his work; he is on his way back to London.'

'Is he happy?'

'About the numbers, sure. But did you hear about our other little incident?'

'No.'

'The woman Judith got herself shot.'

'By whom?'

'Frankie's trigger men. It was a mistake.'

'How is she?'

'Dead.'

'That's not good.'

'No kidding. Will it affect the IPO?'

'Depends. We'll sure as heck have to down-play it.'

'Really.'

They talked a while longer. Finally Tisch said, 'Look, try and keep the lid on. No more violence.'

'I'll try,' said Feaver. 'It may not be easy. The gunmen are still around.'

'And planning an encore? I hear you. Is there any way you can neutralize them?'

'Got to find them first,' said Feaver tersely.

'Understood. Give it a shot anyway. I have great confidence in you.'

'Yeah, right.'

Carlton rang off. He was in the car park down at the marina. He left the phone in his jeep and walked back to the slip.

After the long journey home from England – fourteen hours via Miami and San Juan – he was relaxing in his favourite way, messing about in boats. Grey stubble matched the hair on his skinny brown chest – he had not shaved since London and the Berkeley.

He could easily have afforded to buy a plane of his own but he did not like the idea. He hated flying, on a footing with a visit to the dentist. The runway at Tortola Airport was rather short anyway, which Tortolans liked; it kept holiday makers from flooding the island.

But also, Tisch hated making a show and, if you owned a jet, that was unavoidable. Publicity made him nervous. Like the Stressmans in London, he was very security conscious. He had installed a silent alarm perimeter around the Tortola house along with many burglar alarms but the best security, he firmly believed, was a low profile. If you had a jet, the word soon got round. When travelling alone he actually flew business class, never in first class, and sometimes even wore a pinstripe suit and carried a laptop computer, both items that he despised, as a form of protective colouring.

Today he was pretending to scrape barnacles off his yacht, Goneril, which had been hauled out of the water. Her smooth hull didn't really need it – people at the marina cleaned the hull regularly and did a good job. But by getting his fingernails dirty he eased his guilty conscience as a fully paid-up member of the leisured classes.

He thought about what he had just heard. He had better plan ahead.

He went back to the jeep, dug out his phone and called a number in Gibraltar.

Louis Razzo, manager of the Acme office in St John, was having dinner at Alfredos with Beverly, one of his reservation agents. He had been trying for some months to talk her into bed and things were starting to look hopeful. They had just polished off a couple of prime local lobsters washed down with an expensive hock. After dancing around the subject a bit, he was about to proposition her in earnest when he sensed someone standing behind his chair. It was Captain Tom Truro.

Louis sighed. 'What can I do for you, Tom?'

Truro grinned. 'Sorry Lou, I need some help.'

'Yes?'

'You rented a Lincoln to someone. We want to know who.'

'I'll get on it first thing in the morning.'

'Tonight, Lou.'

Louis controlled his irritation. They were members of the same golf club, after all.

'We have several Lincolns.'

'White?'

'Okay, we have one.'

'Who rented it?'

'It's not banged up, I hope?'

'It's going to need some serious work.'

'Damn!'

'Hey, lighten up. The insurance will pay.'

'That's not the point. They raise our rates every year. At this rate we'll be lucky to get any coverage at all. What happened?'

'That's what we're trying to find out.'

Lou returned to the office reluctantly. Opening his files under Truro's watchful eye, he pulled out the contract.

'Here you go. It was rented by Diego and Lourdes Cato, husband and wife – he rolled his eyes – they're at the Henderson villa out by Foye's Point.'

Truro nodded. 'I know it.'

He was already out of the door.

Back in London the next day, Angus Mackie took a mid-morning break from polishing his report and telephoned Nicco Stressman. The young banker was sipping coffee with two senior colleagues in the partners' room at Wheatsheaf Court.

'Welcome back, Angus. Good trip?'

'Och, like the parson's egg, good in parts.'

'Let's hear the good.' Stressman flicked the speaker switch so that his partners could listen.

'Great quality of earnings, few question areas. Profit growth likely to be sustained, so far as one can predict these things.'

Stressman's partners, who were also his uncles, nodded approvingly. They had discussed Casino Caribbean at length when Nicco had brought it to them and had liked the idea. Senior partner Bruno Stressman had joked a mite sourly that it was nice when earnings were driven equally by addiction and greed. What sounder basis for success could there be?

Stressman nodded. 'So what's not to like?'

Angus explained about Judith and the shootings.

'Did you say AK47s?' asked Uncle Philippe, the Capital Markets partner.

'That's what they were, according to Kon Feaver.'

'And who is this person, Feaver?'

'A chum of Carlton Tisch. He's a sort of fixer.'

Uncle Bruno, who also oversaw the bank's compliance division, looked doubtful.

Nicco Stressman lit a cigarette, trying not to smile.

After Angus had finished, there was silence in the partners' room. It was broken by Nicco.

'Well, Angus, you've been a great help as always.'

'Thank you. I'll send out my report in a few days. I'll see you all get copies.'

'Please do,' said Uncle Philippe.

After Mackie rang off the three bankers looked at each other.

'So the casino will be looking for a new head programmer,' said Nicco.

'Oh, you can always find programmers,' said Uncle Bruno.

'If you pay them enough,' said Uncle Philippe.

'But that's not really the point, is it?' said Uncle Bruno.

'I suppose not.'

The conversation turned to other matters but an air of unresolved tension lingered in the partners' room.

When Inspector Truro and Louis Razzo left the restaurant and went back to the Acme office, Kon and Oliver followed them, keeping a discreet distance.

Leaving Kon in the car, Oliver crept forward until, from behind a bush, he could see through the window of the small office. He also heard everything, including the address of the villa. When Truro emerged and drove away, Oliver hurried back to the car and they followed him.

It became clear that the police chief was heading back into town.

'He's probably assembling a posse,' said Kon. 'Then he'll head for the villa.'

Oliver shrugged. 'Want to nip out there ahead of them, see what's cooking?'

'Why not?'

In minutes they reached the whitewashed residence on the eastern shore. Outside, lit by a sliver of new moon was the Lincoln, sitting on its rims, dusty and bedraggled. The front of the house was dark but there were lights at the back, shining onto the rear terrace. Someone was home.

They could see shadowy movement down at the boathouse. As they watched, a small launch emerged. It shot away from the dock trailing a cloud of phosphorescence and in moments was just a black speck on the limitless ocean.

CHAPTER 26

ICI ON PARLE FRANÇAIS

'T HAT CRAFT is not what I would call a long-distance boat,' said Feaver.

'Just what I was thinking,' said Oliver. 'I think I know where it is going.'

'Where?'

'Guadeloupe. Frankie has a place there, a getaway for his private use. Guadeloupe is eighty miles away and that boat has a range of a hundred miles at the most.'

'Makes sense to me,' said Feaver. 'Let's head over that way.'

Kathy looked doubtful. 'How do we get there?'

'In my plane. It's at the plantation, only five miles from here.'

'One small thing,' said Oliver.

'Well?'

'Frankie is paranoid and his hideaway will be fortified. We may be walking into a trap.'

Feaver grinned. 'Traps can be a challenge.'

'Don't you think we should inform the police, let them handle things,' asked Oliver doubtfully.

Silence from Feaver. The crickets chirped incessantly.

'Did you hear what I said?'

'Oh, I heard.'

'Well, should we wait for the police? They'll be here soon.'

Feaver grinned. 'There's a problem with that. This is Antigua.

The Cato twins are on the way to Guadeloupe. Different countries. Different police.'

'So?'

'So if this gets into "official" channels there will be big delays.'

'Shouldn't things move along fairly quickly?' asked Kathy. 'These are not big countries we're talking about, with thousands of diplomats, just small police departments who are probably used to speaking to each other.'

Feaver laughed. 'Wrong. Guadeloupe is a French speaking island.'

Kathy looked puzzled: 'I thought English was spoken everywhere in the Caribbean.'

'By no means,' said Feaver. 'Guadeloupe is a DOM, a "Département d'Outre-mer" or "Overseas Department" of France. Politically and linguistically it is part of France.'

'But still small,' argued Kathy.

'Not by island standards. It has a population of 450,000.'

Oliver said: 'Presumably its laws are based on the Code Napoléon, the system Napoleon introduced when he conquered territories. That's a lot different than the Anglo Saxon setup.'

'Correct, 'said Feaver. 'From Frankie's point of view, conveniently, it may also make it harder for Uncle Sam to go snooping.'

'Frankie's place is on Basse Terre.'

'That's one of the two main islands. It has an active volcano called Soufrière and some black beaches.'

Kathy looked puzzled. 'The beaches are dirty?'

'No, it's volcanic sand.'

'They have nude beaches too,' Feaver grinned.

'Well, I guess it's up to us,' said Oliver. 'We'd better go there.'

Feaver slapped him on the back. 'Attaboy!'

So they jumped in the car and made for the plantation.

Half-an-hour later, Tom Truro and several colleagues charged into the Catos' villa, weapons at the ready. But they found no gunmen, just two bored *Latina* girls, watching an Oprah rerun. Consuela was heating a Wolfgang Puck pizza in the microwave. They were drinking beer out of cans and might have had a couple too many.

'Hi, girls,' said Truro.

'Hi, sailor,' said Consuela.

'We're looking for some bad guys.'

'There's just us girls here.' She rolled her eyes.

He sighed. 'You know who I mean.'

'You wan' Diego and Navidad?'

'Probably.'

'They left.'

'Left?'

'On a boat.'

'Dit'n take us,' Lourdes said spitefully.

'Where were they headed?'

'Dit'n say.'

Truro sighed. He had no idea where the gunmen were headed – he suspected the girls were telling the truth and didn't know either. It looked like being a frustrating night.

'Ju find them, ju let us know,' said Consuela.

'You bet, said Truro, without enthusiasm.

'Yeah,' said Lourdes, mildly panicky. 'We jus' have our tickets back to Miami and whatever's in the freezer.'

Truro looked round the room, then at his colleagues. 'Guess we're done here.'

With Oliver and Kathy on board, Kon Feaver piloted his plane up from the moonlit sea The night sky was so clear that they could look down from 3,000 feet and see every wave.

Twenty minutes later a thin rim of land appeared, edging the black ocean. They were approaching the coast of Guadeloupe.

Kon turned to Oliver. 'Where now?'

In the dark cabin Oliver peered at the chart, helped by a small directional spotlight.

'There's Basse Terre, the main island. Guadeloupe is butterfly-shaped with Basse Terre being the larger wing.'

'Where is Frankie's place?'

'Near Deshaies, a small town on the west coast. It is three miles north of there. We should touch down close to Deshaies, then cruise up the coast just offshore – it's dark enough not to be noticed. When we get close, we'll moor the plane and approach the house on foot.'

'Got it.' Feaver pushed the plane's nose down and the brief shock as its floats hit the water moments later was almost imperceptible.

They cruised north, staying half-a-mile away out from land. The lights of Deshaies twinkled in the distance but the calm water in between was deserted.

Finally they approached a small private beach and Oliver motioned to Kon to slow down. A substantial two-storey house looked out to sea.

'This is as far as we can ride. Now we'll wade ashore and walk along the beach. We have the advantage of surprise – let's keep it.'

Their approach to the house was uneventful – suspiciously so, Oliver thought, suppressing an uneasy feeling. He was surprised that no one was standing guard.

The lawn running down to the beach was well landscaped with tropical shrubs, so they were able to creep towards the house, using the bushes as cover. To one side of the house was a modern garage, its door ajar. They slipped inside.

Moonlight filtered in. They could see a shiny red all-terrain vehicle with fat balloon tires and, beside it, an open mini-moke in camouflage green and brown. They were recreational vehicles, apparently for joyriding on the beach, although Oliver found it hard to imagine Frankie behaving so frivolously.

'What do you think?' he muttered.

'They're not expecting us,' Kon whispered. 'Let's hit it!'

Leaving the shelter of the garage, they crept towards the front door. There were no lights and apparently nobody home. On the count of three they burst through the door, Feaver ahead of Oliver.

It was immediately clear that they were expected.

Light flooded the hallway as Diego Cato, hiding behind the

door, hit the switch. Oliver felt a gust of still-warm air – the gunmen had not been in residence long enough for the air conditioning to cool the place down.

Navidad Cato crouched in front of them, shirtless, machine gun levelled.

But Kon Feaver fired first with lightning speed. Flames burst from his automatic. Bullets etched a dotted line across Navidad's chest. As the Colombian staggered and fell, blood spurted onto the polished wood floor. Some drops spattered Oliver's shirt.

Diego Cato could only watch his wounded brother stagger and collapse. Given more time to think, he would surely have shot Kon Feaver dead but instead he used his weapon as a club, dealing a smashing blow to the Israeli's temple. Feaver collapsed.

Diego, his face a mask of dismay, watched Navidad's's blood cease to pump. Realizing that his brother was beyond hope, he barged past Oliver and ran from the house.

Oliver knelt over Feaver. The Israeli groaned and moved his head from side to side. His eyes opened and focused groggily on Oliver.

'I'm fine' he said.

'I don't think so.'

'So I'll have a headache. Go get that jerk, don't lose him.'

'We need to find you a doctor.'

Feaver clenched his teeth. 'Don't hang around, go!'

They heard the roar of a motor starting.

Oliver ran outside. The garage door was ajar. It burst open before his eyes.

With a roar the ATV emerged, a shadowy figure atop it, bulbous tires spinning in the dirt.

Oliver clambered into the mini-moke, pushed the starter and gave chase but he was a hundred yards behind. Fortunately the ATV had a loud exhaust, inadequately silenced. He followed the speeding vehicle up a single-track path. Both vehicles bumped and lurched on the winding track, sailing over potholes, sometimes airborne for yards at a time.

The path led higher and higher, narrowing as it progressed. Oliver had no idea where Diego was heading. So far as he could tell it was just mindless flight.

They passed through a copse and emerged, still climbing, on the other side. Scrub and undergrowth gave way to bare rock. Then suddenly he was facing a large crater, a hundred yards across. The smell of sulphur filled the air. Pungent eddies caught at his throat and made his eyes sting. With a shock he realized he was on the edge of Soufrière, the slumbering volcano.

He skidded to a halt on the rim and looked round. He killed his engine and listened but in vain. He got off the moke and peered around in the gloom. The gunman was nowhere to be seen.

Hearing a slight noise behind him, he spun on his heel, just in time to sway backwards as Diego, on foot, ran at him. Oliver quickly side-stepped.

Before he knew what was happening, the Colombian lurched past him, over the crater's edge. As he tumbled into the void, he let out a desperate scream and Oliver glimpsed his face, white with fear. He arched into the crater and fell, bouncing off the jagged walls. Then there was silence.

Oliver drove slowly back to the house. Feaver was in the bathroom, rinsing a towel in cold water and pressing it to his head. But on hearing that the second Colombian was dead, the Israeli pumped his fist.

He made Oliver take him up to the crater again; they stood at the edge and gazed down on the steaming centre.

Far below, they could see the body of the gunman sprawled at the bottom of the crater, sulphurous wisps playing around it, bathed by the moonlight in a white haze.

Oliver gestured down at the crater. 'What shall we do about that?'

'Why do anything?'

'We can't leave him there.'

'Why not?'

'So do we just quit the island?'

'Sure. The sooner the better. Right now, nobody knows we were ever here. Let's keep it that way.'

He tugged Oliver's arm. 'Let's go.'

'Go where?'

'Away from Metropolitan France, for sure. I don't fancy explaining all this to a bunch of gendarmes.'

'Should we go back to Antigua?'

'Then we'd have Captain Truro to deal with.'

Oliver spread his hands. 'I guess Tortola gets the nod.'

Kathy was waiting in the plane when the men came back across the beach and climbed in without speaking.

'So are you going to tell me what happened?' she asked after a minute.

Feaver switched on the cabin light to read his map and she saw the bruise on his temple. She also noticed blood on Oliver's shirt.

'They're dead, aren't they?'

Oliver nodded.

She was somehow shocked. For Feaver to kill was somehow not unexpected, he came from a milieu she knew nothing about, where violence was apparently common. But it changed her outlook towards Oliver. Oliver was supposed to be – she struggled to find the term – normal. Normal people did not kill other people. Even without a blow-by-blow account of events, it was apparent that Oliver had crossed a certain line and that was upsetting.

On the flight back, alone with her thoughts. she felt oddly sad. She was fond of Oliver. Unfortunately, in the last week she had lied to him, annoyed him and generally tested his patience, reducing the chance of any kind of friendly relationship to nil and that was too bad because he was cute – intelligent, good looking, pompous in a British kind of way but she could fix that. She sighed. She was sorry about the way she had behaved but she had only done what was necessary to resolve the situation with her father.

They finally got to Carlton's house at 2am. Mimi appeared in cotton baby-doll pyjamas and silently waved Kathy to one spare room, Kon and Oliver to the other.

Next morning, after a good night's sleep, Carlton Tisch called them out to the terrace for coffee and croissants.

He grinned without humour. 'Do you want the good news or the bad news?'

Oliver rolled his eyes. 'Bad first.'

'Quentin Teague called me from London. Sorry to have to tell you guys, but the IPO is off.'

'What,' asked Feaver, in dismay. 'We kept the lid on any scandal at our end.'

'I know,' said Tisch kindly. 'You did a great job. But unfortunately stuff happens. Yesterday the CEO of an on-line casino based in Aruba was arrested at Los Angeles Airport. He had just arrived from London and was waiting at the airport for a flight to Hawaii.'

Oliver groaned. 'I can guess what's coming.'

'Yeah. He was charged with operating an unlicensed casino that does business in the States.'

'And the stock market took a nosedive?'

'Exactly. Billions of dollars were wiped off the market value of on-line casinos.'

'But what if he beats the rap? You said the law was unclear.'

'It is, but that's not the point. Even if the final decision does favour the casinos, the case will be tied up in the courts for years. Any good news will arrive too late to help us.

Meanwhile, casino stocks are depressed. That makes our IPO a huge gamble and Stressman's partners want no part of it. Most smart bankers would feel the same way.'

'What about the schmuck who got arrested?' asked Kon. There was a note of sympathy in his voice. He had been in a couple of jails and knew how it felt.

'What about him?'

'Will he just rot in prison?'

Tisch shrugged. 'Probably. He may not get bail, he is an obvious flight risk. Especially with Frankie doing a runner so recently.'

'Did you say there was some good news?' asked Oliver.

'Well, Kathy's father is off the hook.'

'Oh, about his gambling debt?'

'Yeah.'

'What will happen about that?'

'Probably nothing.'

'You mean, he can just forget about it?'

Tisch nodded. 'Frankie is in no position to pursue the matter. He's a pariah. Nobody in the US is going to help him collect. If he tries to intimidate the old guy, we'll intimidate him right back. He's a bully, he understands that language. Besides, it's pocket change for him, always was, he was just too mean to realize it.'

'I suppose so, 'said Oliver doubtfully. He had a feeling they might not have heard the last of Frankie.

Carlton had arranged for a senior manager from one of his other companies to take charge of the Casino but it would be a few days before he could start so, afterwards, Kon and Oliver flew back to Antigua to keep an eye on things.

Kathy stayed on Tortola and pondered the immediate future. Now that her father was out of danger, she was at a loose end. There was no urgent reason to return to Florida. She could play tennis with Mimi and maybe go to the beach. Or she might learn to Scuba dive, something she had always wanted to try. She got the name of a diving school in Road Town and signed up for a course of lessons leading to a Scuba certification. She spent the next few days in and out of a pool learning to breathe compressed air from a metal cylinder and hover in the water in a wetsuit with a weight belt round her waist. She learned the rules of 'buddy' diving, whereby divers work in pairs, each checking the other's equipment and always looking out for the other when underwater. On the fourth morning, she did an open water dive and received her 'C Card,' the international certification that entitled her to be recognised around the world as a qualified diver.

Elated, she booked place on a dive boat going out to Cooper Island, a popular diving area the same afternoon. The boat was full to capacity, a dozen divers milling around with their cylinders, flippers and assorted gear. She was disconcerted to suddenly spot the tanned figure of Oliver on the same boat, looking very much the experienced diver in old T-shirt and baggy trunks and sporting a digital dive watch and a knife the size of a bayonet in a holster strapped to his calf. He made his way over.

'You're back!' she said, surprised.

'I came back to thank you for everything you did,' he said grinning.

'That's okay,' she said and paused, feeling awkward. 'I didn't know you were a diver.'

'Nor I you.'

'I'm new at it.'

'You look every inch the pro.' Impulsively, he put his arms round her and gave her a big hug.

'I've been wanting to do that. I could never have managed without your help.'

'You're welcome.'

They reached the reef and the dive master started to marshal them into some kind of order. Oliver turned to her. 'Would you care to be my buddy?'

She half curtsied. 'I thought you'd never ask.'

After Frankie Leon had told the Cato twins to go to Guadeloupe he heard nothing more from them. Initially he was unconcerned but after a few days he began to fear the worst. He called Neville at the plantation and learned that Steele and Feaver were there most days but were telling Neville very little. Neville was curt with Frankie. He was clearly shaken by Judith's death and seemed to hold Frankie responsible. Frankie sensed that he knew Frankie's influence had declined to nil and had finally abandoned him.

He called the agency in Deshaies that managed his Guadeloupe villa and asked them to send a cleaner round to check on things. Half an hour later his phone rang. The cleaner had found the festering corpse of Navidad Cato, riddled with bullets. The manager, Yves, had called the police immediately. Covering his backside, thought Frankie. Yves, too, seemed angry at Frankie. The police were asking questions, none of which Yves could answer. Apparently they had not discovered the body of Diego in the crater but they soon would. That would give them fits, Frankie thought grimly, identical dead bodies. And Yves knew Frankie's identity, which was unfortunate. Soon the Guadeloupe police would talk to the Antigua police and then everyone would be out looking for him.

It was time to leave. He was angry, resentful and bitter, but he did not lose his head. It was tough about the casino and tough about the frozen bank accounts but he had enough money in Belize to keep him going for a few years, thank God; enough to plan a comeback and to get even, but not now. For now, his priority must be to do a good job of disappearing.

He packed his modest bag, went downstairs and checked out. He walked into town and bought a new prepaid disposable phone, ditching his old one in a trashcan; he would replace his phone weekly from now on. Then he hailed a taxi to the airport and for all practical purposes, vanished off the face of the earth.

EPILOGUE

A WEEK LATER Oliver was in his apartment in Road Town, googling the sports news when the phone rang. It was Tisch.

'Can you come up to the house?'

'Why?'

'We need to talk.'

Maybe he's got some work for me, Oliver thought. He'd made no money on the Casino deal. It was an interesting experience, but that was all.

Tisch was on his terrace as usual, a weather-beaten gnome puffing on a big cigar. His Yankees baseball cap was crusted with salt and grime.

He produced a cheque book. 'We have some unfinished business. Got a pen?'

'Money? That's nice. After the IPO wipe-out, I assumed I was out of luck.'

Tisch wrote the check and signed it with a flourish.

Oliver read it and choked. 'Are you nuts?'

'Is there a problem?'

Oliver waved the cheque. 'This is for half a million dollars.'

'It's not enough?'

'Come on! The job took barely a week from start to finish. Why so much?'

'You earned it. Think of it as a down payment on the next job if you like. I may need you to go to Europe in a few weeks time.

'Well, thanks.'

But how had he earned it, he wondered. Tisch was a man who paid by results. And with the IPO cancelled there was no positive result, financially speaking.

Or was there? He looked at Tisch. 'You made money somewhere.'

'I did?'

By way of response, Oliver raised one eyebrow.

'Well,' said Carlton, 'I didn't lose on the episode, if that's what you mean.'

Oliver thought to himself – ask the right questions.

'By the way, what's happening to the Casino,' he asked casually.

'Oh, it was sold,' said Tisch lightly.

'To whom?'

'The Flacks bought it privately.'

'The Flacks?'

'The folks from Gibraltar.'

'They did?' Things were becoming clearer. 'For how much?'

'For a lot less than its value as an IPO.'

'But I thought the Flacks' computer guy had already stolen the key programmes for them?'

Tisch shook his head. 'Apparently not. Turns out he exaggerated when he claimed that. A character flaw of his. Judith, God rest her soul, was smart enough to hold something back. I'm glad she did.'

'The Flacks weren't worried about the scandals or about American legal challenges down the road?'

'Somewhat. But the price discounted all that. Wilf Flack is a businessman. He knows that cash is the name of the game. Casino Caribbean still generates a huge cash flow and he was willing to pay for that.'

'So will Casino Caribbean become part of Flacks?'

'Yes. They need a casino to complement their bookmaking business. As a private company, they are not affected by stock market craziness. And as for a few scandals along the way, that's business. The Flacks are no virgins.'

'So the Flacks bought the Casino,' said Oliver. 'But from whom? The Flacks were the buyers but who was the seller?'

Tisch looked evasive. 'The owners, of course.'

'But who were the owners?' Then light dawned. 'You. They bought it from you, didn't they?'

Tisch shrugged. 'They were bearer shares; what counts is possession.'

'But Jasper Demon had possession.'

'I reached an understanding with Jasper.'

Oliver shook his head in mock exasperation. 'I bet you did.'

Tisch declined ever to say how much money changed hands between him, Flack and Demon but by Oliver's reckoning it was around $500 million, less Demon's commission for delivering the shares. Oliver's own cheque came in pretty handy, come to that. It would not extinguish his bankruptcy, but it would make a huge dent in it.

But, clearly, the winner going away was the short, grey-stubbled financier, smoking a cigar on the terrace of his house on Tortola.

THE END

Financial note:
The profits of *Casino Caribbean* may sound exaggerated but in 2005 a real internet gaming company went public with sales of $978 million, twice the size of *Casino Caribbean*. Just a few years old, it made its owners billionaires.

Neither *Casino Caribbean* nor the people and events surrounding it were inspired by that company or any particular company but they *were* inspired by the remarkable growth in the industry around that time.

ACKNOWLEDGMENTS

I should like to acknowledge the help of Lucinda Stevens, Christopher Stone and Mary Baxter who looked over the preliminary version of this book and suggested dozens of corrections and improvements. The shortcomings that remain are, of course, mine. Thanks above all to the team who pulled the whole thing together: to Sue Berry, my editor, and Anne Wilson, my designer. Thanks, too, to Ed Berry for his sharp cover design.

GRAHAM TEMPEST, a keen squash player and dedicated sun-seeker, now lives in Florida but was born and educated in the UK. His working life has been spent in the world of finance both in the UK and the USA, but there his resemblance to his hero ends!

Visit the author's website at:
www.grahamtempest.com